NASHVILLE: MUSIC & MURDER

NASHVILLE: MUSIC & MURDER

TOM CARTER

ISBN (Trade Paperback): 9780692791523
ePub ISBN: 9780692794494

Cover illustration by Rip Kastaris
Cover design by Rip Kastaris and Holly Jones
Cover photos by Jeff Fasano Photography
Page design by Holly Jones

For Janie Carter, the oxygen in my breath,
and her invaluable assistance in the
writing of my 18th book.

For Diane Evers, Dan Jansson, Randy Register
and Barry Williams—thank you for believing in me
and this book.

Special thanks to Ingram Spark, Pam Dover, Rip Kastaris,
Kasi Williams Morstad, Holly Jones, Mary Lawson,
KORE PR, Jonathan Kayne, Jeff Fasano Photography,
PSU Film & Video, Steve Stafford and Michael Weintrob.

Nashville's Music Row is a neighborhood that began with one recording studio in 1954, and today houses scores of recording studios, celebrities' offices, music publishing houses, rehearsal halls and other real estate where dreams are founded one day, sustained the next and sometimes shattered forever.

Such varied emotions are manifested in the writing and recording of country music songs. Some of their singers get famous, rich and legendary. But eventually, like everyone, they die.

They don't always die from natural causes.

Singer Maci Willis faked another smile, then gazed wearily across a sea of 18,000 jubilant fans. Twenty years ago, she would have given her heart and soul to draw a crowd this size. But tonight, the demanding masses were draining her of everything she had.

As her eyes scanned the room, she heard not the adulation of an army of admirers, but the deafening roar of a thousand lions that had just spotted a solitary gazelle named Maci.

Looking down, she told herself that she could hold her composure together for a few more minutes. The rhythmic stomping of feet told her what she already knew - that people were hungry for more musical manna - and were hoping for a third encore.

With her nod to the band, the opening chords of one of her signature hits filled the arena. Then, as a sea of smart-phones flashed at her, she waved her hand, a gesture to stop the music.

"You probably heard I'm not too big of a fan of these phones," she said.

A few hundred fans who had seen the previous month's tabloids hooted in approval. They'd read the story of how Maci, while dining at a riverside restaurant, was approached by a fan who tried to force her into an unwanted selfie. In one swift, nearly choreographed motion, Maci snatched the boy's phone and threw it into the river. When the press called the next day, her only comment was, "I don't know why they call it a smartphone when there always seems to be an idiot attached to the screen."

Now, in front of a capacity crowd, Maci decided to double down. Rather than address the entire audience, she turned her attention to a pudgy teenage girl in the front row, who was still squinting into her phone as she recorded Maci.

"Darlin'," she said. "You. Open your eyes. You're sitting beneath a thirty-foot Jumbotron. Me and my band are standing here in front of you, larger than life. And your mama paid two hundred dollars for that seat. And now, you want to squeeze us all down into a teeny, tiny, four-inch screen.

"Well, I'm waaay too big for a four inch screen!"

The crowd roared in support of Maci. When the Jumbotron captured the image of the young offender, it finally dawned upon her that she was the target of Maci's remarks.

"Honey, just look at yourself," said Maci in a voice that blurred the chasm between sarcasm and concern. "You're scarcely fourteen years old, and you're already at least thirty or forty pounds overweight, maybe more. That ain't living, darlin'. Put down that stupid phone. Throw it out. Get out of your chair. And get up on your feet and dance!

"In fact, everybody, put down your phones!" Maci yelled to the audience. "Get up on your feet! You didn't come here to see Samsung! You didn't come here to see Apple! You came here to see the greatest female singer alive—and to hear the best songs in the history of country music! Now get up and dance!"

The band instantly ripped into the opening bars of the third encore. Maci had worked the crowd into such a frenzy that only a few noticed the glistening tears rolling down the chastised girl's reddened face. Just as two other teenagers left their seats to console her, the Jumbotron cut away from her and back to Maci, and the cries of the crowd reached a new crescendo.

Winding down from two hours of singing and shuffling across a 40-foot stage, Maci took a deep breath. The sprawling screen above the platform magnified the sweat that beaded on her brow. Her normally erect posture was slightly bent, as if she carried not just the weight of the night's performance, but of the entire world's.

"Maybe not the entire world," she thought to herself. "Just thousands of fans, a production crew of sixty, and five truckloads of equipment. Plus a sizeable part of the country music industry."

Outside, additional Jumbotrons on the façade of Nashville's Bridgestone Arena thrust Maci's voice and image out to the throng of fans without tickets. Throughout the evening, she'd intermittently talked directly to the sidewalk followers, who for the most part were a bit more drunk that those inside. A drone-mounted camera occasionally panned the crowds who came to life each time they saw themselves on the massive screens. One man shot the moon to his fellow fans and a few women flashed their breasts.

The frenetic sea of Maci's fans stretched down Broadway for two blocks, nearly reaching the bank of the Cumberland River. From that vantage point, most could neither hear nor see Maci's show; they'd come primarily to drink and mingle with other folks, and occasionally they'd contribute their own song and dance. Temporary beer stands had taken root in the middle of the road, which had been closed off to accommodate the crowds. In each booth, bartenders poured a steady stream of ice-cold lagers for the mob, who had come as much for the beer as for the music.

"You folks outside should have scooped up some tickets from the scalpers," Maci shouted into her microphone. "The cost would have been outrageous, but I'm worth the money!"

The lilt in her voice hinted that her energy was waning like a jet aircraft leaking fuel. Even so, her little asides ignited smatterings of applause from both inside and outside the arena.

"How much more do these people want from me?" Maci mumbled off microphone. "How much more can I give? Let's see what the old gal's got left."

Lifting the microphone to her lips, she blasted out the first few words of "Come and Get It," her chart-topper from nearly fifteen years earlier. As the band joined in, the audience once again rose to their feet. Maci crossed the stage, dragging the spotlight with her, toward her steel guitarist. Feigning astonishment, he leapt from his seat on cue, and Maci playfully pushed him away. Sitting in his chair, Maci sloppily played a three-string verse without a chorus, and then jumped atop the borrowed chair where she wobbled back and forth to the delight of her audience.

Just as she expected, a hefty faction of the crowd mimicked her movements by jumping up and teetering on their seats. Unaccustomed to balancing on their chairs, people were laughing, spilling beer and falling like leaves in a windstorm.

Holding her microphone to her waist, Maci made sure her admirers could see, but not hear, her exaggerated breaths, which were worthy of a boxer after going twelve rounds with Muhammad Ali. The theatrics once again worked the crowd into blistering ecstasy as the lights began to fade.

"Bye bye, folks," she thought as the darkness embraced her. "I'm leaving my stage, leaving it without an ounce of remaining energy. Time for y'all to go back home to your bored and boring lives."

Precisely as the curtains dropped, the room's semi-darkness was shattered by the burst of the arena's house lights which pierced the air like a thousand tiny suns. Their idol gone from sight, fans squinted into the glare, contorting their faces like animals surfacing from a long winter's hibernation. Many hummed or sang as they headed toward the exits. Most were smiling, and a few were teary eyed from having finally seen a living legend. The Queen had left her throne. There was no High Princess in the wings. The music had silenced, and so had the listeners' world.

Or so they thought.

Before the fans could leave, the arena was thrust into total blackness. Scattered exit signs eerily dotted the darkness like flickering fireflies. Some fans wondered aloud if there had been a power failure. Then, in a flash, the surprised audience released a collective gasp as spotlights sliced through the ocean of black. As the crowd slowly realized what was happening, their murmurings rose from unexpected joy, to unbridled jubilation to outright nirvana.

"Nobody returns to the stage four times!" shouted the announcer through the sound system. "Except for Maci Willis!!!!"

Like shoppers squeezing through a Black Friday turnstile, the departing fans wrestled madly to get back to their seats.

"The show must go on—again!" yelled the announcer. "You won't miss what you don't see, so you'd better see what you might miss!"

Shouts, sometimes profane, resounded from fans, especially those bottlenecked inside the exit tunnels where ushers struggled to herd them back inside.

Then she appeared.

Alone in seven spotlights, Maci stood motionless as she was lifted through the stage floor, bathed in an aura of pastel footlights. Then, as the band played the opening chords of another signature song, she began to frantically dance in place with the fervor of a barefoot child on a tar roof.

"You didn't think I'd leave without singing my favorite song, did you?" she screamed into her earset microphone. "You ain't getting rid of me that easy. I'd NEVER leave you!"

Separated from their assigned seats, the confused audience shifted like a jigsaw puzzle whose pieces had sprung to life. As the band began to play, Maci ripped away her designer gown, flashed her legs beneath her mini-dress and the musical madness became as loud as New Year's Eve at Times Square. The crowd, startled yet joyous, unanimously wondered how long the show would actually go on.

Except for one fan. He knew exactly how long.

Having followed Maci's touring extravaganza through three cities, he'd memorized the show down to its smallest detail. He knew this encore was truly the last. He knew just when Maci would strut across the stage, and exactly when and where she'd stop to pose for one last flurry of photos like a gloating minstrel. Like a legend finally at rest.

Like a perfect target.

While the houselights had sent most of the crowd to the exits, he waded against the plethora of fans, working his way closer to the stage. He knew the arena well; the route backstage, the nearest exit, the gateway through which he could sink safely and silently into the night.

Like a child seeking a hidden toy, he slid his hand gently under his black, all-weather coat to reaffirm the presence of his .357 Magnum whose steel jacket bullets could penetrate an engine block. Patting the weapon's cold steel contours, he marveled at its sleeping power which he would soon awaken.

"The entire crowd'll want to kill me," he whispered to no one. "But that won't be personal. They'll want to kill me because I killed her."

Like a salmon battling its way upstream, he wove his way through the widening flow of torsos engulfing him.

Still too far to see Maci clearly, he repeatedly glanced upward at the Jumbotron as he inched toward the stage. The face he saw no longer had the youthful glow that had filled her early album covers. He could see the streaked mascara and the tired lines on her face that resembled creases on silk.

"Maci's exhausted," he told himself. "She needs to rest. She needs . . . me."

He drifted, lost in the crowd, moving slowly but methodically closer to the stage. As the song entered its second verse, he smiled wryly, realizing he could now ignore the Jumbotron and look straight into Maci's eyes.

"I love you, Maci," he yelled, his voice buried beneath the blare of the music and the roar of the crowd. "I understand your songs better than all of these simpletons!"

As he continued his journey toward destiny, his excitement over seeing Maci was matched only by his disdain for the audience. They were fools. They didn't understand Maci. They didn't understand her or her songs. Not like he did. Idiots. All of them.

Maci and four backup singers slipped into an a cappella refrain as the band members raised their hands high to kindle a round of unified clapping throughout the arena. Not content to merely clap, the crowd began to stomp their feet in time with the music. Feeling their cadence through the soles on his boots, he knew the crowd's emotions were rising. As were his. None of them realized how close they were to the end of Maci's show, and of her life.

But he did.

An unimpressive row of security ushers, dressed in canary yellow sport coats, stood rigidly a few feet apart from each other, forming what passed for a protective line in front of the stage and the performers standing on it.

"Useless geezers," he smirked aloud, safe and smug in the knowledge that his spoken words still could not be heard above the din and fray. He could announce his plans aloud and no one would hear. He shook his head at the inept, unintimidating guards. "A Girl Scout could get by you. Maci deserves better than a handful of escapees from an old folks' home."

His heart raced. He was now close enough to count Maci's finger rings, and was more energized than ever. His voice beginning to rasp, he couldn't hear his own words this close to the stage, no matter how forcefully he shouted.

Realizing he was no longer struggling amid the masses, he drew a deep breath as he turned to gaze at the people in the front row, who rhythmically danced in place. Like the Pied Piper, he would soon abandon everyone on the ground floor before scaling to his lofty perch, and taking his place onstage aside his beloved Maci Willis.

"I'm closer to Maci than anyone else in the hall except her people on stage," he said, congratulating himself.

His starstruck eyes suddenly filled with lust, he barely noticed the nearby security guard waving at him. For a moment, he was tempted to leap up, grasp the lip of the platform, and pull himself onstage.

"Not now," he told himself. "Move now and they'll stop you."

The guard continued to wave.

"Me?" he mouthed as he pointed to himself, faking confusion.

The glorified usher nodded and signaled for the misplaced man to come to him.

Forcing a smile, he walked slowly toward the yellow coat and the old man wearing it. As if seeing a long lost friend, he thrust his arm around the fellow and pretended to yell into his ear. Moving stealthily, he slid his hand into his coat's inside pocket. With a magician's sleight of hand, he quickly found his Taser and dropped the guard.

Maintaining his grasp on his prey, he called out to two of the nearby guards.

"Need some help here," he shouted. "Looks like heatstroke."

The two guards discretely eased their companion to the ground, trying their best to not distract attention from the show.

A drunk from the front row, deciding that a dousing of liquid was the best way to revive someone, flung the contents of his plastic cup into the fallen guard's face. Upon seeing this, two more guards left their posts to drag the drunk away.

With five guards out of the way, half the stage was now his.

"Hell's bells," he shouted, his voice still inaudible to the crowd. "I was expecting a challenge. Seems like you clowns are actually trying to help."

A shiver ran through him. "Like you're trying to help," he said. "Like it's meant to be. Like it's destiny."

Glancing at his watch, he counted in time with the beat as the music approached its bridge into the third verse.

"Three . . . , two . . . , one . . . ," he shouted. "Showtime!"

High above the arena, a thunderous cloudburst exploded from the ceiling, raining colorful, vibrant foil confetti upon the crowd like blessings from Walmart.

Despite the full saturation of stage lights, he knew the torrent of tinsel would conceal his movements as he pulled himself onstage in one quick, coordinated maneuver.

There, behind the cascade of colored paper, illumination and glitter, he slowly rose, invisible to the audience. While the crowd was swept away by sensory overload, his focus sharpened. His entire world was now reduced to Maci, his gun and his hand.

Her back turned to him, he watched her take her first step to stage right. There, she'd halt to wave goodbye to fans, lingering for a moment in a frenzy of camera flashes. He waited until she struck a photo-worthy pose, which she'd hold for several seconds, just as he'd seen in her last two concerts. Inhaling slowly, he steadied his breath as she hit her mark at stage right. He vowed she'd never make it to stage left.

Holding his breath, he pointed his gun squarely into the back of her heart. His thumb cocked the hammer as he made a mental note to squeeze, not pull, the trigger. Resting rigidly on his knees, he felt his forefinger easing toward him.

The impact of the policeman's tackle ignited the shooter's reflexes. His elbow buckled and his grip tightened as the officer collided with his arm. The force knocked the stalker violently to the floor, sending the pistol sliding across the stage.

The officer had acted quickly—but not quickly enough. As his head hit the platform floor, the shooter saw a spurt of blood and hair from the left side of Maci's head.

Amid the blinding spotlights and the relentless storm of tinsel, most of the audience had failed to see the three-feet-long flash from the weapon's barrel. Those who discerned a policeman wrestling a man to the floor assumed it was another case of an overzealous fan trying to get too close to the star.

But onstage, it was a nightmare come to life. The stagehands and musicians had been close enough to hear the cannon-like blast of the weapon. A few of them joined in the melee, helping the officer subdue the stalker. Others started to join, but were stopped mid-step by the sight of a fallen Maci Willis, whose head lay in a widening pool of crimson.

On cue, the thicket of confetti stopped. People in the higher seats, along with everyone viewing the Jumbotron, saw the ongoing skirmish taking place on the stage.

And they saw the fallen Maci.

The crowd emitted a bone-chilling chorus of shrieks, as if the entire arena had been cast into an inferno. The music ceased, the house lights were raised, and everyone under the cavernous ceiling could now see the four-man fracas at stage right, violent and unexplainable.

As the shrieks gave way to shouts, sobs and pandemonium, Maci's sparkling dress reflected the spotlights that were still swirling in time to the now-silenced music. Only the scurrying of first-responders was able to lower the arena's volume, and a concerned, unintelligible murmur filled the air. In seconds, Maci was hoisted upward by emergency personnel, while the stagehands and musicians fumbled about helplessly, equally torn between the urge to look and the urge to look away.

From the first row to the top tier, confused and terrified fans fell into a hush. For the first time all night, the arena was silent.

When nights are long and sleep is elusive, Randy Sorenson lies under a blanket of nostalgia, comforting himself within its sentimental warmth. Inevitably, his thoughts always lead him down the same familiar path, as he regresses to age six and his eager walk beside his mother on his first day of first grade.

During the sluggish wave of insomnia, his memory ushers him back to his mother's love, a protective shield on that long ago day. He can still feel the pity he held for the smaller kids, the five-year-olds entering kindergarten, a scary, foreign place where children are told to close their eyes and take naps.

He'd done the same when he was little. But now he's a first-grader.

His recollection is also accompanied by a sense of six-year-old independence. On that day, he felt he'd joined the ranks of "big" people, those who could be trusted to carry their own lunch money. Locked in his dream, he hopes his mom doesn't place the coins inside one of her handkerchiefs, especially the one with flowers. He's afraid the other boys will think the hankie belongs to a girl, not to his mom.

Then the dream takes a turn, to the part he doesn't understand. This first day of *real* school is making him happy, but his mom is crying. Why? Everybody knows that the first day of first grade means you're grown up. Why isn't she happy?

He asks her about her tears. She shakes her head and says she's catching a late summer cold.

Now in a deep sleep, Randy's dream becomes a nightmare.

Inside his frayed psyche, he hears the screeching of tires that skid beside his six-year-old stance, and he sees the fright in his mother's eyes. The loose coins clink across the pavement as the hankie falls from his hand. Without warning, two strangers bolt from the unfamiliar car, yelling and cursing at his mom as they grab her and drag her into their car. Randy yearns to help, but realizes he's too little. Instead of running to her aid, he stands silent, wetting his pants. The car carrying his Mom peels away, and its two taillights shine bright red as they round a corner. Red is Randy's favorite color, but not now because it's blurred by his tears. He falls to his knees to hunt for his lunch money.

Then, through his moistened eyes, Randy sees another light. It too is red, and it swirls atop a black and white car on whose side "POLICE" is written in big, bold letters.

The car with two colors and a red light suddenly smashes into the bad guys' car. The police car is surely driven by a policeman because Randy saw that on "Law and Order," Mom's favorite television show, although he doesn't know why because Spiderman isn't in it.

Running closer to the bad guys' car, Randy sees Mom with one of them in the backseat. She's still wrestling with the scary man, and still losing.

A policeman with a deep voice jumps from his smashed car. The cop bumps his knee as he exits, and draws his gun as he limps toward the other car. Randy saw something like that on television too.

The policeman yells loudly, spraying spit as the words leave his mouth. Meanwhile, Randy's mother rushes from the car. She picks him up and squeezes him so hard that he thinks he's being punished for dropping the lunch money.

Mom tries to turn his head away from the policeman as he pushes the two men on their car's hood. But Randy peeks and sees the policeman hit one man with a long stick. He doesn't tell Mom what he sees because she might get scared.

"I love you, Randy," Mom says. He wonders why she keeps saying that. He already knows it because he's smart.

He's entering the first grade.

✦✦ ✦✦

Eighteen years later, Randy remembered the dream, and found himself immersed in the same feeling of joining the ranks of the big people. Standing anxiously, he moved one step closer to the podium, as the line of the Nashville Metro Police Academy's trainees stepped forward, one by one, to receive their diplomas. Wanting to savor the moment, to hold its essence for life, Randy remanded each of his five senses to collect every little detail of that morning. Earlier, after breathing in the reek of cheap cigars and Aqua Velva from his fellow male recruits, he opted to mix with his female classmates, determined trainees who smelled mostly of fragrant soap and shampoo. Inhaling deeply, he lingered in their scents as he committed them to memory.

Randy felt himself blush as he stepped before the teary police captain who curtly handed him his diploma. The captain was a law enforcement legend, a two-fisted bruiser who once arrested four men alone, knocking out three of them in the process. The fourth suspect raised his hands and pleaded, "Officer, I'll confess to everything if you won't hit me again."

The next day, the local newspaper headline proclaimed: "Bare Knuckled Cop Knocks Bare Truth Out of Suspect."

On this particular morning, that same burley officer struggled to suppress his emotions when facing Randy, a strapping and handsome graduate. He knew first-hand that Randy's only fistfight to date had been inside a fraternity house, a place he presumed was inhabited by sissies, bookworms and spoiled rich kids. And even among that lot, his son lost the fight.

"I've never seen you cry before dad," Randy whispered to Captain Ezra Sorenson. "Not even on that day you rescued Mom from those guys on my first day in first grade. This is the most important day of my life, except for maybe the day you married Mom, and the day you adopted me."

The captain stared into his son's eager face, and for a moment was uncharacteristically speechless.

Just as Randy was confused by his mother's tears eighteen years earlier, he now marveled at the softness and vulnerability that spread over his father's weathered and gruff visage.

Returning to his seat, Randy breathed a short sigh, then shouted "YES!" as the commencement's benediction came to an end. The trainee was now an official rookie policeman.

The male rookies shook hands, and gave brief hugs to the female graduates. Everyone chatted rapidly as they realized that a new chapter of their life was about to begin. They were no longer classmates; they were now joined together as brothers and sisters, or maybe something closer, in an exclusive pact of law enforcement.

"Let's get drunk and arrest each other!" shouted one rookie. "That way, we'll all get a 'collar' on our first day of duty!"

Captain Sorenson pretended not to hear the barb.

Randy's own expectations for the day ahead were clear: He'd ride with a veteran cop on today's second shift, which started at 3:00 pm. At least, that was his assumption. Unknown to Rookie Sorenson, his dad had other plans.

"Given your grades at the academy, I didn't have to pull too many strings to get you out on the street on the same day you graduated," said Ezra. "And, I've managed to obtain a special detail for you."

"Your mother and I know that Maci Willis is your favorite singer. And we know you couldn't make it to her concert because tickets were sold out, and besides, you have to *work*."

Randy noticed the emphasis on the word "work."

"So what are you saying, Dad?" asked Randy.

"Well, Rookie Sorenson, you're going to see Maci's show from the stage as part of her police detail. Get there early. There'll probably be a meeting between her private security and the cops. That's customary in these things."

Randy smiled. Two dreams were coming true in one day.

"Congratulations Son. This will be your first day of duty, but it won't seem too much like work. Don't get spoiled. Cause after this, you're in for a stretch of traffic duty."

Trying to maintain an air of professionalism, the overjoyed dad told his son he'd see him tomorrow, and ordered him to have a good time—minus fun—at the concert. Randy had no idea what he meant, and knew the confused phrasing couldn't be found in any of his police academy manuals.

"Take good care of Maci. Make the department and your old man proud."

As the veteran turned away, Randy saw tears in his eyes.

Only once had Randy ever seen his dad get sentimental. Now, he'd seen it again.

Using his thumb and forefinger, Officer Randy Sorenson nervously creased his already pressed trousers as he prepared to climb the backstage steps, up onto the stage where Maci Willis stood inside a show-closing shower of confetti at Nashville's Bridgestone Arena.

He and three other officers—two of them rookies like himself—had earlier been asked to remain on the concrete floor several feet below Maci's performance stage. The foursome would be instructed when to mount the back of the stage and onto the platform.

"Until then, Maci doesn't want the crowd to see anyone on her stage, except for her and the band," said a production assistant, a skinny man with wire rim glasses who constantly waved a clipboard. Upon his signal, the policemen would walk to the wings of Maci's stage, escort her down eight steps and into her idling limousine.

"You men must not say a word to Ms. Willis," the bespeckled man said emphatically. "She'll be exhausted, and more than a little irritable. If possible, try to refrain from eye contact with her. After being seen by thousands of people, she just wants a little privacy. Don't feel slighted. I've relayed these identical demands to her limousine driver too."

As a fan, Randy tried to see things from her perspective, but to him, the requests still seemed a bit on the snobbish side.

The fidgety man had suddenly assumed the persona of a drill sergeant, and began to shout to Randy and the other cops.

"Okay—heads up. Get up the stairs and to the back of the stage. Meet Maci as soon as she steps out of the lights. Right after this song. Go and be invisible."

Annoyed, the lone veteran cop asked if he and the others should wear blackout drapes, to prevent people from the trauma of seeing a non-celebrity.

Huffing like a three-pack a day smoker, the little tyrant's lips spread into a thin line.

"Well!" said the pseudo dictator. "I've never . . ."

"Yeah, I'm sure you haven't!" interjected the older cop with a smile.

Fearing his first day on the job was taking a less than professional turn, Randy stepped in to defuse the tension.

"Let's do this!" he shouted over the sound of the music.

Almost in cadence, the uniformed quartet walked upward from a concrete floor towards the outskirts of one of the most lavish and dramatic productions in country music history.

Within seconds, Randy approached the perimeter of a kaleidoscope of falling colors amid music loud enough to register on the Richter Scale. As both a rookie and a fan, Randy found the scene overwhelmingly thrilling.

The four lawmen, still in single file, held their ground outside the reach of Maci's swirling spotlights.

"This is like a hundred flashlights twirling inside a walk-in closet!" Randy shouted to no one.

Partially blinded, he raised his palm over his eyebrows while searching for Maci among the musicians and background dancers. As his eyes wandered, his gaze was caught by a man in a trench coat kneeling at center stage.

Although Randy had never seen Maci's show, he knew the stranger was eerily out-of-place. Randy had only been a policeman for part of one day, but his 24 years of life told him the entire scenario was threatening.

He glanced upward into the rafters, and looked instantly back to the stage where the figure was now raising a gun toward Maci.

"What the hell?" he yelled.

Adrenaline took over as Randy charged the gunman, hitting him like a hockey player checking an opponent. Upon impact, he both heard and felt the discharge of a high-caliber handgun.

"I'm not supposed to be inside Maci's lighting," Randy thought, and wondered why the notion crossed his mind at a time like this.

The music abruptly stopped, and gave way to the hysteria of thousands of people who'd watched the horror inside their line-of-sight or across the Jumbotrons. From his vantage, Randy couldn't see the giant screens and the blood spewing from Maci's head.

Everything was so fast, so loud and so frantic.

Forgetting any police training, Randy was running entirely on impulses. He knew he was out of control, but felt at ease with his instincts.

As the young cop pinned the struggling gunman to the floor, another policeman joined the ruckus, wrestling a loose hand away from the shooter, and making sure it held no threat.

Randy shook free enough to yank the handcuffs from his belt. Mustering his strength, he pushed the suspect's hands together, then slapped the cuffs around each wrist, securing the captive's folded palms before him, as if in prayer.

In an instant, Randy and two other cops yanked the suspect up and toward the backstage steps that they'd ascended a minute earlier.

Randy led the sprint of the shooter and three cops down the backstage stairs, and left the fourth kneeling beside Maci. Shoving the gunman forward, Randy tightened his grip under the man's shirt collar.

"YES! WE'VE GOT THIS!" the rookie shouted.

As if bewildered, the officers and suspect halted in their tracks, and then walked around Maci's limousine just as a giant garage door noisily opened to let the lawmen and captive exit.

"Hey man, where'd you park?" shouted one of the cops to Randy.

"Just beyond this door!" he yelled.

"You got him!" said the cop, semi-smiling.

"Yeah, you made the collar," said another officer. "You take the maggot to jail."

His hands cuffed before him, the suspect was guided by Randy and another officer toward the waiting police car.

"Do the honors!" one cop yelled at Randy. "Put the geek in the car!"

For the first time all night, Randy recalled his rookie's manual, and pushed downward on the suspect's head to ease him into the back seat. But the captive didn't comply.

Bending slightly at the knee, he thrust upwardly to intentionally lacerate his head on the rim of the squad-car's steel roof. Blood seemingly spewed everywhere.

"That was intentional!" yelled a cop at Randy. "Get him to the hospital!"

Disoriented by the sheer frantic pace of events, Randy was glad someone else was directing this real life drill.

"What about the ambulance?" shouted Randy.

"It's for Maci!" he was told. "Leave it! Drive the guy to the E.R.!"

Outside the arena, a dozen people had gathered around Randy's police cruiser, peeking and gawking through its windows like shoppers at Christmas. Dozens more were running toward the vehicle, like moths beckoned by its silent red lights. Randy ignored the onlookers peering through iPhone's, making videos of the arrest.

"Hey buddy," Randy shouted to a fellow rookie. "Give me your undershirt!"

"So, you get the collar, I get the laundry bill," said his colleague.

"Just stay in the back seat with him," Randy said to a cop. "Use your shirt and apply direct pressure to the cut."

In seconds, the siren pierced the air, parting the crowd like the Red Sea.

Reaching toward the dash, Randy pressed a button to direct dial the Municipal Hospital ER three blocks away.

"I've got a suspect with a head injury!" Randy yelled into the receiver. "I think he'll need stitches!"

"Roger that," replied a voice. "But get here fast because this place is about to go crazy. You won't believe this but Maci Willis has just been shot at Bridgestone Arena."

Having never experienced an injury beyond a skinned knee, Officer Randy Sorenson had never entered a hospital Emergency Room in his life.

"Where are we supposed to stand?" he asked another rookie. For a split second, Randy thought about waiting for the two officers behind him, but decided that waiting contradicted the whole point of an Emergency Room.

Having no firsthand experience, his only reference point for how an ER worked were old television shows. He'd watched a lot of "Grey's Anatomy," and couldn't recall a single scene where a cop walked an injured suspect by his arm.

"I've got a suspect with an injury!" Randy shouted to one of the nurses behind the desk.

At the arena, Randy had walked assuredly, like a man with a purpose. Now, he realized his pivoting head and uncertain steps practically screamed that he had no idea where to go or what to do. He feared that he might be intruding on someone's life-saving procedure, that he might displace something vital for a patient whose injury was slightly more serious than a skinned knee.

"I'll just tell them I called earlier and talked to someone here," Randy said to another cop. He wished he'd gotten the name of the dispatcher who'd ordered him to the hospital.

Now leading his suspect by hand, Randy entered another pair of two-way doors, and into the frenzied heart of the Emergency Room. He felt like a bit player in a theater of organized chaos. Harsh lighting and the pungent stench of antiseptics filled his runaway senses. To Randy, this felt like a terrible place to die.

Most of those who scurried about wore sky blue scrubs, while a handful donned tan attire. Nurses versus doctors, Randy guessed. Everyone wore a plastic nametag and a stethoscope that swung like a pendulum with each user's movements. Amid the indistinct murmurs and occasional barked orders, the words "Maci Willis" occasionally surfaced. He wondered if she'd made it, and if his response had made any difference.

"You must be Officer Sorenson!" said a young man with an acne-covered face.

"How did you know?" Randy asked the greeter.

"Uh . . . your nametag," the attendant replied, smiling.

"Oh," Randy thought. "It's my first day of . . . everything."

Embarrassed by his ineptness, his unfamiliarity with his surroundings and his obvious newness to the job, Randy felt the coloring of his face deepen by three shades of crimson.

"That's okay," the man with pimples replied kindly. "Just as long as you know your own name."

Randy wanted to tell him that every worker has a first day, and today is his. He wanted to proclaim that he didn't come here to chatter; there was a job to do.

Instead, he swallowed his humiliation and simply explained his situation.

"I just arrested this man. He resisted and hurt himself. Can you help him?"

"Yes, hurt himself," said the worker with a quick wink. Randy wasn't sure if the young man was a nurse or attendant or orderly. He introduced himself as "Theodore," and stressed not to call him Ted. From nowhere, he insisted he loved Julie Andrews' lead in "Sound of Music" more than Carrie Underwood's.

Confused, Randy raised an eyebrow. "Is this part of the hospital's admittance procedure?"

Theodore huffed, and Randy knew he'd lost the minimal ground he scored seconds ago.

He and Randy walked silently with the suspect into a room behind a thin cotton-blend curtain. The rookie wondered why hospital curtains were so thin, almost to the point of transparency, and just how patients had any privacy.

"You may step right outside the room," Theodore said as he applied restraints to the gunman. "You'll be only three or four feet away from your suspect, er, patient. You can stick your head in any time you want. I'm not a doctor, but I think this cut will need stitches, but you and your prisoner should be out of here quickly."

Randy, now joined by Keith Shultz, another rookie, reluctantly left the room and stood outside the flimsy cloth wall. There, they could easily monitor the prisoner through the virtually transparent curtain.

On his first day as a policeman, Randy had made one of Nashville's highest-profile arrests in years. His dad, his mom, and even Maci Willis would be proud of his actions. Of that he was certain. It was a sign, in a way. After ten hours on the job, he knew without doubt that becoming a cop had been his true calling all along.

The ambulance siren was still winding down when the gurney carrying Maci Willis was slammed through the two-way doors of the emergency room.

Knowing that the eyes of the entire city would be on this patient, a doctor and two nurses had stood by, awaiting her arrival in the ER driveway. There, on a slight slope, a nurse exchanged the ambulance's morphine drip while the gurney was hustled toward the ER.

Five medical personnel charged into the ER hallway where a nurse pointed to Room One. Randy watched every moment, committing each movement to memory, so he would know exactly what to do the next time his job led him here.

Before he finished his thought, the doors burst open again.

Like buzzards converging on roadkill, a cadre of hustling print and television reporters flooded in, adding to the chaos. Raising his eyes across a field of turning heads, Randy thought the entire setting resembled a pep rally whose members weren't cheering to win a game, but to save a life - Maci's.

"She must not be hurt too much," Randy said to Officer Shultz.

"Why do you say that?" Shultz shouted over noise.

"Listen," said Randy. "Tune out the other voices, and you'll hear Maci."

Randy smiled the instant Shultz's eyes sparkled. Maci's voice was unmistakable—and unmistakably angry.

"Who's running this place!?" she demanded. "First some idiot shot off my ear, thanks to my crack security team. Then, you use my gurney as a battering ram to get in here. Let's hope my doctor's not a veterinarian!"

"I read an article the other day that described Maci Willis as the Songbird of the South and the Bitch of the Universe," Shultz smiled. "She's got the world in her hand. What's her problem?"

Randy wasn't sure whether or not Shultz was expecting an answer, nor did he care. His thoughts were immersed in gratitude. Although he'd never actually met country music's most heralded diva, he now felt that he and she were irrevocably connected, in a way. Maci's voice had often sung to him in wee hours, when most of the world was asleep. In return, he'd stopped the man who tried to silence her forever.

"Earth to Sorenson," said Shultz.

Randy shook his head. "Sorry," he said. He didn't want to share his thoughts, so he shifted to another one. "I was wondering if my first day on the job would be the highlight of my career. Like, if it'll all be downhill from here."

The legs of a wooden chair screeched loudly against the tile floor as a man wearing a suit and tie pulled it to a stop, then stood atop the seat.

"Everyone in the press . . . everyone in the press please!" he shouted. "Follow me down the hall, where we'll be issuing a brief statement. Please remember hospital policy: No photographs or digital filming is permitted without authorized permission. And no photos or filming of any kind inside the ER. Each of you needs to be ready to show your press credentials."

The man stiffly stepped from his perch, turned and attempted to lead a swelling press corps whose members didn't move. With cell phones pressed to their faces, the journalists were adamantly staying with the story, and stood firmly outside Maci's cubicle.

A cotton-blend sheet was Maci's only barricade between her and the reporters and a waiting world.

"All you're going to get is a picture of a silhouette," she screamed. "Give me some peace. Some son-of-a-bitch shot me, but that's not as much of a pain as you people are. Get away from me and my temporary room!"

None of the reporters moved, not even when doctors told them to, not even when a security guard approached, armed with a cell phone in one hand and a sandwich in the other.

Randy counted nineteen journalists mulling around outside the curtain encasing Maci, waiting feverishly for a print-worthy quote, whether touching, profound, profane or outlandish. He was sure any development, no matter how trivial, would be online within minutes. Maci probably knew this, and Randy felt she should be more discriminating in her choice of words.

He wondered if her behavior might be attributed to the morphine, or if it was simply Maci being Maci.

"I've never been inside an emergency room," he said to Shultz. "I thought patients had some kind of privacy. Look at what the press is doing to her! I'm twenty feet away and can hear everything she says."

So could his suspect.

Perhaps it was stress, or first day jitters, or the chaos of the moment, but Randy had left the detainee's hands cuffed in front of himself, not behind his back, as procedure required.

The suspect now lay alone and unattended in Room Two, also a flimsy cubical he could exit easily once unrestrained.

Slowly, he pulled his cuffed hands to his chin, then slid them to the left where he unfastened a buckle that bonded his back to the bed. He looked through the flimsy cloth door of his room, watching as Randy and Shultz stood transfixed on the press corps surrounding Maci's cubicle. As gingerly as a gymnast, the prisoner slowly and methodically sat up in his bed. Careful not to grunt, careful not to cause his bed to creak, he eased his cuffed hands toward the buckle of the strap that secured his knees.

Had Officer Randy or Shultz turned around, the suspect's mime-like maneuvers would have instantly ended. The cops would have charged into the room, handcuffed him behind his back, and possibly, for good measure, given him yet another wound to stitch.

But the rookies' eyes remained fixed on the press as the suspect pulled the lower restraint buckle's metal post from its leather eye. He tenderly let the belt's straps ease away from each other. Slightly raising his feet, he pivoted slowly, slid from the bed and inched toward the officers' backs.

A few feet away, still outside Maci's cube, the reporters had begun to loudly argue with one another.

"Hey man!" yelled one journalist. "You're with the print media! You don't need to stand where you can see Maci! You can photograph her later! We television people have a deadline! My boss wants a remote story from the scene! Get out of my shot!"

"Look at that!" Randy said to Shultz. "They're arguing over who gets to stand closest while Maci is telling them to scram. No wonder people think the media are jerks."

Randy's words and the clamoring of the reporters were more than loud enough to conceal any sounds the suspect's footsteps may have made.

"You need to walk over there," Randy said to Shultz. "Tell those reporters to hold it down. Where did that PR guy go?"

Shultz's downward glance told Randy he didn't want to get involved, and he didn't move.

"Hey man," Shultz said. "I'm a newbie just like you. I don't think you can give me orders."

Still holding his breath, the prisoner took another silent step toward the backs of two officers.

Shaking his head, Schultz shrugged and reluctantly stepped toward the arguing reporters. Randy said something in jest, and their distracted tone told the suspect now was the time.

As the echo of squabbling reporters rose, the suspect slowly pulled the sheet past the middle of Randy's back. His breath about to burst, he thrust his handcuffed palms directly at Randy's pistol.

In one motion, he unlatched the holster's snap and put both hands on the butt of Randy's gun. Instantly, Randy jumped forward, a jolt that pulled the pistol out of its case.

The captive stepped backwards, awaiting the split-second when Randy would, on reflex, turn to face him. Instead, he immediately shot beside the back of Randy's shoulder. Had the shooter waited another half second, Randy would have turned around and the bullet would have penetrated Randy's chest.

The shooter fired another round into the ceiling, igniting louder screams as he darted toward the media people.

"Gun! Gun!" someone yelled. "Grab him!" screamed someone else. "It's the guy who shot Maci!" bellowed a third voice.

The gunman was in full stride toward Maci, who lay on a bed where doctors crouched beside her. The singer had no visible protection, not even the lawmen who were charged with saving her life.

The shooter fired toward Maci, and in his haste shot wide to the left, where the bullet blew into the drywall. He stopped, exhaled forcibly, and yelled at Maci, whose head was already turned directly toward the thin curtain, the only restriction between her and a man with a gun.

"I'm sorry, Maci," he yelled, his voice breaking with emotion. "I don't want to kill you. But you asked me to. God help me, but you asked for it!"

Those were his last words.

His head partially exploded by the impact of a police-issued .38 Special hollow-point bullet. Shultz, bent at the waist, cocked his pistol again and braced like a lightning rod anticipating the next strike.

Maci Willis lay screaming, protected only by the men in scrubs coiled and screaming on the floor beneath her portable bed.

3

Max Abernathy splashed another dash of Ralph Lauren Polo Blue on his freshly shaven cheeks, and slipped into his most expensive cheap-looking shirt. He felt silly wearing skinny jeans, but they were all the rage among twentysomething's on Nashville's Music Row, and Max had floated into senior executive status by always looking young. Peroxide hair, bracelets, a diamond stud in his nose and intentional holes in his jeans rounded out his faux-adolescent uniform.

He pitied the idiots in show business who chose not to emulate youth. In the entertainment industry, failing to act young was the beginning of the end. Peering into his mirror, he focused on his surgical nips and tucks, and lightly grimaced. Soon, it would be time to have a little more work done - a moderate lift of his previous lift.

"Joan Rivers was born young," he remembered his surgeon joking, "and she died looking younger."

Yes, Max possessed more than his fair share of vanity, but there was another, more practical reason for his iron grip on his last vestiges of youth. As producer for several young singers, he'd learned he could capture their trust by emulating their fashions.

The male vocalists were that shallow, the women that desperate. And in less than an hour, he'd visit with Maci Willis, the diva of desperation.

He exhaled forcefully to brace for his pending presentation to Maci, Meacham Records' aging icon at age forty-four. She was the most temperamental artist he'd ever met, and her mood swings had understandably grown more unpredictable since someone tried to kill her.

"A bullet almost to the brain could dampen anyone's day," he said to himself. "Then again, she's so hard-headed that . . ." He immediately realized the insensitivity of his comments, but didn't really care.

His life with Maci's volatile emotions had been an exercise in glorified babysitting. He was tired of smiling at someone he couldn't stand. But that came with the territory when you manage a middle-age woman who's going on 16. Max couldn't count the times he held his tongue, or tally the money he'd skimmed from the sale of Maci's 50 million albums.

Extraordinary talent. Unnecessary drama. That was Maci.

During her recovery from the shooting, she'd ripped a bulky bandage off her reconstructed ear and hurled it at a surgeon.

"Photographers are chomping at the bit to see who can get the first picture of me!" she yelled at the doctor. "Can't you fix me up with something that doesn't look like a Kotex taped to the side of my head?"

Her stitches exposed, Maci claimed they itched, and scratched the fragile sewing until she bled.

"Look at this mess!" she fumed at nurses. "Who's my surgeon, Jack the Ripper?'"

Those and other gems had made their way into the tabloids, thanks to the ingenuity of the more enterprising reporters. Some of them pretended to be relatives of patients in rooms near Maci's hospital room. Others slipped a few bills to the orderlies in exchange for carrying a digital recorder in their pockets. One reporter was rumored to have donned a priest's collar so that he could freely make the rounds. Simply getting close to her was enough to publicize her tirades.

In preparing for his meeting with Maci, Max had sent her a tall basket of assorted fruits and condiments. After ripping its cellophane wrapping, Maci had it delivered back to Max at Meacham with an attached note.

"After all the money I've made for your toy record label, you send me a sack of groceries? Try again!"

Max persuaded Meacham officials in New York to buy her a BMW sedan.

His morning drive to work did little to rally his spirits. He had a request, a proposal, to put before Maci. If she said yes, all would be fine. If not, he'd have to tell her the truth: That it wasn't a request at all, but an edict that had come down from Meacham's New York office. An order. And Maci was simply going to have to live with it.

"This," he moaned, "is not going to be fun."

Accompanied by her personal secretary, Maci entered Nashville's Meacham Building for the first time since the shooting. Max heard her long before seeing her, as she bounded down the hallway complaining about its aroma.

"This hall smells like a Men's Room where the men missed the urinals," Max heard her say. "Who's in charge of deodorizing this place, Terminix?"

Maci's employee opened one side of the double doors that led to Max's lavish office. The carpet was plush, the furniture bore a rich luster and everything smelled of wealth.

Maci strode into the room as if it were hers, swaggering like Marilyn Monroe on a red carpet.

Four department heads at Meacham's Music Row office, two secretaries, a transcriptionist, a hostess and Max rose to their feet.

"Are you standing for me?" Maci chimed, in mock gratitude. "If so, keep standing. I took a bullet for this record label. I wouldn't be surprised if it was a publicity stunt to sell more of my records! Which one of you planned it?"

She pretended not to see Max's jaw tighten with disdain.

"If I'd hired a hit man, I'd certainly have found one who could hit your beach ball-size head," he thought.

"Maci, dear . . . ," said Max, warmly. "We've missed you. Sit down and tell us how you're feeling."

"You've all read the papers," she snapped. "Max, you're the only person here who came to see me in the hospital. Of course, that was mostly to flirt with the nurses. But guess what? They're nurses. They can spot your STD's a mile away."

Max again forced his best fake smile. "So nice to have you back."

"Maybe nice for you," Maci quipped. "But I don't want to be back. I told you I wanted to be left alone for a month or two, yet you hauled me in here."

"Well first of all, I know I speak for everyone here when I say we're so glad you're all right," Max said. "And I . . ."

"Never mind . . . I didn't come here for lies wrapped in small talk. Cut to the chase and tell me what this record label's sharks want from me now?"

Setting niceties aside, Max cleared his throat and took a more somber tone.

"Okay, Maci," he said, drawing a deep breath. "To the chase. The guys in New York want you to do a publicity tour in the wake of the shooting."

"Publicity tour?" Maci replied. "Am I supposed to publicize shooters, and say everyone should have their own?"

Obligatory laughter came from a few members of Max's associates, but their chuckles quickly subsided the instant Maci frowned.

"No Maci," Max said dryly. "Right now, you're news. As frightening as it was, your incident was repeatedly covered by national and international media. Footage of your social media coverage went viral. You've been on the cover of all the *right* magazines."

"You're telling me something I already know."

"I know, I'm sorry," said Max, shyly. "But the guys in New York want you to 'humanize' your trauma."

"Don't you mean 'monetize' my trauma, Max?" Maci scoffed. "You people really kill me."

"Maci," Max frowned. "They want your story to go from mass coverage to local coverage in major and medium markets. They believe readers and viewers attach more credibility to local reporters than they do to national or international reporters."

Maci's absent response prompted Max to continue talking.

"In New York, you'll be interviewed by ABC affiliate WABC-TV as well as the *New York Times*. In Chicago, it will be the CBS affiliate WBBM-TV and the *Chicago Tribune*. In St. Louis, you'll be interviewed by NBC affiliate KSDK and the *St. Louis Post*. You get the idea."

"I get it," said Maci interrupting. "You want me to relive the worst moment in my career over and over and over. Does Meacham think they'll sell more CDs and downloads off my pity party?"

"In a word, yes," Max replied. "That's exactly what they think. A sympathetic fan is a buying fan. History has proven that. Look how many records Elvis sold after he died. The same with Hank Williams back in the 1950s. The same with

Buddy Holly. New York thinks hearing your story, in your own words, in face-to-face interviews will sell a boatload of product."

Maci didn't move, and her stoic demeanor emphasized her words when she finally spoke.

"I won't do it," she said, almost in a whisper.

A slight sound of a man clearing his throat was the first to pierce the silence.

"Maci, I know what happened was horrible," Max said. "But if there is one single, positive thing that could . . ."

"No!" Maci interrupted. "Here's what I think . . . I sell records because I appeal to peoples' emotions, but pity isn't one of them. I sell records based on my voice and my talent, not on my bad luck. I'm not going to be a spokesperson for tragedy. It's negative promotion. I'd look like I'm trying to make a buck off a deranged shooter—which is exactly what you're proposing."

Maci slammed her open palm down on Max's desk, and the room's silence grew to deafening levels. Max knew he was wasting his breath and his time. Over the years, he'd often argued with Maci, but had rarely won. He only got his way whenever he managed to make Maci think that his idea was her own.

But this idea wasn't hers or his.

It came from Meacham's national corporate offices not as a consideration, but as a demand. The public has a short memory, and New York was demanding that Maci launch an emotionally charged publicity tour while, in their words, there was still blood in the water. When Max finally spoke, his tone startled even himself.

"Maci, look," he breathed. "I'm just the messenger here. New York isn't *asking* me to *ask* you; they're *telling* me to *tell* you. Hotel suites have been booked in sixteen cities, a private jet has been leased, and limousines are scheduled. You've got to do this, or . . ."

"Or what, Max?" Maci shouted. "Are you going to kick me off Meacham? I've been on this label long enough to sell more than fifty million records and counting. And I didn't sell one song because some maniac shot off my ear. Do your New York bean counters know how much money I've made them?"

"Yes Maci, they know exactly how much," Max's replied emotionlessly. "And of those fifty some million records, only 450,000 were from your last two albums."

Maci glared at him, speechless.

"No one stays on top forever in this business, Maci," Max said, "and your popularity is waning. New York definitely wants to keep you on Meacham, but you've got to help this label help you."

"My career is getting cold, is that it, Max? Is that why I drew a sold-out house with people lined up outside the night I was shot? Just how do you explain those numbers?"

Staring directly into her eyes, Max could feel the gravity inside his next sentence.

"Maci," he said, slowly. "You filled that arena because two younger and hotter artists were your opening acts. Everyone in the crowd under thirty was there because of them. If they hadn't been on the bill, you *might* have filled the floor seating, and not much more."

Pausing briefly, Max looked into Maci's hurt and angry countenance. "I didn't want to tell you this, but New York was getting ready to let you go after your last tour. And then this shooting happened and, once again, you became a household word. Maybe, just maybe, your curse was your blessing in that New York is going to subsidize another album, but only if you do this interview tour."

"Really? Well let me tell you . . ."

"There's nothing for you to tell me!" Max snapped, his voice growing stiff. "You've been on probation with your slacking record sales for more than three years. You're in the music business, and the key word is 'business.' You can do this press tour, or you can walk out of Meacham today for the last time."

Maci's spirits sank quietly as Max eased back in his chair.

"I love you and I love the records we've made together," he continued. "But my hands are tied. The decision is yours. I hope you make the right choice, and that you make it now."

Like a Phoenix rising from the ashes, Max slowly stood and told the numbed gathering they were dismissed. For the first time, he realized that only he and Maci had spoken. The others' silence underscored his contention that record companies have too many people on payroll.

As the last of the Meacham employees left, Maci and her personal assistant fumbled to their feet.

"When is this tour supposed to start?" Maci said in her calmest tone of the morning.

"On Monday. Five days from now."

Defeated, the singer smiled in disbelief. "Five days? Couldn't you have made it sooner? I have nothing scheduled in the next hour."

"I'm sorry," breathed Max. "But New York wants this thing in motion while that shooting is still in people's minds," Max said.

"Yeah," Maci replied. "I guess it would be awful if we waited until I was over it."

Max said nothing.

"So when do I leave, Sunday night?"

"Yes."

"Okay. I'll be at the airport. Email me the departure time. I don't want a Lear Jet. I want something larger."

"You'll have it."

As Maci and her companion walked silently back to her car, an idea came to her, a parting shot that just might get her out of her self-pity tour.

"Go start the car," she said to her associate. "I'll be outside in a minute."

She could tell her assistant wanted further explanation, but none came.

Back inside Meacham's Nashville building, Maci could hear people talking inside open doors as she passed their offices en route to Max's. The jingling of her bracelets told her she was walking too forcefully. She assumed Max was still in his office, and presumably still alone.

Her knuckles whitened when she almost knocked, but didn't.

Instead, she heard a part of a playback of her fiery meeting with Max. He had recorded their entire dialogue. Puzzled, she listened and felt the strange irony of eavesdropping on a conversation she'd just had. Without knocking, she quietly walked away, down the hall and out the door of Meacham Records.

She knew she'd given in to Max. She knew she'd be back. But she knew nothing as to why he'd secretly recorded her spoken words.

Lester Patterson stepped back and let his gaze drift across the dizzying array of Maci Willis photographs that lined the walls and ceiling of his dreary apartment.

"It's like a museum," he said to himself. "Not even the Guinness Book of World Records has something like this."

Earlier that day, his six-year-old collection was completed as he tacked a page from *People* magazine over his last bare spot of drywall. Lester could now look into hundreds of pairs of Maci's eyes from anywhere he chose to sit, stand or lie. He felt her eyes embrace him wherever he walked beneath his leaking roof.

Whenever he stood close to a wall, he'd turn his head right to left in order to view the full panorama of Maci. Sometimes he wondered if he should've arranged the photos differently. By year, maybe, or by size. But the more he considered it, the more he believed he'd gotten everything just right.

Lester knew his accomplishment was a masterpiece. He wished the world could see it. But that would somehow make it less special. Less private. Instead, secluded inside his tattered one room apartment, he chose to keep Maci to himself.

His landlord had rules against too many nail holes. There were lots of rules, but Lester knew the only one that seemed to matter to the landlord was that his $45 a week be paid on time. Early on, Lester had figured out that the best way to keep the landlord out was to continually bring up the leaky faucets and faulty air conditioning. The landlord had no intention of fixing things, or hearing about them, so he simply stayed away.

But that wasn't quite safe enough for Lester. So, as an added measure of precaution, he secretly changed the existing locks and added two more of his own, thereby sealing the sanctuary that he'd created for his beloved Maci and himself. Somehow or someway, he just knew she'd one day visit his home and her shrine. Then, she'd want to live with him forever, the only man on earth to love her enough to tirelessly and meticulously seize pictures from an endless array of newspapers, magazines and online printouts. He was certain she'd be smitten by the effort and sacrifices to preparing this place where she already lived, even though she'd never arrived.

Often, while staring blankly at his now hallowed walls, Lester yearned to tell Maci about how his pictorial creation came to a standstill when he was banned from Fayetteville's public library after a nosy librarian noticed him slipping a copy of *Time* under his jacket. He had to take it, as it contained two pictures of Maci that he'd never seen.

"I'm not a thief!" he yelled at the librarian. "I'm a collector!"

The librarian told him he could never return. But instead of calling the police, she simply let him go, as Lester knew she would. People always made allowances for him, because he was different. He had to be, as so many doctors, and even his own mother, had said so.

Throughout childhood, he'd put up with schoolyard taunts like "Dummy," "Retard" and "Moron." But he knew he was none of those. His mother had told him. "Slow" was the word she used. He was just a little slow. And slow didn't mean bad. A slow walk, a slow day. His favorite Maci Willis songs were the slow ones. Maci understood slow, and he believed she surely understood him. He heard it in her songs. Maybe she recorded them just for him.

On quiet nights, Lester would dream of showing Maci just how brittle and delicate some of the pictures were. Those made with the library's bubble-jet printer had been smeared against the press of his kisses. Others taken from newspapers were crisp and yellow with age.

Recently, he'd added new dimensions to his exhibit by recording her television appearances on DVDs. But that turned out to be a risky venture, and nearly brought unwanted attention to his shrine when the police came.

"The DVD got stuck in the machine and it wouldn't play," he envisioned himself telling Maci. "I got upset and my neighbor said I was hysterical and he called the police. I'd never call the police on you or me, Maci. That might get in the newspapers and prevent us from living a lifetime of happiness."

"I met the police at the door and told them they couldn't come in, Maci."

"We can come inside if you'll let us," one cop said.

"But I told him you hadn't been here yet, Maci, and that I didn't want anyone to see the exhibit before you did."

"The police told me to 'keep the noise down,' and then they left," he continued explaining to the invisible celebrity. "And when they walked down the stairs, I heard one of them say, 'a retard like that living here on his own.'"

Lester had wanted to yell back to him that he wasn't a retard, but they'd just told him to hold the noise down.

"I'm not a retard," he said under his breath. "I'm just slow."

"If I were retarded, I couldn't make a place like this," he said, resuming his monologue to an imaginary Maci. "I told the police that all people get mad when their DVD players don't work."

"One of the policemen asked if I wanted to spend the night in the center at the Arkansas Institute for the Mentally Challenged. Did you see how I just said all of those big words correctly? I knew he was impressed that I could say all of them. But I didn't go with the police anywhere. But I've already told you that, Maci."

Lester drew a tired breath. He felt he shouldn't talk anymore to Maci. She wasn't present, but he knew she could still somehow hear him. He had to prepare for the night's show, and he hadn't even warmed his curling irons.

Sometimes, when rehearsing by swirling around his single room that held his bed, sink and commode, Lester grew dizzy. That must be what stage fright is like, he thought. He was sure Maci underwent the same ordeal before each of her shows too.

Perched atop an orange crate, Lester reached up and pulled the curtains apart. He then turned off every light in his apartment except the forty-watt bulb above the toilet. His home was beyond modest, and the commode set in the open, like toilets in jails. When he saved enough money, he intended to build a partition around it so Maci wouldn't be embarrassed when she used it. Construction would be easy. How hard could it be to nail a sheet of plywood upright against the walls?

"If I were retarded, I wouldn't be so self-sufficiency," he said.

After rolling up some heavy paper he'd found in a covered dumpster into a tube, he attached it to the light bulb, creating a primitive spotlight. He then turned the suspended bulb delicately, so that it would shine onto his makeshift stage. Sometimes, if he stood just right, the light would blind him.

Maci experienced the same blindness each time she was in a real spotlight on real stage. He was sure of that. He was confident the glare prevented her from seeing anyone in the audience, except those in the front rows. He too could only see a fraction of the faces that lined his walls, all of them likenesses of Maci.

"Time is getting away for us, Maci dear," Lester said, seeing the darkness outside. "It's almost eight o'clock, the time you always start your shows. I can dash these curlers and brush out my hair in no time. My dress is ready and my makeup is just like yours in *Redbook*. The show'll be ready to start in just a minute."

After rustling into his dress and wig, Lester slipped a CD of one of Maci's live concerts into the player, whose soundtrack included the shuffling of the audience's feet as people took their seats.

Standing outside the glow of the spotlight and teetering on high heels, Lester spoke in unison with the recording's announcer.

"Ladies and gentlemen, you've come here tonight to see and hear the most popular female country music star on the planet. I could recite a mountain of statistics on her countless record sales and awards. But you don't want to hear numbers, you want to hear music. So without further adieu, here's the legendary Maci Willis!!!"

Music and applause simultaneously exploded from the CD while Lester remained in the wings, tucked behind his chest of drawers. He never stepped onto his stage and into the spotlight until the applause reached its loudest point. This, Lester thought, was the instant that they got to see Maci for the very first time, like a dream coming true right before their eyes.

Slowly, he made his entrance onto the torn linoleum at the center of his rotting floor. Having repeatedly seen a television production of Maci's concert, he knew just how to prance and dance, something he never did outside his tiny room. As he attempted to sway in time to the music, his right heel broke.

"'But the show must go on!'" he heard Maci say to him.

So Lester continued, struggling to hold his balance. He felt like a pirate walking on a peg leg. Whenever his right foot dropped on his broken shoe, it thumped on the floor, throwing both his timing and his concentration off.

He'd ruined the opening. That much he knew. He wondered if Maci had ever had anything like that bad happen on stage. Fumbling his lyrics, he quickly became teary and his eyeliner began to run. Surely his audience was laughing. Worse than that, Lester knew Maci was disappointed, maybe to the point of tears, as he failed in tonight's effort to be one with her.

Distracted, he looked away from the spotlight only to notice the rolling pin that doubled as his hand-held microphone still sitting in the sink.

"Good grief," he said aloud, "I've been singing but no one could hear me?"

For a moment, Lester toyed with the idea of leaving the spotlight, grabbing his mic and saving the show. But as his foot slipped from his broken shoe, he breathed a sigh of defeat. It was too late. The night's performance was a complete disaster. He charged from the spotlight toward the CD player and abruptly flipped the power switch off.

The instant silence sent a chill through Lester, and he forcefully yanked the wig from his head.

His show for and with Maci was not worthy of her. He'd tried to make it as perfect as her and he failed, as he always did.

"I'm trying, Maci!" he yelled. "I'd give my life for you. And all you've ever asked of me is that I take yours! Why!? Don't you know that if I take your life, it would be like taking my own?"

Still wearing the long dress that hid the numerous runners in his pantyhose, Lester sobbed as he dropped onto his single mattress on the floor. He snatched his only pillow and grabbed a handful of its casing in each of his fists. Then held it over his face to stifle his cries, pressing it firmly enough to nearly suffocate himself.

The old and worn pillow tore, and feathers floated through the darkened stench. He gave an irritated swat to each feather that touched his face, and his mouth filled with the taste of his tears. His weak sobs had broken the silence, but not enough to drown the words in his head.

"Kill me," he heard Maci say again. "Kill me."

"Why would you want to tell me to do that, Maci?" he pleaded. "All I ever did was love you."

⊹─⊰ ⊱─⊹

As the late morning sunlight seeped through his burlap curtains, Lester awoke to find the broken shoe next to his pillow, a reminder of the previous night's disastrous performance.

Three failed shows in as many nights had taken their toll on him. Thankfully, there would be no more shows until Friday night; he only worked on weekends, just like Maci, unless she played Las Vegas. And there were no upcoming Vegas dates, as Lester learned from her monthly fan club newsletter. He knew that other people received her newsletter, but his copy was the only one that had a lipstick imprint on the cover. He put it there every month, on the same day it arrived in the mail. Each kiss was a different color. Lester thought of Maci and wondered if each of her kisses would be the same, or if they would be different every time.

Through half open eyes, he stared at the walls and across the floor. His wrinkled dress lay on the floorboards. He decided he'd have to hand-stitch the seam above the garment's waist that had once again unraveled. It was easy to spot, even from several feet away, as it was sewn with white thread, the only color he had when it initially split.

Like the aftermath of Maci's real shows, Lester's linoleum stage sparkled with glitter. But rather than foil confetti, this glistening was made by ice cream sprinkles he'd bought at Kroger. He liked the glitter, but wished the show had come out better.

Sitting up, he realized that he'd worn his pantyhose all night long, and that a full-blown tear had formed from his right knee to his waist. It was his only pair. The nylons had to go, or people in front rows at Friday's performance would certainly see them.

Lester rolled an inch or two off of the flat and filthy mattress and onto the floor before awkwardly rising to stand.

By early afternoon, he'd taken his last bite of sausage and pancakes. He couldn't afford to eat out often, but each Monday he went to Waffle House to celebrate the conclusion of another weekend of shows. He ate the same meal each Monday, at the same place, on the same stool.

For the rest of the week, Lester stayed at home, or took scraps of food from the kitchen at the lavish Royal Dettwiller Hotel, where he washed dishes four days a week.

Lester's boss knew about the pilfered food, which Lester warmed in a skillet set on an electric hotplate. The boss also let Lester take ice inside a plastic sack that he put inside a Styrofoam container whose scarred exterior said "Go Razorbacks." He allowed Lester to take bathroom tissue, plastic tableware and some of the soaps and toiletries from the maids' carts. Lester liked his boss, and he knew Maci would like him, too.

The Royal Dettwiller Hotel was the oldest and most luxurious hotel in all of Fayetteville. It also had the finest food; Lester knew this because he read those very words on the menus, which were updated every week. The inside changed, but "The Finest Food in Fayetteville" always stayed on the cover.

Lester was good at what he did, a master of loading and unloading authentic bone china and Waterford glassware into a commercial dishwasher and dryer several times each shift.

Sometimes, between loads, he walked through the kitchen with his index finger pointed under his name embroidered onto his cook's smock. His name was also sewn on his tall white and starched hat, which confirmed he was special, as no one but he and the head chef wore that particular type of hat.

Lester was expecting yet another predictable Monday, no different from the rest: a hot and sweating grind made tolerable by the music from the transistor radio he kept near the dishwasher. He never raised the volume and never sang along, except low and to himself whenever Maci sang.

Although they couldn't hear the music above the rumble of the dishwasher, his co-workers could tell when Maci was singing. They saw Lester's lips moving, and sometimes they applauded and complemented his voice. Once, the boss himself whistled, and Lester hadn't even known he was listening.

"You and Maci oughta go on tour," his boss said.

He wanted to tell his boss that that's exactly what they did every weekend, in a way. But he didn't.

At 4:30, Lester emptied out both the washer and dryer in anticipation of the mountain of dishes that always followed the early dinner crowd. With both machines off, he could easily hear the radio announcer, whom he normally ignored.

But two words from the announcer shook him from his daydreaming and drew him in, ". . . Maci Willis."

Lester's ears instantly perked. Against rules, he turned up the volume and stopped, as did everyone else in the kitchen who noticed the sudden spike in the radio's volume.

". . . will be interviewed by KNWA-TV's own Sharinda Montell at 3:00 p.m. this Thursday, live from the Royal Dettwiller Hotel," the disc-jockey said. "On what's been called an "Interview Tour," Maci will tell fans in Fayetteville and throughout Central Arkansas all about the recent attempt on her life. Minutes after the shooting, Maci's assailant was gunned down by a policeman only a few steps from Maci's emergency room bed. I'm sure her story will be fascinating. Time permitting, listeners can call in to speak to Maci live. Don't forget, 3 p.m. Thursday, a live interview on KNWA-TV with Sharinda Montell and special guest Maci Willis."

Lester leaned against the kitchen's damp tile wall in disbelief and slid to the floor. He wondered if he'd imagined the story, but knew it must be true when he noticed the other kitchen staff whistling to him.

"Here's your big chance, Lester!" yelled someone.

"Maybe you could sing for her!" shouted another.

"I know," said one voice louder than the others. "We'll make a special entree for her. And Lester can take the food cart to her himself."

It was too much for a sound mind, much less Lester's. Lost somewhere between shock and elation, he began to sob quietly, then wept joyfully and uncontrollably.

"You all right, man!?" someone yelled.

"That's right, you fine!" shouted someone else.

As the calamity died down, one of Lester's co-workers stepped in and began loading dishes into Lester's machine. Two more stepped up, scooped up the dirty plates, and made idle chitchat with Lester until there was nothing left to wash inside the entire kitchen.

5

In all his twenty-five years, Lester had never known a day to pass so slowly. Each second seemed to drag on, yet at the same time he worried that Maci would arrive before he could figure out what to say.

He remembered her saying in *US Weekly* magazine that honesty was the foundation of a strong relationship, and all week long he had tried to think of something honest to tell her. Admitting that he'd stolen pictures of her from the library was the best he could construe.

Blaming his slow mind, he struggled to remember a word he'd heard previously, a word for a person who took things but couldn't really help it. He knew the last part was "maniac," but couldn't recall the first. It was something like "Cleo." He then got stuck on "Cleopatra," but assumed she wasn't a thief, because she was somebody famous.

As he grew increasingly frustrated, he decided that all of his thinking was wrong. He was no stranger to days like this, but this day was special. Today he was meeting Maci.

Swilling the last drop from his well of courage, Lester returned to Fayetteville's library where the musty scent of books reminded him that he was forbidden to enter. He slipped in through the service entrance, just as he always did at work. Service entrances made him feel secure, no matter what the building.

Lester knew there were hundreds of words in the library, maybe even thousands, and he wondered if even the librarian would be smart enough to help him find the right one. Should he openly apologize for stealing pictures of Maci Willis? The librarian knew he'd taken two photographs, but there were at least a dozen others he'd pirated away. Should he apologize for those as well?

A loud voice jolted him from his thoughts.

"Lester!" the librarian behind him said sternly. "You know you can't be trusted in here!"

"I know, and I'm going to leave as soon as you tell me the word that means people who take things that don't belong to them, and they do that all the time."

"What?" Do you plan to steal again?"

"Probably, but I won't do it here."

"What? Lester, you're becoming a kleptomaniac!"

"That's it!" That's the word!" he shouted, in a room posted with 'Quite' signs. "That's the one. Can you write it down for me?"

The woman stared at Lester, not in anger, but with a look that merged frustration with compassion.

"Come with me," she said quietly

Lester knew by her tone that he, too, should speak softly, so he lowered his voice to a whisper.

"I'm going to meet Maci Willis today," he said as he followed the librarian to her desk. "I want to tell her as soon as I see her that sometimes I take things when I shouldn't. Here's why. Did you know that first impressions are the ones that last the longest? And that Maci likes honest people? Maci will know I'm honest if I tell her that I steal. I think she'll like me for that, on accounta she likes honesty."

For years, the librarian had known that Lester was locked in a world of childhood innocence and always would be, no matter his age.

"Well, if you want to be honest, you *have* to stop stealing," the librarian responded as she reached for a pen and a Post-it note.

"Well, I'm not going to steal anything today," he said. "And maybe not anymore. But I did last night. I picked flowers for Maci from your outdoor space. You know . . . that place where dogs pee and people put out cigarettes. I hope nobody ever throws a cigarette that hits a dog. Dogs won't run from cigarettes when they're in their peeing position."

A brief grimace passed over her face as she handed Lester the note. "Out you go, you kleptomaniac."

He thanked her as he glanced at the letters, and whirled away so quickly that he never saw the benevolent woman's softening stare.

⁘

Lester's day-old flowers were wilting, and not even the humid air in his work area seemed to help. He stepped back from the dishwasher's rising steam and looked toward the windows. Today washing dishes was the last thing on his mind.

He felt a little embarrassed that the cooks had to step in and do dishes during his meltdown the previous night. They were nice people, and they all declined his offer to repay them by helping them with their cooking.

"I don't like this job but I love the people who work here." Lester intended the words for himself, but the kitchen's high ceiling amplified his words. For the second time that day, he failed to notice his coworkers smiling in his behalf.

"Lester" said Leroy the meat cutter, "this here is your day, man. You cain't be takin' no wilted flowers to Ms. Maci. These here flowers done look like you peed on them."

"No I didn't, said Lester, "but a dog probably did. That's what I told the woman at the library."

Leroy shook his head. "Isn't no matter. We done went to the gift shop and the lady there gave us these here roses for you to give to Ms. Maci."

As Leroy extended an arrangement of American Beauty roses, Lester felt their softness without touching them, and thought they were more wonderfully red than a fire engine in sunshine. He could have cried, but didn't; men aren't supposed to, and he'd already done that the previous night.

As if forming a conga line, Edgar, the salad chef, approached Lester behind Leroy, gripping a wooden clothes hanger from which draped a new chef's coat. Ironed beyond perfection, its starched crispness could easily pass a military inspection. Above the chest pocket was a hand-sewn word—"Lester."

"We done got you this here new coat, and see yonder you got a new chef's hat," said Edgar, hoping Lester wasn't too overwhelmed by the coat and the stitching.

"Look here, man, you gonna take Ms. Maci whatever food she orders. And when you walk in, you be looking like you own this here hotel. Now don't you let Ms. Maci fall in love with you, thinkin' you got lots of money."

Lester's smile faded to a look of dire concern.

"She might want my money?" he asked slowly. "Or expect me to have some?"

Having spent his youth in poverty and four years in prison, Edgar was no stranger to the pained, worried look on Lester's face.

"I's just funnin' with you, man," he laughed. Lester laughed too, although he didn't know why, except that Edgar had laughed first.

Just because he was about to meet the love of his life didn't preclude Lester from washing dishes. Besides, his drifting, daydream-filled mind needed something to do, and he knew it. He went about his duties, but at a far slower pace than normal; he had no intention of breaking a sweat, not before meeting Maci.

"Turn it up!" someone yelled. "Look at the television!"

Lester and his buddies stopped as the television screen showed a live remote of Maci and two other people disembarking from a private jet. Lester stared as the wind played with Maci's hair. She smiled warmly while gently waving at the screaming fans who had gathered on the opposite side of a chain link fence.

"Look at her boobs!" said one of the busboys.

Lester's anger was instant.

"That's mean and you're a mean person for saying that!" he snapped. No one argued with him, and the kitchen grew unusually quiet as the crew watched Maci's short walk to her limousine. The camera watched the car pull out of sight, while the announcer reminded viewers that she'd be interviewing at three o'clock from her suite at Fayetteville's landmark Royal Dettwiller Hotel.

As the news program cut to a different story, all eyes in the kitchen were trained on the smitten glow that surrounded Lester. On one level, they felt sorry for him, yet at the same time envied his ability to feel the childlike excitement and elation that they'd lost long ago.

They also knew that Lester's life had been hard, and had been even when he'd lived with his mother and dad. It only grew harder when one left the other, and both left him. He could have been bitter, but wasn't. To Lester, bitter meant unsweetened tea.

But even when abandoned, Lester still was not alone. The kitchen crew was his family, or at least he loved them as such. He'd even thought about letting some of them come to one of his secret concerts with Maci, and with free admission. But he decided most people wouldn't understand, because they couldn't see and feel Maci's presence the way he could. Besides, he'd thought, his dress was soiled and worn out, and there weren't any good seats for an audience to sit in.

"Hey Lester," boomed Sam Mullins, the head chef, whose deep voice resonated above the kitchen clamor. "I made a new menu this morning. Do you know any of those guys in our public relations department?"

Lester shook his head no. He didn't know who Sam was talking about, and wasn't really sure what "public relations" meant.

Ignoring Lester's confusion, the chef said the PR people had written a letter from Lester Patterson to Ms. Willis.

"Look, here it is inside a see-though envelope," he said.

"We'll slip it out and you can sign it."

A frozen smile on his face, Lester strutted across the room with all the pride of a spring peacock. His hand began to shake ever so slightly as he placed pen to paper and carefully wrote his first and last names.

"Ooooops," he said, "I didn't write 'Love' before I wrote my name."

"No matter, Lester," Sam said softly. "I think Ms. Willis will know that."

✦ ✦

Lester never felt closer to Maci than he did during her television interview, which was occurring live just seven stories above his head. Silently wishing he had x-ray vision, he now stared into the ornate and beveled copper tile ceiling of the kitchen, wishing he could see see through it and see Maci.

He was glad she did her interview at 3:00, two hours after the kitchen's lunch rush and two hours before the dinner scurry. Entranced by the kitchen's elevated television set, Lester and the rest of the kitchen crew watched in an almost eerie silence. It reminded Lester of the library that he'd visited on his way to work.

Suddenly, the kitchen grew even quieter as Sam pulled the electrical plug from an outlet, shutting off Lester's giant dishwasher.

"It's your big day," he whispered to Lester. "No need to wash dishes right now."

Someone on television said that Maci's interview exhibited "grace under fire," and Lester had no idea what that meant. But he thought she was her special self, even when Sharinda kept asking her personal questions.

"At any point, did you think you were going to die among gunfire inside the hospital emergency room?" she asked Maci.

"That's none of your business!" Lester said, not realizing the loudness of his voice until after the words had left his mouth.

For a moment, he thought he might cry when Sharinda asked if the tragedy might compel Maci to leave show business and public life. He felt himself stiffen as he awaited his idol's reply.

"Sharinda, I've been blessed to work very hard for many years, and I've loved bringing joy to millions of wonderful fans," Maci said. "I can't disappoint all of those people just because one person tried to take my life. And as long as people want to see me, I'll do all I can to see them."

Lester applauded, hoping the others would too.

"See how she is!" he said to no one and to everyone. "Maci loves everybody! Look how kind she always is."

Once again, he'd shattered the quiet but this time he didn't care, and neither did anyone else. In that high-ceiling room, Lester applauded for Maci while a few of his friends joined in, applauding for him. At that moment, he felt sorry for anyone who wasn't named Lester Patterson.

"We've been talking today to country legend Maci Willis," said Sharinda. "This same broadcast will be replayed at eleven o'clock tonight. Maci, thank you for your heartfelt words during what has surely been a very difficult and emotional time."

"Thank you, Sharinda," said Maci. "My best to you and to all of my Arkansas fans."

The screen faded to black, then abruptly cast forth a fat man in a bow tie who was yelling about a "cream puff" of a car that could be bought for twenty-nine hundred and ninety- nine dollars today and today only. And, with every car purchased, the buyer would get one-fourth side of beef and ten chickens. Most of the crew returned to work, save for a busboy and line cook who seemed intrigued by the deal.

Lester wondered how anyone could think about cars or chickens or anything else when they'd just seen and heard the most important person in the world, or at least the most important person in his world.

But he didn't dwell on it. He'd been told that Maci would be ordering after the interview; in a matter of mere minutes, she would be calling the kitchen for room service.

"She'll order now on accounta she knows we're not busy," Lester said to himself. "She knew we were busy awhile ago watching her on television. She'll want to eat supper before she gets on the plane and goes somewhere else to talk on television tomorrow."

As the kitchen returned to it's normal scurrying and clamoring, Lester grew more nervous and impatient. Needing to take his mind off the wait, Lester ignored his boss and activated the dishwasher, then loaded up the few odd plates and glasses used by guests who'd eaten between meals.

A gigantic clock with Roman numerals hung from the north wall of the kitchen, and Lester watched as the second hand approached twelve. He still didn't know how much longer the wait would be.

Neither he nor anyone else in the kitchen spoke Lester's unspeakable fear: that Maci might not be hungry, or had possibly made arrangements elsewhere. Seeing the dwindling spirit of his employee, Sam edged lightly into Lester's work zone.

"Hey man," he said. "Let's try this one more time. You can never rehearse too much."

Without making eye contact, Lester stepped a few feet toward the shining chrome food cart that one of the busboys had hand-polished earlier that day. He pulled it from its resting place, into the main aisle of the kitchen.

"Now show me what you're going to do when you see Maci," Sam said.

Lester obediently retraced the movements he'd been adamantly rehearsing. During his trial runs, he'd actually been allowed to push the cart across the broadloom carpet of the seventh floor hallway and into the plush suite where Maci now rested. Pretending he was inside her room, he eased the cart to a slow, not abrupt, stop, just as Sam had shown him.

Then, stepping to the right, not to the left, he locked the cart's wheels into place before raising the chrome dome that covered food that wasn't there, but would be, just as soon as Maci or one of her people ordered it.

"That's good man," Sam said. "You got that down real smooth."

By 4:46 p.m., Lester had run every soiled dish and glass in the kitchen, as well as his pocket comb and change, through the washer. The television crew had loaded their van and pulled away from the hotel's circular driveway.

But there was still no word from Maci upstairs.

Growing more anxious by the minute, Lester stepped out of his work area, and began placing the dishes, glasses and silverware in their proper places. It wasn't his job, but he didn't care.

The best day of his life was beginning to feel as if it might turn into the worst. For whatever reason, Maci wasn't eating, at least not from the kitchen whose lovelorn dishwasher had planned on meeting her for days, and had fantasized about meeting her for years.

Sensing Lester's growing despair, Sam gave out a loud, single clap of his hands.

"That's enough!" Sam shouted. "If Maci won't call on us, we'll call on Maci. I want to put together a fruit plate. Everyone likes fruit, including Maci Willis, I'm sure. Also, take the cake out of the fridge so it will start to warm."

"Cake?" asked Lester.

"Yeah kid, we made a cake for you to give to Maci," Sam said. "It's says 'Love to Maci from Lester.' She'll adore it. All women love sweets. And sweet talk."

Lester beamed like a new penny glistening in a fountain. Once again, his work family had shown him how much they thought of him. Looking into the reflection of his smiling face in the cart's sparkling dome, he realized he'd never felt so happy—never.

"It's time, Lester," said Sam. "Leroy, you come along and let's get Lester on the elevator and down Maci's hallway. Who knows? Maybe she's a bride in waiting and doesn't even know it."

Lester naturally blushed, and the blush grew even deeper from his knowledge that everyone saw it. Sam realized that Lester's kind yet simple mind had probably never heard anyone else imply that any woman might be interested in him, let alone Maci Willis. While Sam felt happy for Lester's obvious joy, he began to wonder if he'd unfairly raised the hopes of Lester's childlike heart, and given him an expectation of something that might never come to pass.

Sam forced a smile. He was only trying to make Lester's difficult life a bit more fun, if only for a few minutes.

But maybe he'd tried too hard.

Sam told Leroy to hold the elevator door as he and Lester began wrestling the food cart across the deep carpet of the Royal Dettwiller's seventh-story hallway, and beneath the row of ornate lights that had hung overhead for more than a century. The two men said nothing, but Lester's glee was contagious.

"This is as far as I go, Lester," Sam said. "That's her suite. Just knock, and when someone answers, tell them you've brought culinary delights as a gift from the Royal Dettwiller. Say it. 'Culinary delights.'"

"Culinary delights,'" Lester repeated as he ran his hand over his hair. "That's something good, isn't it Sam?"

"It's a fancy way of saying really good food."

As Lester's nervousness grew, he also felt gratitude for Sam, for his efforts in making this moment happen. "I wish I had a brother, Sam," he said. "And I wish he was you."

"You do have a brother, and I am him."

"Really, I never . . ."

"Lester, you need to deliver your culinary delights."

"Okay Sam, here I go," he said, uttering *culinary delights* all the way to Maci's suite.

Sam turned back toward the elevator and motioned for Leroy to join him.

"I wish we could be flies on the wall and see Ms. Maci when she opens her fancy door," said Leroy. "But we cain't. This here is Lester's dream. We best let him enjoy it all to hisself."

Sam nodded and said nothing as the elevator doors slid shut.

Two men who'd aided, abetted and loved a challenged manboy rode downward without speaking. Their days of nurturing Lester were finished. Now, they could only see their graduate with Maci Willis through the eyes of their imaginations. On the first floor where the elevator doors again opened, the men glanced at each other twice then walked all the way back to the kitchen.

Still, they didn't speak.

The barely audible squeaking of the cart's errant wheel came to a stop as Lester arrived at the door that separated him from the love of his slow, humble life. Glancing into the chrome covering the cake and fruit, Lester licked each of his palms and pulled them hard across his hair. Without hesitation, he knocked on the door of the high-priced suite that would be Maci's home for a few hours.

He didn't have time to become uneasy, as someone opened the door while he was still knocking. He assumed the man was a bodyguard who protected Maci, or maybe someone with a record company. For a second, he thought about thanking him for taking care of her, but decided to save his words for Maci.

"May I help you?" said the man wearing a suit and necktie, attire Lester had never worn.

"Yes sir," said Lester, who visibly squirmed at his shaking voice. "My name is Lester and I've brought koolnurries from the Royal Dettwiller to Ms. Maci."

"Uh . . . okay . . . I guess," said the man. "Stay right here."

As the man ducked from view, the hydraulic door closed slowly behind him, leaving Lester standing alone beside his food cart in the quiet hall. Almost instantly, the door opened again and the gentleman asked Lester to come inside. The challenged waiter took a step backwards, lowered his head, and struggled to push the cart as it transitioned from the plush hallway carpet and into the luxury suite.

"I wish Sam or Leroy were here to help," Lester said beneath his breath.

As he pushed, the cart picked up speed and he had to make a conscious effort to slow its momentum and stop it in the center of the room. Breathing short, excited breaths, he looked at the three interior doors that lined the spacious room and wondered which one Maci was behind.

"Hello," he said, to the woman reclining on the sofa in a Royal Dettwiller terry cloth robe. White cream was smeared across her cheeks and forehead, and her eyes were made to look as large as eggs by her thick-as-soda-bottle eyeglasses. He'd never seen such flaming red hair, flat and matted, obviously from having been pressed beneath the blonde wig that lay crumpled on the couch's arm.

A half empty glass of wine sat on the coffee table, next to a half empty bottle.

"I brung these koolnurries from the kitchen 'cause they were made special for Maci Willis," explained Lester. "Should I take them to whatever door she's behind? I know all of her songs and everything about her."

"You know her, but you don't know how she looks?" said the woman with an irritated tone. "I'm Maci Willis!"

"You?" he said, slightly smiling. "Are you funnin' me?"

"You'll think 'funnin,'" she breathed, shaking her head and sitting upright. "Alright. Just leave the cart and go."

Lester was overwhelmingly confused, as if he were standing at a fork in the road not knowing which way to go. He squinted and stared hard at the woman.

"You can't be Maci Willis, because Maci likes me," he said. "She and I are . . .

"What the hell?" shouted Maci.

Lester stopped. Her voice sounded like Maci's but he was shocked that she would cuss.

"Jim!" barked Maci to her road manager. "Go to the kitchen or front desk and tell them not to send anymore geeks to my room. First some nut tries to shoot me in Nashville and now I've got some kook with a fruit plate. Handle this, Jim. Damn it, handle this!"

"Yes, ma'am," Jim said, but instead stepped out of the suite. Lester looked down at the carpet, then glanced at Maci.

"What are you staring at?" she asked angrily.

"What's a 'kook'?" Lester asked sheepishly.

"Look in the mirror, you idiot!" she retorted. "You're a walking-talking kook."

"No, I'm not," Lester said, his face reddening, his eyes filling with tears. "I'm 'Lester.' See, my name is sewn right here under my pocket. My friends had it sewed and they had this new coat starched so I'd look my best when I told Maci that I love her and now we're finally together."

Furious and fearful, Maci abruptly stood and pointed toward the door, splashing wine across the carpet in the process.

"Oh no," said Lester, his own volume rising. "I've got a towel on this cart. Where is it? Where is it?"

He snatched the linen towel that had covered the knife intended to cut the three-layer cake.

"JIM! JIM! He's got a knife!" Maci screamed like a banshee.

"He left," Lester said, innocently.

"Besides, I won't kill you, whoever you are, because I won't kill anyone except Maci," Lester yelled. "I won't kill her until she tells me to again. That's my surprise for her. I haven't told anyone, not anyone, because that's Maci's and my secret. And this here is just a cake knife with a big blade but I could . . ."

Maci leapt onto the top of the sofa and screamed for help.

With the divan elevating her like a stage, and hearing her voice boom, Lester suddenly realized he was talking to the *real* Maci Willis. His emotions ran haywire as he began to inhale excitedly.

"Maci!?" he yelled, struggling to be louder than Maci. "It is you! You told me to kill you and now you're acting up because I will. Do you know how many days my friends and me have got ready for this day? One of them shined and polished that knife. You haven't even looked at the cake. See, look," he said, and raised the cover on the personalized dessert.

"You're insane!" she screamed. "You're retarded!"

"Jim . . . anybody . . . help me!"

Her words stopped Lester like a bullet, and he stuttered toward his next words.

"D-do you want to change your mind and not die together like you said?" said Lester, choking back the tears. "Tell me, really tell me what you want me to do and I'll do it. You know, you have to know, how much I love you, and I know you love me. You had to see that in all of our shows."

The room fell silent as an ashen-faced Maci desperately plotted her next move. In a voice as low and as slow as she could muster, Maci poured her pure brown gaze directly into Lester's eyes.

"You'll do anything I ask?" she asked in a smooth, emotionless voice.

"Anything, Maci," replied a teary Lester. "You know that. And I haven't told anybody about us and what you want."

"And what do I want?" asked Maci.

"You know," said Lester, half in disbelief. "About us being together in death, so we can be together forever."

Maci's unblinking eyes held their gaze as she processed his words. After a moment of silence she resumed her slow, monotone delivery.

"I have changed my mind," she finally said, glancing at his embroidered name. "Lester, instead of me going first, I want you to go first, so you'll be there to meet me on the other side. Don't speak. Just do it. Do it right now if you love me. And when I see that you love me enough to die for me, then I'll kill myself and we can be together—forever."

"Forever?" asked Lester.

"Forever," said Maci, her eyes still locked on his.

Lester had envisioned this moment many times, but it never looked like this. And he couldn't believe it was unfolding spontaneously and today, of all days.

"But what about your fruit? And the cake?" he asked.

"Should we eat and that could be our last meal and then we'd be ready?"

"Lester," Maci said, slowly shaking her head. "We've already waited too long. Just. Do. It. Now. Then we can love each other forever. Who cares about food when we can begin eternity at this very moment?"

"I knew you loved me!" Lester said with nervous joy. "I knew you loved me! But I didn't tell anyone, and only you and I know about our nights together!"

His head swiveled as his eyes ran rampantly looking for a way to the afterlife. He'd always been told that ladies go first, but that didn't matter now. Maci had told him what she wanted, and that's what he should do. And as frightened as he felt, he knew Maci was right; they'd waited long enough.

His stared blankly through the suite's towering window, which stretched from floor to the ceiling. He saw the awe on his own face in the solid pane's reflection. He realized he'd never seen glass that tall. Then he realized that it was more than a window; it was a door that he and Maci would use to leave this world together.

"Follow me, Maci," Lester said, almost giddy.

Pushing with all his might, Lester thrust the cart into motion as he gripped its smooth, shining handle. Later, investigators would measure the length of imprints on the carpet, and estimate that the cart was rolling at 3 miles per hour when it crashed into the plate-glass window. Lester's hands were still clutched on the handle, in a literal death grip, when it hit the ground.

After the seven story plummet, virtually all of Lester's blood had seeped from his shattered body and into the asphalt, creating a dark pool that was dotted with bits of hand-cut fruit and chunks of cake.

Lester's face was no longer distinguishable, and the cart itself was only barely recognizable. A large chunk of the cake had been thrown clear, still inscribed with the words "Love to Maci." The rest of the inscription was lost in the carnage.

Investigators surmised that Maci was loved, but they didn't know yet by whom.

I saac Thompson stared into the rearview mirror of his limousine, fidgeting with his necktie and tugging at his mustache. The look on his face was mostly one of tired and helpless irritation, the kind he always felt when forced to drive a passenger who was wealthy, rude or condescending. In his brief encounter with Maci, he'd found all three.

He'd driven her and her small entourage to the Royal Dettwiller Hotel earlier in the day in hopes that he'd get to watch her live interview. He'd seen the big cameras on TV, and in magazines, but he'd never seen them in real life.

He didn't get to see them that day either.

Ms. Maci, as he was told to call her, ordered him to stay in the car where he watched her on a tiny screen above the backseat. He'd lived in life's backseat all of his life, he thought. This was just another day.

Isaac held his post for four hours without a food or restroom break. In another hour or so, Maci's group would arrive for their return trip to the airport. He'd probably never see Maci Willis again. And, he decided, he'd also never listen to her music again.

He tried not to dwell on her rudeness, but for some reason he couldn't get past her ordering him to unload her baggage onto a cart, a job that belonged to the bellhops. But when she found that none were waiting to meet her, she told Isaac to take care of things. Isaac knew that some rich people get mad when common folks aren't at their beck and call, but Maci had a huffiness about her that grated on him.

"Why is a man your age still driving a limousine?" Maci had asked, during the trip from the airport to the Royal Dettwiller. "You must be at least seventy. After that many years, surely you could have made something better out of yourself."

Stunned, he looked into the rearview mirror, only to see her smirking. He didn't see anything wrong with being a driver, but passengers like Maci made him wish he'd chosen a different path. He therefore turned the mirror to the faces of the other passengers, who were staring out the windows, as if they might escape their embarrassment by pretending they hadn't heard.

Maci then demanded that Isaac turn the thermostat down to a chilly sixty-five degrees. That was too cool for comfort for him, and he guessed it would be for the other passengers as well. Not that it mattered; Maci complained that the heat had moistened the skin behind her knees. She said she didn't feel fresh, and not feeling fresh would surely hamper her interview.

"I probably won't shine like I usually do," she had said to Isaac, and then waited for his reply that never came.

He just shook his head.

"I can't wait to get away from this witch," he said as he continued his wait, sitting alone inside his limousine outside the hotel.

Without warning, a loud pounding emanated from the trunk. Isaac turned his eyes to his rearview mirror, but saw no one in its frame. The pounding grew louder, and he realized that it was coming from near the bottom of the chassis and inching toward him. Drawing closer, the open-palm slaps on the side of the car shook Isaac to a state of alarm.

"Open the door! Open the door! For God's sake open the door!" gasped a voice in a muffled scream.

Instinctively, Isaac pressed the power lock to ensure his safety. Peering into his side mirror, he felt himself gulp at the sight of a woman in a bathrobe crouched close to the ground, as if using the vehicle as a shield.

The woman, now on hands and knees, began crawling toward the driver's door. Without thought, he leaned against his seatbelt and stretched toward the glove box where his pistol was hidden beneath his manual and loose papers. As he pulled it from the dash, his thumb found the hammer and he prepared to cock it.

He peeked again into his side mirror and saw only two bare feet, their heels pointed toward the back of the vehicle. Whoever it was, she was directly beneath his window. He raised himself until his head touched the car's ceiling.

Like the hand of a drowning swimmer emerging from the water's surface, a hand shot up and slapped against his window. He softly cocked his pistol and waited for the redheaded stranger to rise into the opening of its barrel.

He knew he had to protect himself, but had no wish to go to jail. From his vantage point, it seemed to be a homeless woman, or a mental patient. Thinking quickly, he decided it was smarter to warn rather than shoot.

"Get away from the car," he yelled through the raised glass. "This car is private property!" Pointing the gun away from the window, he slowly pulled its trigger and eased the hammer back into place.

The oily red hair moved up to his window, and Isaac found himself face to face with a disheveled woman who was shouting his name and unintentionally spraying spittle on the window's gleaming glass.

"How do you know me?" he yelled.

"It's me . . . Maci . . ."

Taken aback, he looked carefully at the smudged face. There was no hint of the primped and precisely made-up blonde he'd seen earlier. But it was, indeed, Maci Willis.

His pistol still un-cocked and now nestled by his leg, Isaac slowly opened the driver's door while gripping the armrest.

The door slightly ajar, Maci flung it open, dove across Isaac's lap, and scurried to the passenger seat like a distressed dog who'd been rescued. As she sat up and reached for the seatbelt, her robe opened to reveal her panties and nothing else.

"Get me out of here!" she screamed. "Go . . . go . . . get moving!" In the last few seconds, Maci's voice had gone from crazed to urgent. Isaac knew there was trouble, but was clueless as to it's nature. Without thinking, he began dialing 9-1-1.

"Don't do that!" she demanded. "Just get me out of here! My record company paid you, I'm your boss and now, damn it, drive!"

His senses clouded by confusion, Isaac simply did his job. He started the car. Looking again to make certain it was Maci, he absorbed her slovenly, unkempt appearance. For the moment, he no longer felt she was a peg above him. The absence of shoes and clothes and the missing blonde hair that everyone knew had yielded to semi-nudity, smeared mascara and hysteria. He felt superior; he'd never be seen in public looking like that.

As she began to settle and regain her composure, her voice returned to the tone that Isaac had heard earlier that morning in his car, and an hour before on his television set.

"Where are we going?" Isaac asked.

"How much money have you got?" Maci said after a few seconds of silence.

"What?"

"Money! I need money. How much have you got?"

"Well, uh, let me see," he replied, contorting himself in his seat as he withdrew his billfold.

"Don't drive while you're counting." She said nothing as she grabbed Isaac's wallet and began to count. Seventy-three dollars.

"This Visa, is it your only credit card?"

"Yes," he said, now visibly perturbed. "That's none of your business."

Abruptly, she raised her head.

"Look, you know I'm good for a thousand times anything we can charge on this" she said. "What's your credit limit?"

"Well . . . I guess about four hundred dollars."

"Four hundred?" she said in disbelief. "What's the point of having . . ." her voice trailed off in exasperation. She tried to envision being that poor. She knew she had been at one point, but she had buried those memories as best she could long ago.

His eyes forcibly fixed on the road, Isaac knew someone as self-centered as Maci had no idea she'd just insulted him again. He also knew she wouldn't care that she had.

Maci thought for a few seconds. "Okay, Isaac, here's the deal. I got into a scrape back at the hotel, and I ran, and no one saw me. And, even if they had, they wouldn't have recognized me like this. Any more than they'd recognize Johnny Cash without his black clothes."

"So where are we going?" asked Isaac. At the end of the day, at then end of any day, that's what it always came down to for a chauffeur.

"I want you to call your dispatcher or whoever you report to," she directed. "Tell him after taking me to the airport;

you picked up a guy who's offered to pay you three thousand dollars to drive to Chicago. Be sure he thinks your passenger is a man. When we get to Nashville, I'll have an address where you can take me. I have cash there. I'll give you the three thousand, and another two thousand that your boss doesn't need to know about."

"Look," said Isaac, "I ain't asking why you're in this shape. Whatever it is, it's your business. But I can't go running from Fayetteville to Nashville . . ."

"Yes, you can!" she yelled, cutting him off. "And you will! How many times do you get a two thousand dollar tip? You'd walk away from that just because you're afraid of breaking a rule? Now I know why you'll always be stuck behind the wheel, driving around people who aren't too scared to take a little risk."

An uneasy silence filled the limousine, and several seconds went by before Isaac broke it.

"Okay," he breathed. "Nashville."

"Isaac," she intentionally pronounced distinctively. "For the next few hours, you'll be the only person in the world who'll know the whereabouts of Maci Willis? And I want to keep it that way. Because the entire world will be looking for me, if they haven't already started."

Isaac nodded. "Only now the tip is five thousand."

"Five?" Maci asked, raising an eyebrow.

"Three thousand buys the drive, and five thousand buys the silence," he said. "After all, I don't want to be stuck behind this wheel forever, no matter what you think about me."

Macy shook her head and smiled to herself, half because Isaac had actually stood up for himself, and half because she would've readily paid him ten times that.

Later, as twilight faded to dusk, he noticed the glint in Maci's eyes when she occasionally glanced his way. There was something about it, he thought, that's for sure. He could feel her eyes slip right through him. Maybe that's what people meant when they talked about star quality, he thought. Or having "it."

"This is going to be something I'll always remember, isn't it?" he finally said.

"That makes two of us," Maci said. "Just take me to Nashville, and you can take your time driving back. Take the money and have some fun along the way."

She had mentally seduced her driver. She'd realized that the moment he picked up his cell phone and called his dispatcher. Afterwards, she asked if she could borrow his phone for a moment, then flung it out the window of the moving car.

A squint of anger appeared on his face at the thought of losing his phone. But it vanished when Maci smiled and said, "Now it's just you and me, Isaac," in a warm and friendly voice.

That's when she knew she had him. That he could be trusted. And she could imagine how flattered and surprised he'd be when she showed her trust by closing her eyes and drifting off to asleep.

Looking into the mirror, Isaac saw the tired look in his eyes. Somehow, the look was nowhere near as tired as he felt. He shuffled in his seat as he entered stalled, bumper-to-bumper traffic of Nashville's morning rush hour. Before leaving Fayetteville, Maci had made him drive by his house to exchange the limousine for his car, a non-descript eight-year-old Mercury that drew no attention. She laughed to herself when she and Isaac pulled away from his wood frame dwelling, a one-bedroom bungalow that wasn't nearly as valuable as the limousine hidden in its garage.

He'd counted six stops for coffee that Maci had demanded, claiming the caffeine sharpened her wits. He only knew that it soured her breath.

As if trying to find details of an approaching tornado, Maci had incessantly tuned the car's radio dial from one station to the next, in search of any update on her or her incident at the hotel.

In those moments when the nervousness subsided, she felt an occasional rush of adrenaline, and she pictured herself as a fugitive on the lam like Bonnie Parker. But the fantasy was quickly reeled back to reality when she looked at her seventy-something driver, who was a far shot from Clyde Barrow.

The details on the radio were sketchy. The press offered conflicting theories that Maci had been kidnapped, or had committed some crime, or was fleeing out of fear for her life. But they all painted Maci as someone who was in a fragile, if not crazed, state of mind, still recuperating from the memories of a gunman who had tried to kill her, but instead died before her eyes.

During the wee hours, the late-night commentators had named Maci the elusive "Heartthrob of the Heartland," and another dubbed her the "Missing Minstrel." Maci didn't like either moniker, and felt the lack of creativity perfectly illustrated why those announcers were working the overnight broadcast, instead of prime time.

Each time that an announcer intimated that she might be involved in some form of wrongdoing, Maci quickly switched the dial.

"Where's there's smoke, there's fire," said one faraway radio announcer. "But with Maci, forget the smoke. Her life has suddenly become an out-of-control wildfire. We can see the smoke, but no one knows where the source is."

Maci liked the imagery, and told herself there might be a song somewhere in that line.

Within the dimness of the car's interior, Isaac saw Maci's ever-so-slight smile each time the radio dial landed on a story about her.

She, in turn, didn't notice Isaac, or detect his growing concern that he may be involved in some sort of crime.

Given the absence of facts, most of the transmitted stories raised more questions than they answered. Mostly, the weary driver wanted to know just what "scrape" Maci had encountered at the Royal Dettwiller.

And so they traveled, the famous fugitive and her fatigued and unwitting accomplice. Maci figured that he was mentally preparing alibis and decided that she should interject before he came up with something too far fetched.

"Look, Isaac," she said. "If you're worried about any trouble, don't be. I don't think I'm in trouble, and you're certainly not. Just tell people that I wanted to get away, and I offered you a lot of money to drive me."

"But what about throwing my phone away?" he said.

Maci shrugged. "Just tell them I'm a bitch," she said. "Even my manager will back you up on that one."

Isaac had to agree. His thoughts turned back to his unregistered gun, and whether he should toss it out as well. If things got really bad, he could say that it was Maci's, and that she'd forced him to drive.

As the sun rose higher, he was growing uneasy about the money and how such a large amount might look to police. The thousands of dollars began to seem less like a payday, and more like evidence. A good district attorney might build some type of case against him, he thought.

"You know, in show business, there's no such thing as bad publicity," she said, her eyes locked on the white lines of the interstate. "This whole thing could turn into a great movie!"

For Isaac, Maci's way of thinking was too surreal and too self-absorbed. She seemed less concerned about the reality of her situation, and more concerned about what she could get from it.

Had he not seen it with his own eyes, he would not have believed that a person could swing from hysteria to cold calculation in one short road trip. He'd heard of drastic mood swings, and had even encountered one or two, but this went far beyond that.

"This don't feel right," he said under his breath.

"Were you talking?" Maci said, turning toward him.

"No. I guess I was just thinking out loud." He paused a moment, then added, "We're well inside the Nashville city limits, and you haven't told me where I'm supposed to take you."

"I'll let you know where to turn."

"I know you think people don't recognize you," he said, "but people are going to notice a barefoot woman in a bathrobe. And if the police see you, they're gonna want to talk to you."

Her face became blank. She'd covered the details, but had ignored this particular part of the big picture.

"I suppose," she said pensively. "I don't guess I'd be invisible while dressed like this. What are we going to do?"

"Well, Ms. Maci, I don't know."

"Hmmmph" she breathed impatiently. "I don't know why I'd I expect otherwise. I'm thinking about all of the maniacs that want to kill me. Why would I expect a man who's charging me eight thousand dollars to use his head and figure out how to get me safely where I'm going?"

"Well . . ."

"No 'well,'" she yelled. "I'm sure you're just thinking about how you're going to spend your money. Who cares what happens to Maci, right?"

"Well, I . . ."

"Never mind, I'll handle this, the way I handle everything. You're so slow you should be the president of a record company."

"How you do that, Ms. Maci? How you go from quiet to mean in one second, and why do you want to hurt the only person on earth who's helping you right now? It ain't fair."

She hesitated for a moment, astonished that someone of Isaac's lowly status would talk back. As if seeing an apparition, she caught a momentarily glimpse of her selfishness, and didn't like the view.

"I don't have to be fair and I don't have to be nice!" she deflected. "I'm Maci Willis. You might not like her, but I don't like Maci either, and that's fine. I have so many people feeding off me, that it's perfectly okay if I try to find people I can feed off of in return, and who can make me happy. And anyone who doesn't understand that can get out of my life. And if nobody's there, that's okay. I don't need anybody, let alone a failed limousine driver."

Again, Isaac felt his humiliation turning to outrage, but kept it in check.

"How do people who have everything manage to turn out so angry and mean?" he asked.

"That question doesn't deserve an answer," came the instant reply.

That was fine with Isaac; he hadn't expected one.

She was totally disarmed by his near silence, not because he had nothing to say, but because he no longer cared. She was a spoiled and hollow human being and she knew it. Her irritation lay in the fact that she'd let Isaac know, too. And now he'd joined the ranks of those who had encountered the real Maci, and simply didn't care either.

"I've got to pee," she said abruptly. "With all of the coffee I've had, you should know that. There's a Truckstop about a mile ahead. Just pull in there."

"How you going to get out in your housecoat and bare feet and go to the ladies' room without being seen?" he asked.

"I'm not getting out of the car," she insisted. "You go inside, buy a half-gallon of milk in a cardboard container, empty it out, and bring it back to me. I'll do my business right here in the car."

Isaac realized that she was speaking without thinking, that she was driven by her impulses. But urinating in his car took the depth of her insults to a new low. Maci sensed his anger and tried to ease the tension.

"You're right, Isaac," she said, as if listening for what she might say next. "I can't risk getting out in daylight, dressed like this. I just need to get through the next twenty minutes, and we'll be out of here soon. Just hang in there a little longer. It'll all be over then."

In all the years he'd spent mastering the music business, Max Abernathy thought he'd endured every brand of neurotic personalities and crises that the industry generated. He was more than an esteemed executive; he was also a "fixer," someone who had the skills to clean up the messes left behind by his stable of luminaries, who lived under the unrelenting scrutiny of a ravenous press corps.

Several of his acts had committed crimes or misdemeanors worthy of a night or two in jail. But none had ever gone to prison, and not because they weren't guilty. Max knew just who to call, who to beg, who to schmooze and who to pay.

He'd once managed an adulterous star who was literally caught in the act by his wife. Standing behind her, Max saw the naked truth himself.

Crushed by embarrassment, the wife might have otherwise swallowed the emotions brewing inside her and convinced herself that it meant nothing. But there was a difference between private shame and public humiliation, and the seventy-six people at the video shoot prohibited her denial of her two-timing spouse. Her husband was a serial cheater, and she and the entire crew knew it. She also knew that in show business, gossip travels faster than electricity. By sundown, her invasion of this tryst would be the talk of every restaurant and bar in Nashville's Gulch and other trendy neighborhoods. Of this, she had no doubt.

Max worried not only about the press, but also about the commercial, speaking and endorsement deals that a scandal would undo for his celebrity singer/actor.

Responding entirely by reflex, Max told the distraught wife that the adulterer she saw was actually a stand-in actor for her husband's video.

"You and I saw the stand-in from thirty yards away," he continued. "That's far enough for you or me to mistake him for your old man."

"It's hard to believe, I know," Max said in front of the crew. "He's a ringer for your husband. Come back and see for yourself."

"You're a liar and so is the bum I married!" screamed the devastated wife, while furiously waving her purse. Max knew the bag probably held a legally concealed weapon, like half of the purses on Music Row. He didn't want anyone, including him, to be killed by a jealous and crazed wife. Most of all, he didn't want his star to be killed, not after he'd persuaded Meacham to spend $500,000 on his latest music video.

As the wife stormed off, Max was close in tow, replacing his logic with synthetic sympathy. Stepping closely behind her, he began a lament about the pressures that engulf celebrity wives.

He knew he was finally tugging her heartstrings when he saw her hardened eyes start to soften.

"People have no idea how much pain celebrity wives must endure," he said, his phony tone still approximating compassion. "They say the road is tough on performers, but it's twice as hard on their families. The wives are left at home running a household and telling the kids that Daddy loves them, even though he's constantly gone."

Gently, he placed the woman's hand in his, moving so smoothly that it did not seem out of place.

"The big shot star gets all of the applause, and the wife gets the all the silence. The star spends the best part of his life taking bows and earning money. The poor little wife spends the best years of her life waiting for him. It just isn't fair, and a lot of wives break down. That's why I have always admired you. Because what really makes a success in show business is a strong wife. If strong wives were measured by one to ten, you'd be an eleven. I know, you're hurting, and I can feel it. I can feel your anguish. Imagine how many marriages would be saved if more women were like you."

"People don't know, they just don't know," she said, finally breaking down. "I try my best, but sometime it's just so hard to stay with him."

Max held her gently as he tried to mentally tabulate what damage a divorce would do to any pending endorsement deals.

"I know you try," said Max. "Look, let's get out of here. Let's have a cup of coffee and talk a bit."

As the two left the video shoot, the wife realized Max had tried to gallantly allow her to save face, by again swearing to the crowd that it was her husband's double they had seen.

Few people knew exactly what transpired that evening. Some say Max had a profound heart to heart with the wounded wife. Some say that the two engaged in a few hours of revenge sex, while others say that money changed hands, or that the wife was given the deed to a Gulf Coast condo, off the books.

All anyone knew for sure was that the wife was back at home the next day, answering calls from the press.

"Yes," she said with a giggle. "For a moment my head shot through the roof, before I realized it was his double. When you see the video, I can guarantee you won't be able to tell him from my husband."

Max had done his job. Once again, a wife could truthfully tell a lie, and her high-profile marriage, the endorsement deals, and most of the community property would remain intact.

But that was twenty years and seventy-five pounds ago. Today, anyone would laugh at the idea of having revenge sex with Max. He was different now. Everything was different now. The business was less freewheeling and more high-strung, and held more pressure than Max's thirty-one years on Music Row had prepared him for. Emotionally spent, he lacked the mental resources he once had, and he knew it. His associates knew it, too.

⁜ ⁜

As an entertainment news junkie, Max could scarcely tear himself away from the non-stop coverage of the missing Maci. On the three broadcast and four cable news channels that played silently on the flat screens in his executive conference room, Maci was simultaneously nowhere and everywhere in old videos.

Max was astonished at the number of texts and voicemails on his iPhone, a private number that most people didn't have. He was glad he'd turned off its ringer. He skimmed a sampling of the messages, and virtually all of them demanded to know the location of Maci Willis, and right now. For the first time in all the years he'd known Maci, he truly didn't know her whereabouts.

Together, they'd launched a multi-million dollar career, but at the moment he didn't have ten cents' worth of information as to her location. All he could do was listen and wait, as breaking news reports claimed that Maci had been an eyewitness to a suicide in her hotel room. But the reporters stopped short of sympathy, saying that Maci had fled the scene without calling authorities or alerting medical personnel.

Max could ignore phone calls from the press, but not from his bosses in New York. They demanded that he find Maci, and called every twenty minutes to check his progress.

"You and that out of control hillbilly are making this label look like an asylum," said Walter Robbins, president of Meacham. "Get that airhead under control, and get her in front of the cameras. I don't care what happened. You just make sure that everyone feels sorry enough for Maci to go out and buy her albums."

Max was on sensory overload and could barely process what Robbins said. He mostly remembered how the big shot's voice rose louder with every sentence.

He tried to gather his thoughts as he began to wade through his growing list of unopened emails.

"Circumstances surrounding the death of Lester Patterson are consistent with suicide," said an email from Agent Richard Shale, chief agent for the Nashville office of the FBI. An identical letter was hand-delivered to Max by someone who left the missive at the front desk.

"Suicide," the memo continued, "is a felony. Usually, suicide is an unenforceable law, because of the perpetrator's disposition. But conspiracy to commit suicide is enforceable. Because she left the scene with no explanation, Maci Willis is a person of interest in a conspiracy in Lester Patterson's suicide. If you have any knowledge of the whereabouts of Maci Willis, we ask that you contact our office at once."

Max had read the communication multiple times, but didn't respond. He knew the agent wanted updates, and he had none. Neither did anyone else at Meacham, or so they claimed during an emergency staff meeting.

Max and his office had told the FBI all they knew, which was virtually nothing, just as Max had emphasized when agents came to his house before sunrise.

Max noticed his normally steady hands trembling when agents walked into his office for the second time that day. If he didn't produce information on Maci soon, Shale would ask the U.S. District Attorney to issue a warrant for Max's arrest for harboring a fugitive from justice. If that failed, the agent could surely procure an arrest warrant for conspiracy, he'd earlier threatened.

"The federal attorney might not file charges," Shale explained, in an earlier telephone conversation with Max. "Whether he does or does not, the warrant will still be public record. I'll personally make sure all of those reporters get a copy."

"I haven't done anything," proclaimed Max.

"I've heard that before," Shale retorted. "I don't know if this is a crime or a publicity stunt, but I'm not buying that she just disappeared.

"Look, I don't know where she is."

"If you think you're going to sell records off of this, think again," Shale huffed. "Just picture the headline: 'Record tycoon protects singer connected to a mentally retarded fan's suicide.' That won't play too well. Best-case scenario, the charge won't stick and you'll lose your career. Worst case, the charge will stick and we'll let the judge decide. What's it going to be?"

Max shook his head. He didn't want to go to prison, and he didn't want his legacy to be disgraced by a crime he didn't commit.

"Look, I tried to find Maci," he said. "She's not answering calls. But when I find her, you'll know the very next minute. I gave you guys her cell number, thinking you find her by locating her phone. But one of you said the device was found on the ground inside the Fayetteville city limits. What else can I do?"

Shale left Max's office with a look that announced he'd soon be back. The doors to his office slid shut, muffling the noise of the reporters.

His office now locked, Max let his bloodshot eyes scan the walls that showcased more than four dozen gold and platinum records. Slowly swiveling in his executive chair, he tried to shut out the sounds of the reporters and collect his thoughts.

As Max stared blankly across the room, a courier slid yet another pink "call back" message under his door. Max didn't care enough to stand up and walk the twenty feet to read its contents. There were at least a dozen identical slips of paper impaled on his desk. He didn't care about them, either.

"*USA Today*," he said to no one. "*New York Times, CBS Evening News, Tennessean* . . . can't live with 'em, can't live without 'em."

One by one, he crumpled the messages and tossed each paper ball out onto his seemingly ankle-deep carpet. The man who'd held the press on a leash for years now had no clue as to how to hold them off.

"This must be how a nervous breakdown feels!" he yelled, slamming his fists down on his desk.

Someone pounded on his door.

"Max, are you all right?" shouted a concerned voice. "Let us in Max! Let us in!"

"Get away!" he yelled back. "I'm okay."

"Are you sure?"

"What part of 'go away' don't you understand?"

For an instant, Max's torso jerked, as if he were suffering a minor seizure. As he silenced himself and breathed deeply, a bell signaled the arrival of another text message. At first irritated by the interruption, he suddenly realized that he'd silenced his phone earlier that day.

Then, a ringtone chimed through the air.

"What the . . ." he looked about, realizing that the sound of the bell had come not from his vest pocket, but from somewhere behind him.

Mystified, Max began easing toward the phantom ring that seemed to originate from inside his desk. Listening closely, he followed the sound to a bottom drawer of his seamless desk. Like a child looking for a spider, Max slowly opened the rarely used drawer, where he kept trinkets given to him by fans and vocalists—the type of useless gifts bordering on junk that he sent on special occasions to people who weren't special to him at all.

He started to close the tiny museum when the invisible phone rang once again. This time, he let his hand follow the sound to its source. His fingers landed on the frame of a small flip phone. The phone rang again before Max could raise it.

Whoever called had blocked their name and number. There was no hint of the identity on the phone, but the message told all.

"I have a marking shaped like a triangle behind my right knee. Text back if you can talk."

Few people other than Max had known about Maci Willis' birthmark; he'd made her hide it during the photo shoot for one of her first albums.

His hands shaking uncontrollably, Max struggled to hit the letters on the small, TracFone.

"I'm alone," he texted.

The next thirty seconds seemed like hours. Max nearly dropped the phone when it rang.

"I planted that TracFone you're holding, and others just like it, throughout your office," said a distant and raspy voice. "I'm on a TracFone too, and as soon as I get off, I'll give it a bath. So don't think you or the law will find me through GPS."

"Maci?!" Max exclaimed. "Are you okay? Where are you? Do you have any idea how many people are looking for you, and the trouble you're in?"

"You're asking questions, you're not letting me talk," she replied. Max, someone tried to kill me again, this time in my own hotel room. Now Max, you need to think long and hard about how you're going to save your career and my life. I don't know what's going on, but at this point I don't trust anyone. Don't try to find me; I'll contact you when I think it's safe."

"Maci!? Maci!" He raised his voice loud enough to be heard in the hallway. Instantly a series of knocks rapped on his door as he looked down to see yet another text.

"Throw away this TracFone," it read. "Remember, I put others in your office. I'll call again soon."

Max knew nothing more than he knew five minutes ago, except that Maci Willis was alive.

＊＊＊

Certain that they'd heard Max call out for Maci, some of the more enterprising reporters decided they needed to find a passkey to his office.

"Where's the janitor?" one of them asked.

"Probably outside smoking a joint," laughed one of the office admins.

The jab, like most good jokes, was rooted in truth.

"Hey, Carl. Looks like they smoked you out," said a Meacham staffer, when the janitor was escorted from outdoors into Max's office.

Without being asked, the half-paranoid custodian explained that he had stepped outside simply to catch his breath.

"I don't want anyone to think I was outside smoking weed," he said.

"Oh, no one *thinks* that," joked one of his coworkers. "If you're going to get high under the parking lot's only tree, you should at least go on the other side of the tree so we can't see you."

Everyone laughed, except the janitor, who'd been terrified from the moment authorities invaded Meacham. He had an outstanding warrant for misdemeanor possession, and he was sure the eyes of the press would soon be focused on him.

"Look, I can explain," pled the janitor.

"No need, Carl," someone chimed in. "You have the right to remain silent, you know."

"We don't care if you smoke a joint or if you grow the stuff in the attic," said one of Meacham's songwriters. "We just want you to use your pass key to open Max's door. He's in distress inside his office. And, if you are holding—did you bring enough for the rest of us?"

"Honest, all I have is this joint I found on the ground," said Carl as he slipped it from his shirt pocket."

"That'll do," said the writer.

The wearisome custodian slowly handed over the illegal cigarette, saddened to be so easily relieved of the evidence.

As Carl slid the pass key into the slot and opened the door, a tidal wave of bodies pushed in like a mob fleeing a burning building. The beleaguered Max looked like the proverbial deer in the headlights, but unlike the deer he had nowhere to run.

"Where's the phone you were just talking on?" demanded FBI agent Dewayne "Dual" Hathaway, who had been waiting among the reporters and Meacham staffers. His nickname had been formed years ago. His investigations almost always produced enough evidence to arrest and convict a suspect in only one apprehension. He was a flesh and blood example of efficient, dual justice.

"I heard it ring, and so did everyone else who had their ear against your door," continued the decorated agent. "I need to see that phone."

Max looked down at his feet, then raised his head and stared seemingly at nothing at all.

"Max, you're already in enough trouble. You don't want to be arrested for interfering with a federal investigation. Give me the phone."

As sheepish as a schoolboy caught red handed, Max pulled the cell phone from his jacket's inside pocket. He was raising his arm when Hathaway jerked the phone from his grasp.

"Now, tell me where she is? I want to know and I want to know now!" the agent demanded.

"I don't know where she is. If I did, she wouldn't be texting that she's going to call me soon. Let's not kid each other. You don't have a thing on me. If you did, I'd be in handcuffs right now. And if you were going to arrest me, you wouldn't have let all of these employees stand around in my office. Do you always gather audiences before each of your busts?"

"Prisons are filled with people who thought they couldn't be arrested," countered Hathaway.

"Well I notice that I'm still here."

"Not for long," Hathaway replied. "Max Abernathy, you're under arrest for interfering with a federal investigation, for conspiring to house a suspected felon and for conspiracy regarding an assisted suicide. You have the right to remain silent. Anything you say can and will be used against you in a court of law. If you cannot afford a lawyer, one will be appointed for you!"

"STOP! Just STOP," said Max. "What do you want from me?! I'm not doing much to help you because I can't. But if I'm behind bars, I can't do anything for you men at all!"

"Everybody out!" yelled the angry agent. "Everybody out right now!"

Max thought that Hathaway's evacuation of the room meant the agent had been bluffing about the Miranda Rights, and that the agent thought he could pressure whatever information was there to be had. Hathaway's softening demeanor also told Max that he finally believed that Max was not aware of Maci's whereabouts.

Small talk in low tones spread among the departing workers, while two cops, a deputy sheriff, and two FBI agents remained inside Max's office. No one seemed to want to speak first.

Moments later, an FBI specialist took the TracFone to a government van filled with investigative equipment parked behind Meacham. A quick examination showed that the TracFone's GPS was useless; that particular service hadn't been activated. He'd traced the phone's serial number and its purchase to a Wal-Mart in a small town 135 miles west of Nashville. As expected, the buyer couldn't be identified.

"We won't find Maci through a disposable cell phone," said Hathaway. "I guess she's smart enough to know that much."

At that moment, a single electronic tone bled through the virtual silence, announcing to the entire room that another text message had been sent. Out of habit, some of the officers checked their own cell phones, but it belonged to no one present.

"It isn't me! Max yelled at Hathaway. "You've got *my* phone in your hand."

The tiny ring sounded again, and everyone knew the sender was issuing more texts.

The two agents took a few steps in the direction of the sound's origin, while a Metro policeman grabbed Max's chair. He pushed it to the office's towering drapes and stepped in its seat to reach behind a massive drapery rod. As if handling a baby, the cop carefully reached over the rod, where he found another TracFone.

"Go to Max's door," said the text, read aloud by the cop still teetering in Max's leather chair. The message had been sent more than once.

Still flustered, Hathaway said nothing when a deputy sheriff opened Max's heavy door into the hallway, as if he'd launched his own investigation. The deputy saw no one, and then took a step into the hallway to clearly look both ways. Then, stepping back to close the door, he noticed a colorful, designer box on the floor. He picked up the container by its bow and carried it to Hathaway.

"Do you know what this is?" Hathaway asked Max, who instantly shook his head.

Slowly, the agent raised the octagonal box and removed its delicate lid to reveal a Styrofoam head that held a shoulder length blonde wig.

"That's Maci's!" said Max and a police officer simultaneously.

"She wore that wig the night she was shot at Bridgestone Arena," Max continued.

"Where did this come from?" said Hathaway. "And what's in this envelope? Get me some gloves!"

The room fell silent as Max and the others watched the agent slowly slip his thumb under the envelope flap. A sizeable lock of red hair fell to the floor. It was taped to a note that Hathaway read silently, then aloud.

"Stop standing around. Find the person who persuaded two people to kill me."

"She's back, maybe even in this building!" shouted Hathaway. He and the other lawmen charged out of Max's office, and sprinted down the hallway while demanding that the building be sealed. Terrified spectators who hadn't seen the contents of the box wondered if they were in danger.

High strung and disorganized, the lawmen were barking orders and yelling in all directions, including at each other.

Hathaway called for everyone to come out of their offices, and to gather in the central lobby.

"Do it now! Do it now!"

Within minutes, five police officers had scanned every room on the ground floor of Meacham Records. No one found anything incriminating, and there was no sign of Maci. An annoyed detective told all employees to go back to their work stations, and to stay there until further notice. He and the other lawmen walked back to Max's office at a weary gait that clearly symbolized their feeling of failure.

"Where did you put the box and its contents?" Hathaway asked Max.

"Nowhere," he replied. "I thought one of you had grabbed it when you stormed out of here."

"I put it down when I went to search the building," Hathaway said. "Here in your office, not ten feet away from your door."

He scanned the floor, and found that only the box's top remained.

"I'm glad I ran down the hall with all of you," Max said to everyone. "Otherwise, you'd be accusing me of stealing it."

"I don't seem to remember you joining us," said Hathaway. "Any of you guys remember that?"

A couple of officers shook their heads no, while the remainder simply stared at Max.

Hathaway's stare told Max that he wanted to talk more, but on his own turf.

"Grab your jacket Max," he said. "We're going downtown."

8

Max Abernathy's fourteen thousand square foot mansion was divided into eighteen lavish rooms, and fashionably decorated by designers from New York and London.

That was just the first floor.

A different room was featured on the cover of *Homes and Hideaways'* monthly edition for eighteen consecutive issues, the most continuous coverage of any home ever showcased in the journal. The regional magazine was a wish list for wealthy and bored women, who digested every caption and photograph, and read each article if it were scripture.

A gossip junkie at heart, Max took sadistic delight at the stories of pressure levied by high-society women against Nashville's leading interior decorators. Many sought accent pieces like Max's—but not identical.

One woman went so far as to tell her decorator that if he didn't capture an ambiance of wealth and sophistication that rivaled Max's home, she'd tell "all of the right people" that he was gay.

"Oh honey," the decorator replied. "Please tell everyone except your husband. He already knows."

Divorce papers were filed within a week.

"Most of Nashville's society women have a mountain of money, but a deficit of taste," Max was quoted in H&H. "Their actions are dictated by Emily Post, and their clothing by whatever Vanity Fair tells them Julia Roberts wore last month."

Only one room inside his pseudo-castle had never been photographed. The basement was an ugly but functional 500 square feet of fortification that could, if needed, withstand the collapse of the entire house above it. No tornado could destroy it, no flood could dampen it and no fire could burn it.

Several magazines had referred to it as the *safe room* or *panic room*. Its four concrete walls, floor and ceiling were two feet thick. The veritable bunker contained a refrigerator, canned goods, a bed, a commode and running water. Not even a power outage could touch the room, as a heavy duty battery-operated generator was set to provide alternate voltage for up to a week.

Max called the room the "Presidential Hideaway," believing it to be as secure as the President's Emergency Operation Center beneath the White House.

Having returned from his trip to the Nashville FBI office, Max sequestered himself in his bunker and activated his cell phone. His builder had assured him that a special element inside the concrete would allow him to place calls to the outside world, but prevent any calls from coming in.

Dialing a memorized number, Max waited in silence as the person on the other end of the dedicated phone line greeted him with the correct password.

"This has got to stop," said Max, in a low voice.

"There have been two attempts on her life. This thing is taking on its own life. It's getting her a ton of attention, but some of the attention is drifting toward me."

"You should . . ." said the other voice.

"Stop!!" Max snapped. "I'll talk, you listen."

"There has to be a third time, and it has to work. Do what you've been doing, but get it right. So far, you've enlisted two psychos. Each failed, and each is dead.

"Meanwhile, she's alive and so is a crowd of reporters, not to mention the cops and federal agents. It's getting too hot for comfort.

"I'm going to push up the release date for her next single and video. It'll draw in her regular fans, plus the sympathy crowd.

"I just need you to make sure that the next try is the last. Get away from the rubber headed, wannabe killers. Find someone who's actually up to the job. Find a mentally distressed personality whose primary glitch is passive aggression toward her, and no one else."

"That's what I did the last two times," said the voice on the telephone.

"Look, all I know is that I'm paying you to get a job done, and I expect it to be done right," Max said, angrily.

He instantly regretted his outburst. After all, they were in this together; he needed to keep his partner engaged and motivated until Maci was dead.

"Right now, I'm still trying to find her," Max said, his tone turning calmer. "So we can stand down until she resurfaces. Meanwhile, I'm going to be busy hiring a few lawyers who can help navigate me through this mess.

"Look . . . I know you couldn't have predicted the other guys would have botched this," he continued. "I guess failing to kill Maci wasn't your fault."

Max rarely showed remorse, but was uncomfortable with what he'd just said. Stopping short of an apology, he took a deep breath and regained his focus.

"Just get this thing back on track," he said. "I'll call you in a few days."

Shutting off his phone, Max wondered how he'd let things go this far. Circumstances looked desperate, but he still had confidence in his ability to fix most anything. He could get away with anything, he told himself, including conspiracy to commit Maci's attempted murder.

A moment after the call's end, Max cast the underground command center into darkness. He smelled the rankness of his own body; he hadn't had a shower since the lawmen had invaded his office. Max decided to drive to Meacham and resume his search for Maci. No one would expect to see him there; the building was normally vacant at night, and no one could enter after eight o'clock without a pass code and approved thumbprint. That much Max knew; he'd orchestrated the security system himself.

At the time, he had wanted to be absolutely sure that he, and the artists on Meacham Records, would always be safe.

9

During business hours, the hallways at Meacham Records smelled of women's perfumes and a slight hint of marijuana. But after hours, their fragrances yielded to abrasive cleaning fluids as the janitors arrived for the nightly cleaning.

On entering tonight, Max wondered why he preferred the scent of Lysol to Chanel N°5. He decided he'd been suffocated by perfumes too many times, by too many women who wore too many fragrances, and nothing else.

Even though the building was his domain, he felt as if he were rudely intruding by making footsteps in the newly vacuumed carpet leading to his office. He apologized to the custodian who was pushing his electric sweeper.

Years ago, Max had set a policy that the janitor must vacuum the carpet before and after each of his visits.

"I want the world to know I'm always making new tracks," Max repeatedly said at staff meetings. "Always remember, here at Meacham we always tread on new territory."

Even though they served him well, Max didn't know the name of any of the janitors, including the man who'd literally followed in his tracks pushing a vacuum cleaner. Max ignored the noise and the person making it. The blue-collar employee had no power on Music Row, and Max was too busy to engage with people who couldn't further, or at least compliment, his career.

"Never interact with anyone wearing a uniform," he once advised Maci, years ago. "People who dress alike too often think alike. They're not innovative, they're just dutiful clones. And that's not who we want to be."

He wondered if she was processing that thought somewhere tonight.

Entering his office, Max made a mental note to tell his assistant to order the janitor to cut his hair. Its length drew attention to its grayness.

"So, it's just me and Santa Claus tonight," Max mused to himself. He made an additional note to have the custodian lose his sunglasses, as the lenses reminded him of a horsefly's eyes.

"I'm running a record company, not a science fiction movie set," he said, knowing the sweeper's noisy motor suppressed his words. "I'm Max Abernathy, not Alfred Hitchcock."

Max knew he was rambling, but he didn't care. He called his outbursts "primal therapy" as prescribed by his therapist. The intention was to say whatever he wanted to say and say it loudly, no matter who heard. He found the practice liberating, and he only had to pay his therapist three hundred dollars an hour to justify it.

"I'm an aging man running a company that caters to youth," he said, the sweeper still loud. "I don't want some over-the-hill hillbilly employee trying to look young with shades as big as Michael Jackson's and hair whiter than Leon Russell's."

Max was tempted to shout loudly, but refrained. No matter. The janitor was wearing ear buds that muffled both the sweeper and Max's complaining.

An admitted micromanager, Max blamed his quirks and hostilities on an Obsessive Compulsive Disorder, especially regarding his demand for exaggerated neatness. Whenever anyone left his office, Max personally ran disinfectant wipes over the wooden arms of the visitor's chair.

He also asked that no janitors, repairmen or other common laborers ever speak to him. He hadn't made that request a rule, but thought he soon might.

Max was rich, powerful, admired and miserable. He had everything a common working person could ever dream of. Yet somehow, they seemed happier than Max, and he loathed their contentment. He'd decided long ago that he disdained all people who quit the pursuit of happiness because they'd already found it. There was always something more to be done or acquired, he believed. There just had to be.

At that moment, he was annoyed with himself for stupidly dwelling on the janitor and his kind. He had more important things to think about. And, even if he hadn't, commoners weren't worth his time.

Now two hours into sundown, he walked quietly across his silent office to open the blinds while intentionally listening to the slight swish of his leather soles against the weave of his Persian rug. To him, the sound was another reminder of his gaudy wealth and status.

As the steady whirr of the vacuum continued, he was tempted to tell the janitor that tonight the noise was too much of a distraction. But he didn't want to contradict his own decree. You have to be consistent with simple people, he thought. Start bending the rules, and you'll have chaos. His dream was for Meacham to be music's version of a military post. In Max's fantasy world, there'd be a clear chain of command, and maybe even mandatory physical exercise.

"Why not?" he often mused. "The Japanese are totally devoted to corporations, and they begin each day with physical training."

After Max had commissioned a company workout facility, someone posted a sign in the lobby that read, "Lose your creativity and excess weight at Meacham." Max personally scanned hours of surveillance video to find the author, but the scribe had been too clever. The rascal had procured a giant, sponge finger seen at sporting events. He somehow moved the forefinger to a middle position, and pulled the enormous hand over his head. Max's four hours of scrutiny yielded no suspects, just a foam-figured gesture designed specifically for him.

Max was trying to focus on a pressing matter at hand when the annoying janitor slowly edged his whining sweeper into Max's office. Never had a custodian entered Max's inner sanctum while he was there. His gut instinct was to evict or possibly fire the worker, but instead he opted to tune the noise out.

His tolerance turned to apprehension when the janitor closed Max's office door without permission, then preceded to lock it.

Deducing that the janitor must be a recent hire, Max decided he'd had enough. Angry, Max walked from his chair toward the janitor. Not wanting to have to yell above the noise, he switched off the vacuum and yanked the earbuds from the worker's ears.

"Custodial staff are not allowed to enter this office when it's occupied," said Max sternly. The janitor looked up, and Max saw his own face mirrored in the oversized sunglasses.

"And it's forbidden for members of the custodial staff to make eye contact with Meacham executives," he said with a rising air of authority. "Look, I don't have time to quote our policy manual to you. Just get out of my office, and find some other floor that needs cleaning."

Rather than obeying, the janitor stood idly, staunchly ignoring Max's words. Suddenly, Max realized that the two of them were the only people inside the six-story building. Not even security personnel were present, having been replaced with electronic surveillance the previous year. Uncertain whether or not he was in danger, Max wished that someone, anyone, would enter Meacham.

"Is there something I can help you with?" Max said, after turning and walking to his desk, intending to put the massive mahogany block between him and his intruder.

"You can help us both," the worker said sarcastically, in a surprisingly high voice. The custodian covered his mouth with his hand, a gesture often used by children who say things they wish they hadn't.

Focusing on the hand, Max was perplexed by the janitor's manicured fingernails and the smoothness of the skin on the back of the worker's hand, which was void of soil, smudges or any signs of manual labor.

Max cleared his throat, and then asked again if he could help the mysterious man, who suddenly turned his back on him. Returning to the door, the janitor rolled a second lock, this one a deadbolt. Now, no one could come inside Max's office, not even if they had a passkey.

And no one could quickly get out.

The janitor slowly walked back across the floor, brandishing a stare as dull as a park statue. Rather than approach Max, the intruder brazenly opened the door to Max's private restroom, whose automatic light bleached his skin like a shut-in who hadn't seen sunlight in years.

Max no longer believed the suspicious worker was a part of the cleaning crew. He knew he was in trouble and he wanted to do something, but wasn't sure what. A pistol lay in the top drawer of his desk, but he was physically frozen as he scanned the imaginary mile between his own hand and the weapon. Max wondered if the intruder had a concealed firearm, and whether any action would set off a more drastic reaction.

"Someone this brazen has to be armed," Max told himself. Finally, he decided to speak.

"Excuse me," Max said, his voice breaking. "You're in my private lavatory. You needn't clean it tonight."

"I won't clean your piss hole tonight or any other!" the janitor replied. Max was certain the speaker had earlier used falsetto in order to conceal his real voice.

"What!?" Max shouted, stepping toward the washroom. "You won't clean my what!?"

For the first time since his entry, the janitor moved his lips into a smile that evolved into a laugh.

"Watch and learn, Sweetie," the janitor suddenly said.

"Stand still, don't be afraid . . . watch and learn."

Max was tempted to run when the intruder turned his back, but didn't. If push came to shove, Max was sure he could overpower the slightly built janitor. Besides, he thought, the guy was breathing heavily, as if merely pushing a vacuum sweeper had depleted him.

His face now turned away from Max, the brazen custodian put his hand in his front pocket. Max stumbled before darting toward that desk.

"Don't go for the gun," the stranger yelled. "If you do, you're gonna be sorry, Fatso."

Max stopped in his tracks, not six feet away from his desk drawer.

"I told you to watch and learn!" said the voice in charge. "How many times do I have to say that?"

Max turned slowly, expecting to see a gun, but instead saw the janitor gazing into the washroom mirror. He withdrew from his pocket not a weapon, but a fist full of cotton balls and a small plastic bottle.

As the janitor flipped the bottle's lid, the scent of rubbing alcohol consumed the small washroom and wafted into the office.

Dousing a cotton ball, the janitor began to briskly dab the alcohol onto his face. The man placed his sunglasses on the counter, and then spent a minute or two emphatically rubbing additional alcohol-soaked balls over his eyes and cheeks. The swabbing moved downward to the intruder's neck, whereupon he tossed all of the soaked balls into the commode and flushed. He returned the lid to the alcohol, and tenderly situated it onto Max's vanity, as if it were an heirloom.

Max was fascinated, but furious with this performance.

"Hi Max," said Maci, removing the white wig from her head. "Miss me?"

Max stared at her in disbelief, and did not answer her question. He couldn't, as he literally couldn't breathe.

Maci Willis fancied herself a layman psychologist without a degree or license, and was convinced she needed neither. All her life she had studied people not through reading, but through her interactions with them.

After decades of seeing millions of fans, and mingling with a few thousand, she was convinced she'd mastered all of the traits surrounding human behavior. Right now, Max's body language, his tone of voice and shifting eyes indicated that his warmth toward her was lukewarm at best. He tried to hide his feelings behind a phony excitement that was akin to someone welcoming their in-laws for a weeklong stay.

"So you're happy to see me," Maci said skeptically. "I'd be happy myself if I saw a white-haired janitor transform into a gorgeous woman and music icon who I feared might be dead."

Max still said nothing.

"Breathe, Max," she said. "I hope you don't faint. I'd need a block and tackle to get you off the floor."

Reeling, Max stepped behind his desk and slowly collapsed into his chair. "Why the . . . ?" he stopped. He was about to ask why the dramatics, but Maci had a history of being overly dramatic.

"Max!" she snapped, knowing her tone would bring him back to reality. "I didn't come down here just to startle you, although it's been fun. I haven't worn that much make-up since back when you signed me up for that movie deal."

"Maci," said Max, somewhat regaining his senses. "Do you have any idea of what type of stir—and trouble—you've caused?"

"Really?" responded Maci. "It's only been on every radio and TV show in the country. Plus you've been sending texts and leaving messages about the severity of my problems. But right now, I just need someone to talk to—and hopefully intelligently."

Max drew a deep breath, as if bracing for a dentist's drill.

"Okay," he said, clearing his throat. "If you've been following yourself on TV and radio, then you know a warrant has been issued for you. The FBI has been here, and so have the police. It's been a mess, because I've been accused of harboring a fugitive, even though I had no idea where you were."

"I just needed time to myself," said Maci. "My world's gone crazy. The police can wait."

"You might think that," Max said. "But it's about more than you. That guy in Fayetteville? Lester something? You were the last person to see him alive. The authorities think you may have assisted in his suicide."

"Max!" Maci interrupted. "That Lester guy wasn't right in the head. Even the news shows are saying that. They said his house was plastered with pictures of me, and he wore dresses, wigs and lipstick like mine."

"Still, they want to talk with you," he said. "Technically, you're a fugitive."

"If they talk to anybody, it should be those idiots in the Royal Dettwiller kitchen. They knew he was obsessed with me, although I doubt they thought he wanted to die for me. And as far as me being the last to see him? How does anyone know? I don't know myself. Lester pulled out a giant knife, started talking about he and I dying together, and I ran like you did the night you were caught with Ray Webster's wife. My driver will attest that I wore nothing but a hotel robe. Doesn't that prove I was in a hurry?"

"It proves you were in a hurry," said Max. "But people can be in a hurry for a lot of reasons."

"When I fled, Lester was alive. How do I know when he leapt out the window?"

"So where have you been?" Max said. "Your house has been empty all week."

"I haven't been to my main house for days because every square inch of my lawn is covered with tourists and media," Maci said. "I have a second place, off the books. The lease and utilities are in someone else's name, and they're paid in advance. And I didn't get it because of this stuff. I've had it for six years. I go there to get away from show business and the people in it, especially you."

Max let Maci's jab roll off his shoulders, as he'd done countless times. "Maci, I know you've been through a terrible time. But things are getting way out of hand. There's a national manhunt out for you. You've got to end this."

"You're the one who wanted media exposure," said Maci with a frown. "Anyway, I know. And I'm going to face the music, pardon the pun. I'm going to walk into FBI headquarters tomorrow morning with my lawyers, unless you turn me in before I get out of Meacham's driveway."

"I have to tell them you've contacted me," he said. "I have to. But where you go from here is your business."

"Now, Max," she said. "Don't act all perturbed. Look at the bright side. You got what you wanted. Thanks to those two psychos who tried to kill me, and to me dropping out, you probably have no idea how much product you've moved.

"On second thought," she added, "you probably do. You probably know to the penny. Maybe my accountant should examine the books, to make sure I'm getting my fair share."

As the room eased into silence, Max suddenly seemed unfazed. Maci decided that it was impossible to insult him. His skin was as thick as an alligator's; it had to be, in his business.

"I don't know what to say," Max finally said. Before he could frame another sentence, she interrupted him, telling him she didn't want to wait for him to gather his thoughts.

"Don't say anything, Max," she said. "People who always have to think before they speak are usually lying, or don't really mean what they're saying. Maybe I let my words fly, but at least they're real."

As Maci headed for the door, Max rose from his seat.

"So where are you going from here?" he asked.

"That's my business," she said. "But tomorrow, I'll visit the FBI and local cops. And after I answer their questions, I'll have several for them. I want those talented sleuths to tell me why two mentally challenged people have died while trying to kill me. Because mentally disturbed people tend to be dependent people. They're also often obedient people. I'm not in law enforcement, but I don't have to be to know that someone or something enticed these people to do what they did. It's not a coincidence. Somebody initiated all of this, and I want to know who. And I'm not going to stop until whoever did this is in prison. Or in the ground."

10

The knock at her sagging front door sent Maci's emotional antennae into overdrive. The caller couldn't possibly be a salesman, she thought. The outward appearance of her remote cabin shouted poverty, and its long, secluded driveway was lined with "No Trespassing" signs.

If a wolf came to this door, he'd surely bring his own meal, she'd thought the first time she saw it. Though it was only twenty minutes from her mansion, it resembled the best house in the neighborhood in a Third World country.

She tried to wait out the knocks, in hopes the uninvited guest would go away. By the fifth round, she knew the knocking would persist until someone answered. She tried looking through the door's peephole, but a previous resident had covered it with tape that had hardened and wouldn't budge.

Mess that she was, Maci nonetheless pulled open the squeaking door, and instantly squinted against the morning sun.

Two men in neckties smiled at her, and she quickly assumed they were members of Jehovah's Witness.

"Good morning, Maci," said a debonair man.

"Religious men are more handsome than they were when I was a girl," she replied.

"Excuse me?" one man said.

"Never mind," she said, giggling.

"I'm Agent Rick Shale with the Federal Bureau of Investigation," he announced. "And this is FBI agent DeWayne Hathaway."

"Well, my name isn't on the mailbox, and there's no car outside. So how did you find me? Or were you just scouring Nashville and doing door-to-door searches for me?"

"May we come in, please?" asked Shale, ignoring her aloofness.

"Do you have a warrant or a subpoena?" she replied, seriously.

"No," said Shale, "if so, we could have entered without your permission."

"I know that! I was just testing you guys about law enforcement."

She instantly regretted her comment, as her wisecrack had held no malice. The light in the men's eyes said so.

Maci sighed. "Come on in," she said. "Into the filth. The domestic staff hasn't arrived yet. Would you like refreshments? Some moldy, month-old bread, or rusty tap water?"

Hathaway grinned again, and Maci thought his smile went well with his blended wool suit.

"We've been looking for you," Hathaway said. "We need to talk a bit."

"Let me get dressed," she said, trying to hide her rising anxiety. "Go ahead and sit in any kitchen chair with four legs. One of them only has three. Be sure you don't sit in that one unless you want to start your day with some tumbling exercises."

Scanning the room, the agents decided to stand and wait in the ramshackle kitchen.

Still nervous, Maci obsessively opened and slammed her bedroom's dresser drawers, hoping to hold off the questions from two gentlemen poised amid her kitchen's squalor.

"I wish I'd known you guys were coming," she yelled. "I'd have cleaned this place, or at least set off a bug bomb. Of course, the only thing that would actually clean this sewer would be kerosene and fire."

Once again, the two men smiled, and Shale let out a muffled laugh that finally gave Maci the response she wanted.

"Found it!" she yelled, still inside her bedroom. "At first I mistook it for two measuring cups, but lo-and-behold, it was my bra! Now if I can only find my jeans. I hope they contain both legs. Found them! They do!"

The men were laughing when she finally entered the kitchen. She liked the way their amicable mood broke the tension. They had endured her insecurities masked in humor, and she loved that.

"So," she said. "I take it you're not here to deliver a pizza."

Realizing that her nervousness was still fueling her levity, she took a deep breath.

"First of all," said Shale, his deep voice finally instating an air of seriousness. "Agent Hathaway and I purposely avoided a warrant. We did that because warrants and subpoenas are public records, and we know that the media tend to equate them with guilt—and agent Hathaway and I don't feel that way."

Maci breathed deeply at the thought that they may have actually acted in her interest.

"Plus, we think you've been through enough stress and negative publicity," said Hathaway. "If you were at your main house right now, you'd see enough journalists to cover a Presidential Inauguration."

Ever so softly, Maci's eyes glazed and Hathaway realized that she understood the agents' motives were in her behalf. She wanted to express her appreciation, he could tell, but sensed that gratitude was something she wasn't used to expressing. He was sure he'd never get a "thank you" card from this hardened woman, but he still felt sympathy for the ordeal she'd endured.

"Off the record, just how did you find me here?" she asked.

"Nothing here's in my name. I rent a lousy car with license tags that belong to the owner."

"I placed a couple of electronic bugs inside a public place," Shale replied instantly. "That is, if you consider Max Abernathy's office a 'public place.' After all, there were so many people in his office last week that it may as well have been Grand Central Station."

Maci wondered if he was trying to convince her or himself about the laws regarding hidden microphones. She wondered if he used a warrant, or if he even had to. In either case, she adored his honesty. She wished he'd pull his hands from his trousers so she could see if he wore a wedding ring, then wondered why she'd even look.

"From our surveillance, I recognized your voice when you pretended to be a janitor. I drove like a mad man to Meacham, and then followed you to this house. When Agent Hathaway and I came here this morning, we left our unmarked car parked a block away in front of vacant lots.

A sign on both of the car's doors says 'Vitality Insurance Company.'"

"Maci, I assure you that your secret hideaway will remain your secret. The tourists' buses might circle your mansion, and take 'selfies' outside the gate, but this place is yours. Everyone, myself included, feels you've suffered enough attempts on your life. If Agent Hathaway and I have our way that will never happen again - ever."

Maci was touched by the genuine empathy. She'd expected the agents to be cold and detached, but found quite the opposite to be true.

"Why, if I wasn't afraid of your guns going off, I'd give each of you a big hug," she smiled. When she finally did, she tried to remember the last time she'd really held someone.

"You guys are so right about the press and the way it hounds me," she said, intentionally changing the subject. "That started long before someone shot me."

"I know," said Hathaway. "I heard a story about a reporter who demanded that you explain why you never got married?"

"I told him I had a husband once, but his wife came and got him," said Maci, finishing the story.

The three laughed as if they were old friends, or new ones or new ones in the making.

"And you know," Maci continued, "he reported it as if it were the truth. Can you believe that reporter took me seriously?"

"I know," said Shale. "I think the headline was, 'Country Music Pillar Having Illicit Affair.'"

"Just how much homework have you guys done about me?" she asked, and then asked them not to reply.

"Well, you've given us a few days to get up to speed," said Shale.

The trio continued resurrecting stories about Maci, including the time she called the White House and reversed the charges.

One recollection ignited another, and Maci somehow felt warmly secure between two men who'd memorized her past, outrageous as it was. She began framing a fantasy, pretending that these two decent men cared about her as a person, not as a persona. She hadn't felt that way since leaving her hometown as a teenager. She wondered what her life would have been like had she taken a normal job, like law enforcement, instead of music. She smiled and shook her head, and one of the agents asked what she was thinking.

"Oh nothing," she said. "Just thinking about all that I could have been, rather than all that I've lost."

"Say," she said, abruptly changing her tone. "Are you guys sure you don't want some bottled water? You don't have to worry. Unlike my life, its seal hasn't been broken."

❧ ❧

Maci felt increasingly closer to the agents. Their politeness, consideration and demeanor were a stark juxtaposition to the ill-spoken, seedy and often underhanded men in the music business.

Later that day, Agent Hathaway put thousands of fans at ease when he told the media that Maci was alive, well and unharmed. When asked when she would be making an appearance, he simply said that she was resting and recuperating at an undisclosed, private location.

She was moved by the fact that an FBI agent had become her unofficial spokesperson. Not only was she comforted by it, but she also knew the media and her fans would regard him as credible and trustworthy.

"The 'country music nightingale' is in fine health, and said she'd like to resume her concert touring soon," Hathaway had said at a short press conference. When asked by reporters if she was currently in the Nashville area, the agent coyly said "no comment."

The agents were quoted as saying Maci had no involvement in or knowledge of the tandem efforts to take her life. They also stressed that they'd interviewed Arkansas investigators who had no proof that Maci was even in the room when a Fayetteville man took his life.

To set the record straight, the agents reiterated that the singer's first assailant shot her with a pistol, but was later killed by a Nashville policeman when the perpetrator tried again to kill her.

Asked why Maci had never been arrested for obstruction of justice, Agent Shale personally issued a press release.

"Ms. Maci Willis did not inhibit a federal investigation, as was once thought," Shale wrote. "She did not disrupt justice, and therefore was never subpoenaed. Early in the investigation, she was a person-of-interest regarding a Fayetteville fatality. That standing was later dismissed. At this point, there is no evidence to support any charge that Ms. Willis was involved in any illegal conspiracies or activities."

When asked where Shale and Hathaway had interviewed Maci, the agents did not respond, except to say that they did not meet her at her Music Row mansion.

Maci felt secure with their presence. But while they may have taken a personal interest in her well-being, the elimination of charges meant that they no longer had a professional interest in her. As the day came to a close,

Maci knew that the men who had protected her would soon be leaving. The only people in the world who knew her whereabouts would leave her just as they had found her—alone.

Suddenly her hideaway cabin began to feel like a jail cell. She was imprisoned by a merciless sadness, the type that often descended upon her yesterday, today or tomorrow.

"How can someone who draws 20,000 people still be alone at the end of the day?" she yelled at her stark and faded walls. "Money. Fame. Mansion. I've got everything, and I've got nothing."

Her words were bathed in self-pity, and she didn't care. There were so many emotions pent up inside her that she had no choice but to let them out. With no one to listen, she expelled them into the air. The more she ranted, the more she wanted to.

"Nobody knows about my hollowness because nobody cares. My fans don't know me. And the people who do know me don't care. They care about the money I make for them, but they don't care about ME!"

Dropping to the floor, Maci curled into a ball and sobbed uncontrollably. Through sheer willpower, she forced herself to separate herself from her sorrow, and focus her mind on other thoughts. This is how it always ended; eventually, she tapped the sadness back down, and smiled through tears. Aloud, she repeated a handful of affirmations she had memorized, which she repeatedly used like Xanax. Even after the melancholy subsided, she continued speaking. Listening to her own voice was better than hearing no voice at all.

She thought about the two agents who had come to look after her. They swore they'd work to prevent any further attempts on her life. But at this point, it felt like a life she no longer wanted.

Silently she began to cry again.

"What if those wonderful agents were here?" she muttered to herself. "Would they be interested in protecting the likes of me now?"

Still weeping, she never answered her question.

11

aci Willis rode atop the back of a convertible limousine that coasted slowly in front of two marching bands. The radiant center of attention, she felt less like a celebrity and more like a paper mache figure perched on a float.

Bars and cafes along Nashville's lower Broadway, the epicenter of country music's tourism, were almost empty, as virtually all patrons had spilled shoulder-to-shoulder onto the teeming avenue, now congested with sightseers aimed at Maci.

As if patrolling for a lost child, two television news helicopters hovered overhead, while reporters from network affiliates did man-on-the-street interviews as half-drunken bystanders pushed and shoved to weasel their way into the television frame.

Her legs dangling on the back of the convertible's leather seat, Maci sat upright on the trunk, with the mayor on her left and Max on her right. Smiling to herself, she realized the irony—one man ocassionally made laws, the other regularly broke them.

The open car led the bands and an army of people from lower Broadway uphill to Sixth Street, where the mob then turned South. People continued left and coiled back to Fifth Street at the corner of Broadway and the entrance to Bridgestone Arena. As the gathering curved through the streets surrounding the heart of Nashville, Maci was inattentive to the route and surroundings. She simply thought the gala resembled a country music Mardi Gras, and after a few moments as the center of attention she was ready to leave. But that's not what others had in mind.

A portable stage engulfed the arena's concrete lawn, where Maci's band, dancers and background singers nervously milled beneath a giant photograph of Maci's face. High above that likeness, enormous letters proclaimed "Welcome Home Maci!"

"Raise that stage three feet off the ground and it'll look like a blimp at takeoff," she shouted to Max.

"Damn," he responded, stupidly taking Maci seriously, "we should've gotten one!"

"Well," replied Maci quietly, below the noise of the crowd, "you're pretty close to resembling one, Max."

She recalled the famous photograph of a drunken sailor kissing an unknown girl on Times Square amid ticker tape while celebrating the end of World War II. She mischievously thought she'd kiss Max, but knew the imagery would be lost on him.

Escorted by Max, Maci walked up the backstage steps and out to her microphone. She knew the crowd would cheer once she surfaced. Max wanted to stay by her side, to bask in the glow of the applause as well, but Maci decided he hadn't earned it.

"Okay Max," she said only to him. "Why not put an egg in your shoe and beat it? I've got a show to do, and if you can't play or sing, you need to step down and join the audience."

She wondered about Max, and if enduring her insults was worth the money he unlawfully pocketed. Sure, in the early days, he'd do anything. But now he was worth as much or more as most of the Meacham's stars, and still he took whatever rudeness they dished out. Given his bloated salary, plus the label's funds he skimmed, she decided her smart-alecky barbs were worth it to him.

Stepping onto the stage, Maci pulled the microphone to her mouth, but her words were drowned in a sea of hysterically cheering fans. After crossing from one side of the stage to the other five times, and bowing while crying, Maci finally held her forefinger vertically across her mouth to call for silence.

As the crowd finally became quiet, Maci cleared her throat.

"A few weeks ago," she said at last, her voice reverberating through the speakers, "I left this arena behind me in the back of an ambulance. Today, I'm alive, well and back!"

The last sentence was kindling for the fiery mob, and renewed adulation engulfed the outdoor air.

"I left this building wondering who'd just shot me," she said, her voice quivering and echoing. "I never got to meet him, not even in a courtroom, because one of Nashville's finest policemen killed him on my behalf. Officer Keith Shultz, please come up here and take a bow."

The surprise sight of the uniformed hero triggered another round of deafening applause. To Maci's surprise, she was secretly jealous, and silently chastised herself for resenting the man who'd risked his life to preserve hers. For an instant, she feared she'd become as jaded and egotistical as Max.

"As I was saying . . . again . . ." she continued. "I left Nashville after that harrowing ordeal only to meet another man who also wanted to take my life. Instead, he accidentally took his own!"

The cheers began to crest again, but Maci quickly interjected.

"PLEASE DON'T APPLAUD!" she ordered.

Without remote cameras and Jumbotrons, only fans in the front saw the beads of moisture trickling from beneath Maci's signature wig, and she felt as if she were in a sauna. Without theatrical makeup, she knew her mascara would soon resemble Tammy Bakker's tearful pleas.

For an instant, she wondered how many years had passed since she'd last performed outdoors, and she made a personal promise to never do it again.

Maci's thrilling comeback show was free-of-charge for the fans, but not for her. It was the most emotionally taxing performance she could remember. Partially faking her gratitude, she felt like an actress who'd forgotten her lines, but brazenly decided to speak and sing anyhow.

Still, she could feel the ocean of gratitude from fans old and new, some celebrating and others worshipping. She was touched by the level of love she could hear in their voices.

"Thank you for showing me how much I mean to so many of you folks," she said between songs. "I feed off your love. And this has truly been a feast."

But her show of humility was fused with guilt more than gratitude, and she was surprised to notice that the hypocritical mix was gnawing at her conscience. Maci yearned to abolish a secret shared by only Agents Shale, Hathaway and her. Earlier in the day, the trio conferenced in a three-way cell phone summit and mapped out their plan following the concert.

"Under the front seat of Max's Mercedes, I planted several imprint kits used to duplicate keys," Hathaway had told Maci. "Throw all of the kits in your purse. You'll need to grab them one by one, so get rid of everything else in your bag."

As she replayed their conversation in her mind, she marveled at how precisely she'd retained his instructions.

She was also told to ride with Max after the concert. That posed no problem, as she would have probably ridden with him anyhow. The catch came later; she was also told to direct Max to Meacham, rather than let him take her to her mansion or to his, at least not right after the show. Hathaway also demanded that no one else accompany Max and her inside his car.

While en route to Meacham, she was told to order Max to stop at a convenience store across the street from the giant outdoor screen that flashes Nashville's coming attractions. It was a landmark; everyone in town knew it, he explained.

"A reality television show is being advertised there today," Hathaway had said, as if she could have possibly missed a screen the size of half a tennis court.

As Max's car approached the large, brightly lit sign, Maci found herself once again replaying their instruction. Taking a deep breath, she told herself she was ready.

As Maci squirmed in the front seat of Max's Mercedes, she wondered if he wondered why she was softly perspiring, despite his air-conditioning. A wave of nausea swept through her, magnified by the fact that she'd eaten nothing that day.

"Man, that was a great show," she said, knowing how phony she'd sounded. To her, all of her shows were great, and she felt it was evident to the point that bragging about it was unnecessary.

"Huh?" Max replied. "Your show? Think so?"

Maci thought his reply was as rude as her remark was fake.

Easing back into the seat, she prepared to execute her instructions. Everything was fine so far. She was in the assigned seat inside the assigned car at the assigned time.

She watched Max's odometer and began counting down the miles.

After five minutes on the road, the giant, electronic screen was in sight. Like an oasis in the desert, the screen became larger with every approaching yard, or so she felt. Silently, she prayed that Shale and Hathaway were already inside the designated store.

"While sitting in the car, how will I know if the agents are even inside?" she wondered. "If they're gone, what will I do?"

Maci was not accustomed to trusting other people, let alone people she'd known for such a short time. She'd seen enough television to know that agents on a stakeout were sometimes found out. Then, there were fistfights or gunplay.

"What am I doing?" she asked herself. "Is there any part of my life that doesn't draw drama?"

She was silently searching for an answer when it became time to take the agents' plan into the second act.

"Max," she said. "I'm not feeling well. Will you stop at that gasoline place, that convenience store up ahead on the right? I need some headache medicine."

"No problem my songbird," he replied, and lifted the lid on the console between them. "Here's some aspirin."

"I, uh, I can't use aspirin," she replied. "I have to have Ibuprofen."

"I've got Excedrin in here somewhere," he said, and fumbled through the compartment while driving. "Works like magic. Knocks out my headaches."

"MAX!! You're swerving!!"

"What the hell?!!" he yelled, quickly looking at the road and pushing Maci's hands from his steering wheel. "See if you can find that Excedrin in there."

The store was now less than a block away and approaching fast. Maci estimated that she had about thirty seconds to execute her part of this lawful "sting." Max wasn't slowing down, and she feared he'd drive past the rendezvous point, leaving the agents' mission aborted.

"Dammit, Max!" exclaimed Maci. "I don't want Excedrin! I just played that free concert for you in this heat! The least you can do is pull this friggin' car over and get me the headache medicine I want!"

Max pressed the brakes and easily slowed the car.

"Whatever you want, Maci," he said in an exasperated voice. "Like always. You want me to get you some tampons, too?"

"I don't need sarcasm, Max," Maci said. "I need Ibuprofen."

Maci exhaled when Max finally turned into the parking lot of the convenience store. Without being asked, he parked next to the gasoline pumps, where the awning shaded his car.

"Was that so hard?" she asked.

"I'll be right out," he said, turning off the ignition as he opened the door.

Maci knew better than to argue with him now.

"Max, honey," she said, slipping into her best imitation of niceness. "Please leave the car running. My headache will get worse if it gets hot in here."

"When the hell have you ever called me honey, or anyone else for that matter?"

"I know, but you're so nice to stop for little ole me and my headache."

"Fine . . . my little lamb," he said sarcastically, leaving the keys dangling in the ignition as he stepped from the car.

The car door clicked shut, and Maci watched as Max waddled toward the convenience store. Now, it was Showtime.

To Maci, the jangle of Max's key ring rang as loudly as a Salvation Army bell. Having turned off the motor to extract the keys, she feared he might glance toward the sedan and wonder why the motor had stopped. She then realized that the engine ran so quietly, that it was nearly impossible to tell the difference from ten feet away, let alone on the other side of stores' brick and glass wall.

"I'm so glad I didn't go into law enforcement," she said to herself as she nervously sorted through the keys.

She glanced at the dash clock, which seemed to flash out each second far too quickly. Reaching into her purse, she opened an imprint kit, and instantly broke a fingernail. She watched in panic as it lodged in the crease of the driver's sunken seat. Frantically, she dug for the errant nail, only to pop another.

"Good grief!" she murmured. "Get hold of your self, Maci. Get hold of yourself."

Glancing upward, she gasped when Max entered the checkout line, his hand gripping something small. Only three customers separated him from the clerk. She couldn't stand Ibuprofen, and dreaded having to soon swallow two pills.

The key ring still jingling, Maci pulled a single brass key off the ring, slowly placed it on the imprint pad, and accidentally smeared the solid paste. She tossed the out of focus print into her purse. Quickly and with a softer push, she made a second attempt to make a clean imprint.

She raised her head, and gasped as Max had moved in line and was now behind only two people. She hoped one of the customers had an arm full of groceries. She silently prayed that one had the type of stupid question that only surfaced in checkout lines, and only when you were in a hurry. Squinting, she realized that one held a bottle of water, the other a soft drink. Both would be out the door in a minute, two at best.

Pulling together all the focus she could muster, she retrieved the keys from the ring one by one and delicately imprinted each. Taking deep breaths to steady her hands, she breezed through the remaining keys quickly, then peered through the store's tainted window. Another customer had walked away, and a rush of adrenaline hit her as she realized that the customer directly in front of Max was Agent Hathaway. Agent Shale instantly appeared and handed Hathaway a few more grocery items.

Maci wanted to applaud. Renewing her focus, she forced her eyes away from the lawmen. She decided to leave it to them to keep Max occupied, and as she did she realized that she was once again putting her trust in someone else.

"Crime may not pay but this undercover stuff sure as hell is fun!" she joked to herself. As she neared completion of her task, a rush of adrenaline hit her like two Red Bulls. "Maybe I can persuade Max to rob a bank, then rat him out."

Maci's euphoria deflated when she glanced up and unexpectedly saw the two agents pushing and shoving and bouncing off of Max. As Shale made a fist, withdrew his arm and swung, Hathaway ducked and Shale connected directly with Max. The bottle of Ibuprofen was thrust into the air as Max grabbed his nose.

Having finished her imprints, Maci slid them into a container, which she then slipped safely inside her purse.

The car engine was running and its air conditioner quietly whirring when Max bolted from the store, took a few giant steps, and opened the driver's door.

"Let's get out of here!" he stormed, and screeched his tires while thrusting backwards. "There were two nut cases in there who got into a fist fight right in front of me. Didn't you wonder what was taking me so long?"

"No," she smiled. "I just assumed you couldn't find the tampons."

"Look," said Max. "They knocked your pills right out of my hand. I'm not going back in there. You watch for another store, and we'll get all the drugs and tampons you want."

"It's just not safe to go anywhere these days," Maci sighed as she shook her head.

"I've got half a mind to call the law on those thugs!"

12

Agents Shale and Hathaway, armed with nine-milli-meter Glocks and an evidence warrant, moved like decisive shadows as they stepped from the darkened woods surrounding Max's gated palace.

"I'd feel like a deer hunter," Shale whispered, "if my camouflage weren't a blue sports coat and tie."

"Doesn't matter to the deer," Hathaway said softly. "They're colorblind. You could wear neon and it wouldn't bother the deer."

"Maybe we should kill a deer then field dress it on Max's wraparound porch. Think he'd mind?"

"This place is so big he probably wouldn't find it for two weeks."

The two smiled at their nonsense. Even though Max's mansion wasn't inhabited, they mutually drifted into silence as they drew closer to the magnificent and sprawling manor.

A crack surveillance team had laid the groundwork for them earlier that day, temporarily disarming Max's security system, and strategically placing tiny microphones throughout the interior of Max's home, just as they'd done in his office and his Mercedes. The crew dubbed their clandestine work the "Maci Willis" mission, as she'd provided the imprinted keys that enabled them to unlock virtually every secluded corner of Max Abernathy's life. One of the keys gave the agents access into Max's hallowed safe room—the basement conclave where no one other than Max had ever entered.

"About the only place we haven't covered are the strip clubs and pickup spots he frequents," one of the technicians said.

"Just as well," said Shale. "Anything we'd get there would be a lie anyway."

⁘ ❧ ☙ ⁘

FBI Agent Joe Mundt had a theory: If you sit motionless and speechless at a bar, no one would see you. Or, if they did, they would act as if you didn't exist. So he sat, still as a statue, on a Music Row barstool. When not on duty, he was a small game hunter, and his buddies had nicknamed him the "Duck Dodger," claiming he could hold a pose so steadily that not even a bird's eye could detect him.

Whenever he was on a stakeout, only his pupils moved, and when they did they darted faster than an old maid's slap.

Tonight, he again held his perch where he occasionally and lazily sipped a cocktail. Though he showed no emotion, he was mildly surprised by the bottom shelf bourbon that had obviously been set before him. He expected better from a place where the customers' attire was silk suits for men, and designer weaves for easy women. Discretely slipping an earphone into his left ear, he glanced to his right, where Max had just eased himself into a booth for the evening.

"What can I do for you?" asked the waitress.

"You can bring me a bourbon and water," said Max. "And, just to make things even, what can I do for you? Do you sing?"

Agent Mundt slowly inhaled. He knew where the conversation would go from there, and believed he could actually sing along to that worn-out pitch. For years, Music Row executives and celebrities had cast this same lure to hopeful women whose musical aspirations were larger than their talents.

"Let me see if I can guess," replied the waitress. "You're going to make me a star?"

A nearly detectable smile curled at the edge of Mundt's lips.

"No," said Max.

"No?" the waitress asked, perplexed by Max's reply.

"No," he said. "I can't make you a star. Only your voice could do that, and I've never even heard it."

"I see," she said with a slight hesitation. "Then we're back to your original question. What *can* you do for me?"

"If you're interested in a singing career," said Max, "I can help you make a demo tape, and make sure that at least three members of the marketing team at Meacham Records listen to it. If they think you have something, they call you in, the process takes over, and you go as far as your voice will take you."

"And if they don't?"

"Like I said," replied Max, "I can't make you a star. Only your voice can do that. All I can do is make sure that the right people sit down and listen for a while."

"All out of the goodness of your heart, right?" she said.

"Not really," said Max.

She looked into his eyes. His response was unexpected, but not surprising.

"Look," Max said. "I can tell you're intelligent, so I'm not going to pretend to seduce you, or to pull one over on you. I'm just going to put something on the table. I have a studio-quality recording booth in my home, with digital music tracks to over a thousand songs. I give you a day with my studio, and in return you give me a night with you. The next day, your demo lands on the desk of Meacham's A&R department. I have the power to hire and fire the entire department, and once again, I can promise you that at least three people will listen to your demo from the beginning to the end."

Mundt was surprised by Max's blunt, straight-forwardness. It was an approach he'd never actually heard previously. Neither had the waitress.

"I, uh," she hesitated. "I don't know what to say."

"And I won't pressure you," Max replied. "I'll be here for three drinks. I'm sure by the third one, you'll have an answer."

Even though it still seemed sleazy, Agent Mundt was mildly impressed with Max's approach. The seasoned music tycoon had successfully straddled the gap between smarminess and honesty. Must be a heck of a salesman, Mundt thought. He knew that industry guys were usually smarter than the women they approached. But Max had made the woman think she was on equal footing with him, by giving her the opportunity to choose what happened next. For the next 30 minutes, the waitress would enjoy the illusion that she was actually undecided and in control. But in both Max's and Mundt's mind, there was no question as to how the evening was going to end.

Mundt had sat on countless solitary stakeouts like this one for years. He practically had calluses on his buttocks from the bar stools to prove it. He both loathed and envied men like Max. For a split second, he felt disgusted by men in general.

As the minutes ticked by and Max sipped away at his drink, Mundt watched the story play out in the waitress' slowly evolving facial expressions. Doubt. Trepidation.

Rationalization. She didn't feel that she was being blatantly played; Max wasn't promising the moon and stars.

He had made a direct, clear promise of access, and it was up to her to sink or swim. There was no reason he wouldn't drop the demo off to his employees. And they'd have to listen.

By the time Max finished his second cocktail, she had the look of an applicant applying for a job she didn't really want—but knew it was a stepping stone to one she did.

"What if this time is finally the time, and my sleeping with this pig might actually get me a record deal," Mundt whispered, mimicking the now-willing girl. The agent shook his head, and told himself that he should be a film director. Why not? He'd learned to anticipate lines before people even spoke them.

As she walked by, Mundt sized up the hopeful waitress. He guessed her to be twenty-two, and probably from outside Nashville. She had maybe done this a couple of times before, enough to grow leery of the come-ons. But she'd caught a big fish now, and his spiel seemed like less of an empty promise and more of a concrete opportunity. She seemed like a nice kid, and Mundt hoped this particular girl would actually get a shot at a record deal.

He wondered if he was getting soft.

"So," the waitress said as she slid Max's third drink toward him. "What's involved in making this demo?"

Max smiled and nodded at her. "A day," he replied. "Twenty four hours. Eight hours in the recording booth, eight hours with me, and eight hours of rest."

"And you'll do everything you said?"

"Yes," he replied.

"How do I know I can trust you?" she asked.

"Because what I'm offering really isn't very much," he replied. "Like I said, I'm not promising to make you a star. I'm promising to drop a demo off. And if, by some chance, you actually *do* have some sort of star quality and can actually sing . . . well, then I benefit as much as you do."

"I see," she said. "So. When do we start?"

Mundt lifted his drink to his lips. It was the same song he'd heard a hundred times before, just a new verse. It was the Music Row way. Tonight, the drama was as stale as last year's news, and he was ready to depart this cash free bordello disguised as a bar.

Slipping his phone from his pocket, Mundt slowly typed a text to Hathaway.

"Time to clear out. Subject should be arriving in 30-40 minutes. Confirm."

He pressed send, and listened as the text disappeared with a faint swoosh sound. His job for the night was done. He stared at the phone. Technology had made his job easier, but it hadn't made it any less depressing. He wondered how a night's work could be this easy and this distasteful at the same time.

"Can I do anything for you?" a voice came from behind him.

Mundt turned and looked into the girl's sparkling eyes. "No," he said, after a brief pause. "Think I'll settle up."

"You have a good night," she smiled.

"You too," he replied, feeling a touch of sadness over a hopeful girl he didn't know, and never would. .

His phone swooshed. "Message received."

Mundt once again turned his focus on Max, who sat relaxed, contented and self-assured, sipping his final cocktail.

"Glad you could join us," said the waitress, sliding a plastic tray and receipt in front of Mundt. "Enjoy your evening."

Mundt looked at her. "You too," he said as she walked away.

Mundt looked at Max, then typed out another text. "Expect a party of two when Max gets home."

Reaching into his wallet, he pulled out a fifty. He left it on the counter, slid off his perch and walked out into the night, his stool still spinning.

*   *   *

Maci Willis lay on silk sheets across a fitted mattress, her comforter tucked around her like a cocoon.

It was only her second night on her cloud-like bed since Max had sent her to Fayetteville, but her lumpy mattress in her hiding place seemed like a distant memory.

In the mental haze of the wee hours, she thought about Shale and Hathaway, who'd entered her hidden retreat as softly as cat's feet, but sported solid steel badges and guns.

She'd never liked cats or weapons.

As she stretched her arms, she realized that the past week had seemed like a year. For ages she'd felt like her life was a melodrama, but her life since Fayetteville had taken things to new dimensions. Surely things had hit bottom, and sound sleep would come tonight. Her fatigue was off the charts, as her mind drifted to the previous morning, when she showered and primped before her two-hour show. All of that was more than enough to make for a draining day. But the charade at the convenience store and the subsequent hiding of key imprints inside Max's office had been enough stress to last three lifetimes. He had repeatedly demanded why he and she had ended a marathon day by stopping at his office. Waiting for an opening to hide her imprints, Maci had been a nervous wreck. But she executed her assigned role, and Max still didn't realize that FBI agents had planted microphones in his office, and now his house .

It all went off like clockwork. The plan was intact, but Maci remained on the edge of exhaustion.

She closed her eyes and tried to drift away. But like an apparition given life, Lester, the feeble boy man, was suddenly inside her head, his baffled, befuddled face unable to understand either his actions or hers. Meeting her had been his dream and his nightmare, played out inside her Fayetteville hotel suite above a rock-hard parking lot, Lester's temporary and open grave.

She wondered if she had brought this upon herself, if the person she had turned into actually deserved this. She wrapped the pillow over her ears, as if that would banish the image of Lester from her mind, and tried to sleep.

Again she saw Lester's contorted face, the countenance of pity that pled for the type of love that could only come from a soul mate. But she knew she was not his soul mate. And when she thought of her soul, she felt nothing but a sad and silent void.

She pitied him. She hated him. But she told herself that none of that mattered. She had acted on a defensive instinct that had ultimately spared a life - her own.

As Maci eased toward sleep, she realized that she, and only she, could have persuaded Lester to push his cart, and the cake he'd made for her, through a tall window and to his demise. She also knew that she and only she could have prevented it.

She reflected more on their encounter in her hotel room, and how she ran away. She wondered if it would have made a difference to him if she had looked out the window, into his pitiful and pitiable dying eyes. Lying in bed, she sensed how he must have looked; his face a steady gaze that never softened. It filled her with overwhelming guilt, the knowledge that she wouldn't look down at the human lamb that lived to look up to her. Then she finally slipped into sleep, where a sordid dream told her she should have done something different, but would not tell her what she should have done.

She awoke the next day, saddened by her dreams, but happy to be alive and in her own bed.

Her bleary eyes began to discern lighted numerals on her bedside clock, and she realized she'd been awakened by a muted ringing. She sobered herself with loud cussing, and heard her words mesh with the muffled ringing of her bedside telephone buried somewhere beneath a spare pillow.

She grabbed its handset as her clearing eyes focused on the table clock.

'Surely that clock is wrong,' she thought. 'Surely I haven't been asleep for ten hours.'

"Whoever this is," she said into the telephone, "better have a damned good reason for calling."

"Maci," a voice said calmly. "I'm deeply sorry for calling this early. But I need to send a car to your house. Please have someone open the gate, and dress as you would for television."

"I've had about enough television to last nine lifetimes," she said. "And who the hell is this?"

"Sorry, Maci, I thought you knew my voice by now. This is Agent Shale."

"Oh, uh, I'm sorry Agent Shale, I guess. Is something wrong? What is it?"

"Maci, thanks to you and your key imprints, we were able to access Max's house and the safe room."

"Okay, that's all good, I think," she responded. "So why are you calling?"

"Max entered the safe room with a TracFone and called someone whose number we recorded and deciphered, then tapped it when the person was still on the line with Max. We want to bring you in to see if you can identify who Max talked to."

"Tonight? I mean, this morning?"

"Maci, we need to know if you can identify this guy so we can apprehend him. We recorded his voice, but that's all we have now."

"Can it wait a bit?"

Agent Shale exhaled heavily. "Maci, we think Max was talking to that voice about the attempts to kill you. We think there could possibly be another try."

Maci's throat tightened and the conversation fell silent.

"Maci, are you there?"

"I'm out of bed," she answered. "The gate will be open, and I'll be at my front door in ten minutes. Just let me splash some water on my face and find a suitable wig."

13

The clutter on Maci's bedroom floor looked as if an explosion had been set off in a second hand store adjacent to a pawn shop.

"And why not?" she said to herself. "Everything else has happened to me this week."

Still sleepy, she stretched before brushing her teeth. After haphazardly getting dressed, she forced a wig onto her head and wondered when she'd last washed her hair.

Almost running down the stairs, she hit the second floor landing and glanced through a window overlooking her front lawn and gate. An unidentified, off-white sedan sat in the driveway. Given its bland color, she guessed it belonged to the FBI.

Once outdoors, she trotted toward the vehicle as it started toward her, and they met halfway between the open gate and her circular driveway.

"Good morning," she said happily, bouncing into the front seat. "I understand you guys think I know someone who murders people."

Agent Shale sat upright in the drivers' seat, while Agent Hathaway sat just as stiffly in the back. They knew Maci was under stress, but had no desire to make light of her situation.

"Too bad we're in a rush," Maci said. "I made a five-course breakfast for you guys. It was a box of cereal and four more just like it."

The agents smiled, and that told Maci they were actually amused, and that they truly liked her, bur probably not much. She wondered if they were allowed to share friendships with informants, or whatever she was to them.

"Now, Maci," said Agent Shale, attempting to change her tone. "We've got some serious business to take care of today."

"I've never been to the Federal Building in Nashville," she said. "I'm eager to see if your offices are like the ones in the movies."

"Well, you'll have to check them out another time," said Shale. "We're not going to the Federal Building this morning. It's a public building, and too many people would recognize you, even if we entered through the back."

"Okay," she replied. "So where are we going?"

"We were hoping we could talk inside your house. We've brought digital recordings of Max's phone calls. The sound quality is very good. If you know the other guy's voice you'll probably know his name."

"Well . . ." Maci hesitated. "You want to talk in my house? It's a shambles. My housekeeper hasn't been here in a week!"

"That won't be a problem," said Hathaway. "It's probably Buckingham Palace compared to the place where we first met you."

Maci smiled and shook her head. She genuinely liked these men who weren't afraid to treat her like a normal person. She considered buying each a new car, but thought that two Corvettes might be a bit excessive. She instead wondered if she really had breakfast cereal.

After driving to the back of Maci's home, the trio stepped from the government issue vehicle, onto the asphalt driveway and stood before a four-car garage.

"I'm sure you guys heard the story about George Jones when he was married to Tammy Wynette," she said to neither in particular. Looking at Hathaway, then returning his stare at Maci, Shale said he didn't think so.

"Well, then you definitely haven't heard it, because it's a story people don't forget," Maci said. "Have you guys ever heard of George Jones?"

"I have," Hathaway replied. "He was the greatest singer and the biggest drunk in country music."

"You're right!" Maci said. "Let me tell you a true story that happened in front of my house.

"Well, Tammy did everything she could to get George sober. So one night, when George had run out of booze, she hid all of their car keys so he couldn't drive to a liquor store. But Tammy forgot to take the keys out of the riding lawnmower.

"So Jones actually drove the riding mower out onto the street in his quest for spirits. He had traffic backed up bumper-to-bumper for blocks, but he just kept puttering along toward the liquor store. I never knew if he got home the same way."

"That would be a MWI," said Shale. "Mowing While Intoxicated."

The two men laughed, if for no other reason than to hide the dread of what lay ahead. In a few scant minutes, Maci would hear a man she'd known for decades, discussing attempts on her life with someone else she might possibly know too.

Once in her kitchen, the agents seated themselves across from each other at circular table in front of a bay window. Hathaway pulled a small recorder out of his pocket and placed it on the table.

"I'm really not looking forward to this," Maci said.

"I know," replied Shale. "But you are looking forward to all of this being over."

Maci nodded. She wanted to make a joke to lighten the mood, but knew it was useless. Not even the late George Jones could have lifted their solemn moods, she thought, not even if he drove a lawnmower through her kitchen.

"I'll let you hear the dialogue between Max and his accomplice," Hathaway said to Maci. "This conversation took place just two days ago. The dominant voice is Max's. There's no doubt about that. But as I said, we couldn't identify the other person. Most of this recording is small talk. But there's a segment where there are indications that Max knew you might face mortal danger. Another part implies you'll face that same kind of danger again."

Maci felt awkward being involved with this level of the investigation. She was out of her element. She wondered if either noticed the slight trembling in her legs.

"All of this will be fine," Shale said to Maci. "We can turn off the recording whenever you want."

Maci instantly felt secure when Shale took her hand, looked into her eyes, and said, "We've got this."

Hathaway pressed the player's button. Max Abernathy's recorded voice was anything but calming. Even through the compact speakers, his word had a sinister ring to them. His tone was a slimy whisper, even during his small talk. Maci thought he needed to clear his throat, but he continued to speak in a quiet, raspy tone.

When boasting about his sexual conquests, Max the record producer and Meacham big shot issued vulgarities in levels of low and disgusting mumbles. He mentioned the cocktail waitress he'd recently picked up in a Music Row bar. But he never mentioned her name. Maci surmised he didn't remember it, probably because he never cared to ask it.

"I can't stand that sickening animal!" she exclaimed, her voice bouncing off her high ceiling. Her tears told the agents that she wasn't afraid, but outraged by the sadist who'd managed her career after inventing her public persona more than two decades ago.

"I'm all right," she said, pausing.

Max continued talking, bringing up a few priceless fixtures inside his contemporary castle. He said he'd bought all of his accent pieces for pennies on the dollar, because he "knew a guy."

Maci's floating eyes told Hathaway that she was mentally drifting, and that she had heard Max's bragging more than a few times previously. She envisioned a bedroom with brass-plated bedposts under a black velvet painting of Max. Or maybe the painting was attached to the mirror over his bed so his women were forced to see it. She envisioned their gasps at the sight, and cringed at the touch of Max the Pig.

"Hey," Max said, his tone still subdued on the recording. Hathaway raised the machine's volume as high as possible.

"You've got to stop what you've been doing, know what I mean?" Max said to the unidentified listener. "Your work was outstanding, and it succeeded. Good grief, you found two guys and both of them tried to take her out. They had perfect psychological profiles."

"And it sure wasn't your fault that both of those misfits were killed before finishing their jobs. But plans have changed. I don't need her dead, at least not for a while."

"All of this publicity has pulled the world's heart strings. They're buying her CDs and downloads like crazy. I want her to stay around for another tour to sell more products, know what I mean? Who knew her burned out career would revive like this?"

"I mean, you know I hired you to do your thing so I could collect on the life insurance policy I took out on her," Max continued. "Ten million was a lot when I bought it. It still is. But that can wait. She can get dead whenever we want, know what I mean? Right now, her shows would fill arenas, just like she filled them in her prime."

"I'm going to arrange for Meacham Records to promote all of her dates. Hell, I can skim fifty thousand dollars off every show. And I've got a 'fix' with her merchandise manager. Man, I'll make another small fortune off her."

Of his own volition, Hathaway stopped the recording.

Without looking, he knew Maci was suppressing the hysteria that was building inside her.

"How could he say those things!" she yelled, exploding into tears. "I thought he liked me and loved me in his own sick way. Why would he . . . ?"

"Maci," Shale interrupted, and slid both of his hands over one of hers. "We're almost through. We just need you to identify the next voice you hear."

She was glad it was Shale and not Hathaway who'd spoken the encouragements. The younger agent seemed to bend the rules just enough to follow his heart, while Hathaway clearly went by the book.

"Look Max," said a new voice on the recording. "We had a deal, and I have ways of collecting, you know that. I mean, if a couple of people can be persuaded to kill Maci, at least one can be persuaded to kill you."

"You'll get your money . . . there's no reason for threats or anything stupid. You'll get your money. I've been sifting cash little by little from Meacham, but with all of this publicity about Maci, I wasn't going to hook up with you until things settled down. You'll get your money . . . how about this week?"

"That will work," said the second voice.

"I just don't need anything else done on any more of her songs. There's plenty of that on her current album. Who knows if other retards with a gun will surface again because of that?"

The recorder clicked off. Maci stared at it as if she were suddenly catatonic.

Both agents stared at her silently.

"Did you recognize that second voice on the recording?" Hathaway finally said, intentionally shattering the silence.

"It's 'Ears' Sullivan," Maci said, without having to think. "Jim 'Ears' Sullivan. He's one of the best engineers in the business, and he's been the engineer on all of my records produced by Max. Come to think of it, Ears has engineered every song I've ever recorded for Meacham. He's nicknamed Ears because he can fine-tune a recording just by listening to the mix. Ears can take a Fender Telecaster Guitar, you know, with its sharp sound . . . ?"

"I don't know about that, but go on," Hathaway said.

"Well, as I was saying, Ears can make a Defiant sound like a Telecaster, and place its slice in just the right places on a recording. Or, he can muffle the same guitar, and let it carry the instrumental lead. He's Max's favorite recording engineer. Max gets all of the credit for producing a song, but it's really Ears that makes the work really shine."

"So what are you getting at?" she finished.

"Let's take a break, Maci. You might want a drink or something to eat before we resume. Agent Shale and I are going to prove to you that Max and Ears arranged the shooting at Bridgestone Arena, and the guy with the knife in Fayetteville. They conspired to kill you—and they might do it again."

Maci ingested a handful of stale potato chips and downed some lukewarm water from the kitchen sink. Staring at her food, the agents politely declined her offer of anything to eat.

"Well, let's get on with this thing," she breathed. "I want to be sure that I live to eat a real meal. What are Max and Ears talking about? And what does it have to do with my records?"

"Agent Shale and I will answer all of those questions and more," said Hathaway. "But first, I want to tell you a little story that may answer some of them. Okay?"

"Sure," she replied, puzzled. "I mean, I guess . . . "

"About sixty years ago, a guy ran a movie projector in a theater in Ft. Lee, New Jersey. In those days, film was twenty-four photographs moving every second. So he decided to experiment by removing an occasional image and replacing it with a photograph of popcorn. It was there, but it was too quick for the human eye to detect. Viewers saw the popcorn, but they didn't know it. But their subconscious minds caught it. People in the audience suddenly had mass cravings for popcorn—which they acted on by buying all the popcorn in the theater."

"They call it 'subliminal suggestion,'" interjected Shale.

"I've heard of that," said Maci.

"Subliminal suggestion is a subconscious suggestion that ultimately manifests as human behavior. In the case of Ft.

Lee, the subliminal suggestions resulted in a big boost of popcorn sales."

"I get it," said Maci. "But what's popcorn got to do with me and my records?"

"From outward appearances, it looks like the people who attacked you acted on their own," said Shale. "But we believe they didn't. We believe the idea was planted in their heads by your music."

"My music?"

"Yes," replied Hathaway. "Or, rather, suggestions that were planted in your music. The subliminal suggestions were buried in your recorded lyrics."

"Based on Max's and Ear's conversation last night, Max had earlier hired Ears to electronically place clips of your speaking voice into your recorded songs—subliminally, beneath the music tracks. The words were your request to kill you. Now, 99.99 percent listeners never heard the words. But only one listener was needed to kill you. And your music is broadcast so widely, it was bound to reach at least one person who was susceptible to subliminal suggestion. Some person who had some form of mental dysfunction. Who possessed a psychotic obsession for you and your music. And, whose mind had some sort of glitch that enabled him to hear and subconsciously process the suggestions buried in your music."

"And Max did that?" asked an incredulous Maci. "With Ears?"

"You've told me that Max lives for money," the agent continued. "And you've told me that Ears has the talent to deeply place sounds onto recorded songs. Between the two of them, that's exactly what they did."

"Max would do a lot of things," she said, shaking her head. "But he would never do that. He and I go back over twenty years."

"I thought you might feel that way," Hathaway said. "That's why I brought this."

He slid a compact disc marked "Evidence" into a portable player and, without explanation, activated a conversation.

"Where did you get that!?" Maci demanded, instantly recognizing the voices. "That's Max and me arguing. He's trying to convince me to do that stupid promotion tour after the Bridgestone shooting. He thought I'd sell a lot of records from sympathetic fans. Instead, I got some jerk who tried to kill me on the tour's Fayetteville stop. Where did you get this?"

"Never mind, Maci . . . listen to what you're about to say."

The recorder couldn't lie. Maci heard herself demanding that she not be forced to do a publicity tour in the wake of the Bridgestone shooting, the most frightening ordeal of her life. She regarded the proposed tour as a greedy gesture to generate revenue for Meacham Records.

"Don't you mean 'monetize' my trauma, Max?" said Maci's recorded voice. "You people really kill me."

Hathaway stopped the recording, and abruptly raised his hand for silence.

"You heard your own voice saying 'kill me,' right?"

Maci said nothing.

"Ears Sullivan lifted your words, in your voice, saying 'kill me,'" explained Hathaway. "He electronically spliced the words into a recorded song you released before the Bridgestone shooting. The result? You unknowingly asked some poor demented soul to kill you. The same subliminal request caught the ear of the waiter in Fayetteville who wanted you to leap from a high-rise window. He thought that's what you wanted."

"Take one *special* fan," Shale injected. "One who is mentally off-balance, and who is obsessed with you, and he might do exactly what he thinks you're asking for. In your case, there were two fans out there who filled the bill."

"This is just too much . . ." said Maci, throwing her face into her hands.

"Here," Shale said. "Listen to your last song, 'Leave Me Then Go.'"

The song poured from the agents' CD player. As cautiously as a child awaiting a jack-in-the-box toy to pop up, Maci moved closer to the familiar arrangement and audio mix emanating from the metal case. Her blank face told Shale she heard nothing but the song she'd released weeks before the shooting attempt at the Bridgestone Arena.

She stiffened as Shale began turning dials that modified the recording and muffled the primary tracks. Gradually, her voice and all instrumentation were gone.

"Now I'm going to raise a track that you didn't hear," Shale said slowly. "But it was there all along. And at least two men heard it, and each responded in a way that cost them their lives."

Like a whisper inside a stadium, an electronic sound hinted at a voice that was so silent Maci couldn't discern it. Still turning the dial, Shale let the volume gradually rise. It was then Maci heard the words - her words - repeating, "kill me."

Like a bolt of lightning, she realized what Max had done. He'd used her own voice—the voice that had made them both rich—to make him even richer, and to orchestrate her own assassination.

The blood seemingly ran from her face. Shale then replayed the song with all audio components in place. Maci's subliminal voice was nowhere to be heard.

"It's gone," Maci said. "But it's still there. But my voice begging someone to kill me is still there, isn't it?"

"Yes," said Hathaway. "It's always been there."

"And maybe somebody else is still hearing it," Maci said, her eyes moistening. "And all this might happen again!"

Her chair fell backwards when she nervously stood, wringing her hands. She took two steps forward into Shale's arms, and buried her uncontrollable weeping into his shoulder.

"I'm afraid so," Hathaway said. "It's still there, on this CD and all the others, including downloads. There are millions of them out there, and there's nothing that I or Agent Shale or anyone else can do to erase them."

Maci's sobbing evolved into hysteria. Shale tried to comfort her, but at the same time said nothing to gloss over the situation at hand. He instead remained speechless, and let Maci's heaving chest rise and fall upon his muscular torso. He held her tightly, and realized his sympathy wasn't mandated in any FBI manual or handbook.

"Maci," said Shale, "the simple reality is that you're not out of the woods yet. There may be other people out there like the first two who responded to your unreal request. And some of them might feel compelled to try to kill you.

They think you'll love them once they do."

14

The high, vaulted beam ceilings of Maci's mansion seemed to magnify her isolation even more so tonight. Sitting in the vastness of her oversized living room, she felt like a minnow lost in an ocean of solitude.

"This is how it's always been," she said. "This is how it will always be. I entertain twenty thousand people, but at the end of the day there's only me. The crowds are easy. Facing loneliness is the hardest thing I do."

She worked to live, and lived to work, and neither gave her any peace of mind. She had everything she ever wanted, but now felt as if she had nothing at all.

With the lights off, Maci eased back into her overstuffed sofa and casually watched the current events unfolding on her television. Few things are brighter than a television screen in total darkness, she thought to herself. Squinting into the glare, she watched as the late night newscast cut to the image of a familiar face.

Her publicist had often said that television adds ten pounds to anyone onscreen. Maci noted that Max indeed looked a tad heavier. His usual arrogant strut was also replaced by an awkward slump. The camera lights reflected off the shining chrome of the handcuffs that locked his hands against the small of his back.

"No comment!" Max shouted to reporters loping beside him outside the Meacham offices.

Maci wondered how so many journalists had learned so quickly of Max's arrest.

The television announcer spelled it out for all to hear: the head of Meacham's Nashville office was being charged with conspiracy to commit murder, a felony punishable by life behind bars.

She couldn't process all of the questions being fired at Max, but a few rose above the clamor.

"Max, are you guilty?" a reporter flatly asked.

"Max, did you arrange the attempted killings of Maci Willis?"

"Max, were you paid by organized crime to have Maci killed? Did you hire a hit man?"

"Max, have you and Maci ever had sex?"

Taken totally aback, Maci felt her lower jaw drop and her breathing stop.

"Why the hell are you asking him that?" she screamed, her voice bouncing off the walls. To her astonishment, Maci found herself defending Max, if only for herself.

"He may have the morals of an alley cat but he built my career and a dozen others!" she screamed.

Still in shock from the day's events, she felt a sense of pity for the man who had orchestrated her rise to wealth and fame. She was saddened to see one of the most powerful men in the industry—and in her life—suddenly rendered powerless and vulnerable.

"Why don't you ask how many records he's sold?" said Maci, still thundering at the television reporters. "And how dare you ask if he slept with me! Be sure that not one of you ever will! Good grief, I'd rather do it with a mannequin."

Maci's rant came to an abrupt stop when the camera zoomed back from Max's bewildered face, and Agents Hathaway and Shale entered the television screen.

Shale opened the backdoor of the very car that had been parked on her grounds earlier today. Hathaway's open hand capped the top of Max's head as he firmly shoved his prisoner into the backseat.

Her sympathy for Max was fast evolving into pity for herself. As if she hadn't been examined enough by the media lately, she now knew that her file footage would be offered to stations all over the world, and attached to the footage of Max being led away in handcuffs. Her mind running in circles, she winced to imagine what the Internet would make of Max's high profile arrest and the questions of whether he had ever slept with her.

She shook her head and muted the sound when a female reporter nearly bolted onto the screen, then began telling viewers what they already knew.

"That's good, honey," Maci muttered, "if you can't find a new angle, just repeat the old ones. That's what they pay you for."

Knowing her moods were vacillating, Maci wondered for a moment if she were losing her grip on sanity. She'd been through too much in the past weeks, and she knew it was taking more of a toll than she wanted to admit. Taking a deep breath, she turned the sound up when the agents once again appeared onscreen.

"Decorated FBI Agent Dewayne 'Dual' Hathaway and Agent Rick Shale had arrived at Meacham Records earlier tonight with an arrest warrant for Max Abernathy, legendary music business mogul and Grammy-Award-winning record producer," said a reporter.

"According to an unnamed source, the arrest was tied to the recent attempt on Maci Willis' life by a shooter last month during the singer's concert at Bridgestone Arena in Nashville. The source went on to say that the FBI intensified its investigation into Abernathy after the mysterious suicide of a kitchen employee who'd just visited Ms. Willis inside a Fayetteville, Arkansas hotel.

"Moments ago, Tennessee Insurance Commissioner William Oswald confirmed that Abernathy had purchased a ten million dollar term life insurance policy on Ms. Willis during a period when her record sales had hit a two-decade low.

"Oswald said the policy was legal, and that Ms. Willis had signed the policy with Abernathy as its only beneficiary.

"FBI agents will likely interrogate Abernathy over his monetary motives for his alleged conspiracy to have Ms. Willis killed.

"Agents are also seeking the whereabouts of James 'Ears' Sullivan, a legendary recording engineer for numerous Music Row record producers, including Abernathy. Reporting for WOLL, I'm Tira Cline."

Maci feverishly looked for the remote control to silence the television once again, then realized she'd thrown it at the TV screen upon the revelation of the ten-million-dollar insurance policy.

Torn between her anger at Max and her greater hatred of reporters, Maci's mind remained in an unstoppable whirl.

"Who knows what kind of life insurance policy I signed?" she yelled. "I've always signed whatever Max put in front of me. I'm an entertainer, not a lawyer. And I'd rather be a two-dollar hooker before I'd ever be a reporter!"

Listening to the depth of her heavy breathing, she stopped short, fearing she'd hyperventilate. She was sure her blood pressure was about to explode. "There was no sense in arguing with the idiot box," she told herself. "Even if you're right, it can't hear you. You can't win."

Desperately, she turned her open purse upside down, grabbing in the dark for anything small. She hoped for a Valium, but found nothing but a half broken antacid, which she furiously tossed to the floor.

Now totally beside herself, she angrily turned her television off. She was mad at herself for even listening to what she didn't want to hear.

Forcing herself from her sofa, she hurried upstairs to the landing and peered through the window where she'd seen the FBI car earlier that day. The crowd outside her locked gate milled about like a spastic picket line, and one member brandished a sign that read, "Leave Maci Alone." Some irony, Maci thought. Still, she appreciated her fans' outrage against reporters.

She wondered how beloved she'd be to those fans if they could see her current breakdown in progress. Her closed window muted their voices, but she tried in vain to discern what they were saying. She wondered if any of them had heard the subliminal voice in her song. Hopelessly confused, she wondered if she was hallucinating on adrenaline, and if that was even possible.

"Are these people really on my grounds, or inside my head?" she wondered.

She needed support, but not the kind afforded by fans who love an image. She needed something real, but she wasn't sure where to find it.

Increasingly delirious, Maci stumbled back down the stairs to the garage. She didn't turn on a single light, and heard little but the distant sound of her television set.

Inside her car, she thought the soft rumble of her rising garage door resembled thunder. The racket was too much for her agitated state, and she responded by prematurely stomping the car's gasoline pedal. Her car's roof caught the bottom panel of the rising door and noisily pulled it from its tract. Frightened, she accelerated further and the car continued to pull the door until it tumbled onto the concrete driveway. Fallen steel, wood and glass were still rocking on the pavement as Maci slammed the car into drive.

Disoriented, she turned on her headlights and charged headlong down the driveway toward the milling fans outside her gate.

She was cognizant that her actions were wrong, but at the same time she seemed to have no control over them. She began blaring her car's horn while barreling toward the crowd stationed between her gate and the road. Flashing her headlights repeatedly from high to low, she closed her eyes as her car sped toward the assembly, praying aloud that God would make them move.

If she electronically opened the gate, energized fans would overrun her grounds and her unlocked house. If she didn't, she'd drive through the gate and possibly overrun some people.

She felt a sense of relief when, through the open driver's side window, she heard someone yell, "She's coming through the gate! Get out of the way!"

The terrified fans chaotically pushed at each other, but miraculously managed to form a widening hole in their ranks. It never occurred to Maci to stop her car, and thanks to the crowd's quick reaction, she didn't have to. She instead focused on aiming her vehicle toward the opening they'd formed for her.

She felt the resistance of the wrought iron gate as she smashed through it. For some reason, she glanced down at her speedometer where she saw the number 42 as she screeched onto the road.

In her rearview mirror, she could see that some of the fevered onlookers were charging onto to her private grounds, just as she'd expected they would. Her taillights eerily turned them into reddened silhouettes sweeping across the dewy grass. Maci thought they were like a gallery painting come to life. Then they were out of sight, swallowed by the darkness that was deepening in her rearview window.

She gripped her steering wheel firmly and headed into the night. She was unsure where she was headed, and for the moment unsure where she had been. "If I had a riding mower, this might be funny," she thought to herself.

She breathed deeply and continued to drive.

15

It was the only place she could think to go. After driving aimlessly for more than an hour, Maci returned to the familiarity of her dilapidated retreat on the other side of Nashville. The night air had a calming effect, and as she drifted back into sanity the entire evening began to seem like a bad dream. She let a few hours pass, then decided to use her old car as a disguise to return to her mansion.

With oil smoke floating from the exhaust, Maci stopped to chat with Leon Smith, her gatekeeper inside the guard shack. She had hired him nearly ten years ago upon his release from prison. He never told her why he'd been incarcerated, and she'd never asked. "I'd rather have an honest ex-convict than a liar who's never been caught," she'd said to him, the day he delivered his employment application.

Now daylight, as he leaned over Maci's driver's window, Leon did what he'd done countless times, and talked with her through the slight opening of darkly tinted glass, while simultaneously scanning her acreage and adjacent street. Passers-by simply thought Leon was chatting with a fan to whom he wouldn't allow entry.

"Well, Miss Maci," Leon said, "I done come to work this mornin' and found the gate plumb knocked down. There's paint on the wrought iron, and it's the color of your BMW. And the way that there wrought iron fell, well Ms. Maci, the driver done come from your house's side of the gate."

"Really?" Maci replied. "Well . . . you know the driver wasn't me."

"How so Ms. Maci?"

"Because the guard shack's still standing, and the house hasn't been set on fire."

Leon laughed and watched the exhaust from Maci's car form a trail as she drove up the driveway toward her garage.

Slowly, her rage from last night had been replaced by a sense of comfort the instant she'd encountered Leon. His welcoming demeanor made her mansion feel even more like home. Even after entering her lavish house, Maci's thoughts remained on her gatekeeper who'd stood inside a guard shack, hot or cold, dry or wet, for over a decade. She wondered where his replacement had been during her overnight rampage, but didn't ask. Instead, she called Leon to ask him to get someone to repair the gate that she'd knocked from its hinges. But there was no need; he already had a man en route.

She felt herself smile when she recalled multiple incidents when Leon stood toe-to-toe with drunks who spat out insults while threatening to climb over the gate to visit Maci Willis.

"Not on my watch!" Leon had always said, his face glaring at the potential intruders.

"Let me on this property old man or I'll whip your ass," a man had threatened Leon one night.

"You won't be in shape enough to whoop a two-year-old when I get through with you," Leon shouted, as Maci heard from her home's open window, and fascinated by Leon's loyalty.

The obstinate drunk swung, Leon ducked then pelted him with a rapid combination of punches. An upper cut knocked him out.

The failed fighter awakened only to feel Leon dabbing iodine on his bottom lip, which Leon had split.

Once, a starry-eyed and very pregnant woman vowed to Leon that she wasn't going to leave the perimeter surrounding his guard shack until Maci came down from her house to meet her.

"Yous don't have to move," Leon told the zealous fan. "It's not against the law for you to stands in that there zone."

For hours thereafter, the two exchanged friendly barbs until the woman's water broke.

Watching from inside the house, Maci heard Leon shout that he'd called 911. An ambulance arrived, but not before the woman delivered a baby on the asphalt beside the guard shack. From his military training, Leon knew how to ease the baby from the mother's womb and cut the umbilical cord. The happy and frightened mother was crying tears of joy when the ambulance took her away, and promised that she'd name the infant Leon.

Six days later, she returned with the child and a birth certificate.

"She'd named her little girl 'Leon,'" Leon proudly reported to Maci.

Giggling, she remembered that her night guard was off duty when she ran through the gate and into temporary freedom the previous night. She hoped she wouldn't have another lapse like that. She didn't know how much it cost to repair wrought iron, but she guessed it wasn't cheap.

"My neighbors and fans are going to think I'm crazy," she said to herself. "Not that that's anything new."

She half-expected her words would make her smile. Instead, she felt a tiny hint of sadness slowly building in her cluttered mind.

For a while, she didn't say a word. Not to herself, or to anyone else, not even to her trustworthy Leon.

"I guess you just gotta go crazy from time to time, to keep from becoming insane," she said, thinking she'd heard a similar phrase in a song.

She realized she'd been talking and singing to herself for months, maybe longer, and feared for a moment that her chatter was symptomatic of mental illness. She made a mental note to ask her psychologist if it was cause for concern. She intended to schedule an emergency session after the previous night's mayhem.

Dreading seeing her shrink, Maci feared the doctor would use words like "neurotic," "psychotic" and "bi-polar." But Maci preferred to think she was simply a chatterbox who talked to herself only because no one else would listen.

Having left her television playing overnight, Maci was greeted as she walked in the main room by an announcer spelling out the agony of psoriasis, followed by a commercial for wart removal cream. She realized that her only dependable companionship lay in the endless string of programs and commercials, and the cheers from fans who still stood outside her property.

"On some days life is awful, on others it just hurts," she said, thinking there may be a song in that line.

She'd never had a loving family, and was fairly certain she never would. "Families are for happy, energetic people who love each other. I'm a worn out, embittered person who loves no one, especially myself" she said, as if debating herself.

Fearfully, she finally met with her psychologist whose clinic she'd nicknamed "Dr. Shrink's Therapy Stinks." The respected female psychologist deplored the disrespect, but that didn't stop Maci from repeating it once each visit.

"What kind of 'shrink' are you if you can't take a joke?" she often asked her. "Besides, you should recognize it as a sign of passive aggressiveness. Or something. I don't know. I have a lot of guilt about my hate, and I hate my guilt. And guilt is the root for most psychological infirmities, right?"

Like a juror during a trial, the therapist never replied. Instead, she responded to most of Maci's comments by sitting and listening. Her silence was infuriating to Maci.

"I want a psychologist, not a deaf mute!" she said. "Shouldn't I be getting well right about now?"

"That's not how this works," the doctor replied. "But then, you already know that."

"I get it," Maci replied. "You want to make me better, but only by the clock because time is money. I get that. After all, each time I leave your office I feel like two cents. And three hundred dollars lighter."

The psychologist hardly smiled. She let Maci rattle on another thirty minutes, then announced that it was time for her to leave.

Maci always hated that.

Her recurring depression and mood swings didn't start or stop at the dictates of a clock. After some sessions ended, she tried desperately to stop her anguish with self-therapy. This usually involved retreating into a few hours of solitude, where she allowed herself to be terrified by reflections of her deplorable father. She could trigger his reappearance by merely closing her eyes. Sometimes, in fact most times, he'd come into her mind without her willingly conjuring his image. Each time he returned, he was accompanied by the secret that she pretended belonged to someone else.

Falling asleep, her mind's imaginary curtain rose on a scene where her unwashed and unshaven father told her she was old enough to play house. Maci was twelve, and the simple phrase "playing house" was sickening by his demand that she touch him, and let herself be touched in return. She had to let him do whatever he wanted. Otherwise, he would tell her mother, and then neither parent would want her. He reminded her of this over and over.

A few years later, her dad said that no household, whether play or real, was good without a baby. As he lay heavily on her, she gasped for air. He told her she was pleasing God for giving Him the chance to make another precious child like her. But Maci didn't feel precious.

Her dad said she'd make God mad if she didn't do her part to make one of his creations. She wondered why a nice person like God expected her to do awful things to please Him.

Frequently, her dad kept her from going to school. "He would be her teacher." During recesses, she and he worked more frequently to please God to help Him make a child. But school soon evolved into a series of constant recesses, and her dad made her do her part even more often so God could make a baby, and not be angry at her.

At age fourteen, her guilt for failing God drove her to confess to her mother, whose reply was instant: She called Maci a liar, and said liars deserve beatings. In the theater of her memories, Maci became numb to the belts, and ultimately numb to the entire world.

When she was 15, Maci saw her dad die after a man shot him for "playing house" with his wife. Unlike Maci, that woman had given God a baby by her dad. That woman was therefore good, and Maci's immature mind told her again that she was a disgrace to God because she didn't make Him a baby. And now she never would, she thought, because her dad died before she was able to please God.

Her mother remanded her to the State of Louisiana, where she lived in a home with older and delinquent teenage girls who didn't fail God the way she had. They claimed her dad just wanted to have illicit sex, and she'd never heard the word "illicit."

Suddenly, Maci's neck tinged as she awakened from her fitful sleep. Wiping her eyes, she eased back into the day, that time where she was always sad or angry or alone. As she washed her face, she was impressed with how well she was able to function and fake her happiness in public. "That's what good performers do," she reminded herself.

But recently, she felt as if she'd been sleeping more and more, even when awake. And so her suppressed pain had begun to arrive and depart more and more frequently. And unlike her doctor's clock, it didn't care when an hour had passed.

+⸙+ +⸙+

The television host's incessant banter was nothing but white noise to Maci, so she changed the station in hopes of some form of distraction. She hated numbing sounds, but sometimes decided they were better than sad silence. This wasn't one of those times. With the flip of a switch, the screen went black.

Suddenly, the quiet was pierced by the ring of her land-line phone, which reverberated beneath her high-rise ceiling. The caller ID screen read "Meacham" above a number with a 212 area code. Maci recognized it as a New York City number, probably Meacham's international headquarters.

She considered not answering, as she hated unexpected calls. Besides, only a handful of people knew her home phone number, and she didn't care to speak to any of them. Still tired, she knew she wouldn't sound composed if she picked up the receiver.

She let the call click over to voicemail. But rather than leaving a message, the caller simply redialed. Despite her inclination to not take the call, she decided the utterly ingratiating ring would continue until she answered.

She watched her shaking fingers slip around the telephone receiver, then placed the earpiece to her tilted head. She said nothing.

"Maci," an unfamiliar and resonate voice interjected after a few seconds. "After all of these years, I think it's about time we meet. I'm Claude Silverman, Chairman and CEO of Meacham Record's. How are you?"

She held her silence.

"Maci," he delicately said again. "Are you there?"

"Yes, I'm here," she finally replied, and flinched at the sound of her own voice. "I mean, I'm fine. Well, I mean I'm fine but I'm here too. Didn't you ask both of those questions?"

Rattled, she considered telling the caller he'd reached the wrong number, but realized she'd already identified herself. Knowing first impressions are most lasting, she guessed that this biggest of the big shots probably thought she needed rehabilation. Or something.

"How are things in New York?" she finally said, trying to move the conversation away from her.

"Well, things were fine when I left this morning."

"Really? Where are you now?"

"I'm outside your gate. Looks like you've had a little mishap here. Your security guard is sitting in a folding chair and people are driving by with camera phones taking his picture. Maybe he'll be Meacham's next big star."

"Not a chance," Maci replied. "I can't let Leon go."

"He's not wearing a uniform," Silverman continued. "Do you think people will show their pictures to their folks back home, and say he's your boyfriend?"

"No chance of that," Maci blurted. "Leon's been here ten years. No boyfriend could put up with me that long."

Silverman chuckled briefly, then his voice shifted to a serious tone. "Maci. We need to talk. May I come in?"

"This place is a shambles," she replied. "I didn't know you were coming. I've never had the Top Dog in my house."

Instantly, she regretted her choice of words.

"Well, I promise I won't bark," he said.

"Well, I'm a wreck, I need to clean up," she said. "Can you come back in an hour? Or better yet, next year?"

The would-be visitor giggled

"Maci, of course I should have called," he said. "But if I'd ask to visit, you might have said no. But we need to talk. Believe me. Otherwise, I wouldn't have flown down here this morning."

She knew her sanity had been shaky for days, but not enough to turn away her label's chief executive, one of American's most heralded music powerbrokers.

"Hand your phone to the guard and I'll tell him to let you in," Maci finally said.

She started toward the second floor landing window to size up her visitor but detoured into a bathroom to spend a few seconds primping.

Fumbling through a junk drawer, she happened upon a Groucho Marx mask, complete with horn-rimmed glasses, a giant nose, bushy eyebrows and mustache.

"Let's just see if Mr. Silverman has a *real* sense of humor," she said, tittering before he reached her door. "And let's hope he's old enough to remember Groucho Marx."

A tattered T-shirt, wrinkled Bermuda shorts and sneakers without socks rounded out her unwashed ensemble. She was sure Meacham's main man had never seen her without her signature blonde wig and impeccable makeup. On their first meeting, she looked less like Dolly Parton and more like Don Pardo.

The bell rang, and Maci leisurely walked to the door.

"Hi there," she said as she opened the door. "Now that you've seen what I look like up close, you'll never spring for the good seats again."

Her opening line delivered, Maci focused on the tall, impeccably dressed man who stood in her doorway. His pinstriped suit belonged in an Armani ad, and his lustrous grey hair had surely been coifed one follicle at a time.

"Well hello," he finally said. "Is Maci Willis here? She's expecting me."

"How could you not laugh at my 'Groucho Glasses?'" she said. "I worked all of three seconds to put this together."

"Pleased to meet you," he said. "Should I call a photographer? We might want to capture this for your next album cover."

Maci stepped back, removed her novelty spectacles and smiled.

"Mr. Silverman," she said. "Please forgive my appearance. I'm dressed like a joke because lately my life has been like one." She shook his hand and, to her surprise, she was actually at ease.

Silverman was accompanied by his much younger assistant, a slender blonde in a shimmering dress. Her suntan suggested she spent more time outside the office than in. Maci was sure the glamorous woman was recruited from a modeling agency, rather than a secretarial pool. As arm candy goes, she was pure Godiva.

"Come on in," Maci said, stepping back from the door. "I'd like to serve you folks something to eat, but I don't have anything. I thought I'd be on tour now, so the stock is low in the house. But you're welcome to whatever you can find in my medicine cabinet."

Maci saw that her guests' smiles were forced, and knew it was time to end her improvisations.

"So, Mr. Silverman . . ." she said.

"Please, call me Claude," he said, interrupting.

"I was just going to say that you didn't fly your jet this morning just to see an unkempt country singer. So, what can I do you for?"

"Maci, he replied, clearing his throat. "You know you're loved at Meacham, and you know you're adored by a sympathetic nation. Everyone extends love in the wake of these horrendous tragedies that have beset you."

Silverman's rhetoric and demeanor reminded Maci of a politician. Nice words usually are a smoke screen for not so nice actions. She wondered what was coming next.

Instead of responding she forced a nod, signaling him to continue.

"We at Meacham don't want to deprive you of pleasing the fans we know you love," he said, feigning compassion. "So Meacham wants to help you get back on the road, and get back in front of your adoring fans. Now, of course, we're mindful of your fear and misery from the two attempts on your life. If I may say, you're literally gun-shy."

His forced, half-smile reminded Maci of a used car salesman. She felt her stomach turn and decided his fashionable clothing wasn't enough to hide his crookedness.

"Excuse me, Claude, are you asking what I think you're asking?"

"I think you should hear me out," he insisted firmly. "No one expects you to go on stage without protection. In fact, your protection will be like a presidential security detail. But Maci, your recent ordeals prove that there's really no such thing as bad publicity. Sentimentality means sales, and fans young and old are swimming in sentiment and pity for you. We at Meacham couldn't have invented this much interest in you, not even if we'd used the best PR firms in the world. Why, only this morning, I talked to our publicity people, and all said the requests for inter-views are growing daily. I'm talking *60 Minutes, Dateline, Entertainment Tonight* and scores of others. And the print media? It's off the charts."

"You people amaze me," Maci said, interrupting. "You know, I had this same conversation, almost verbatim, with Max less than a month ago. He said I'd be safe, and look how that turned out. A mentally challenged man came into my room with a giant knife, then jumped out of a seven-story window.

Sure, I'll go on stage, if you stand on stage behind me."

Silverman's deep breaths told Maci he was slightly annoyed. Her mind made up against his proposal, she none-theless let him continue talking just to placate her label's top executive.

"Maci, work with me here because I'm going to describe a safety precaution that will be the first of its kind," Silverman continued.

"We're prepared to build a special performance booth for you lined with bullet-proof glass, the same stuff you see when you approach your bank's drive-through teller. You can sit on a stool behind a shield of bulletproof glass. Now, of course, you won't be able to dance in your shows, and there won't be any costume changes. But at this point, I think just having you show up is enough to fill most venues."

Maci stared in disbelief. Her inability to process what she'd just heard left her unable to speak.

"Let me get this right," she finally said. "You want me to sit on a stool and sing with my band behind . . . ?"

"No, that's another perk in this idea! You can dismiss the band entirely, and sing your hits to digital tracks. A solo performance. It won't have the punch of a big show, but it'll feel a lot more intimate."

"You want me sitting on a stool? No band? You don't want me to do my famous dancing? No costume changes, which is something else my fans expect? And sit behind glass that will splinter but not break? Have I got all of this right? Essentially, you want me to lip-sink my own recordings?"

"Maci," Silverman shouted, "It's not as bad as it sounds. You remember how hard the beginning of your career seemed. Well, the end is hard, too. And this can breathe new life into your career, and buy you a few more years."

"Well," Maci drawled, "why don't we forget the stool, and replace it with a toilet? I'll need one because this whole idea makes me sick. Yep, I could sit on the porcelain throne and flush the handle at the end of each song.

"You guys in the front offices . . . have you ever even seen my show? Do you know how I can work a crowd to a fevered pitch? Do you realize how many of those supercharged fans buy CDs at my merchandise table? It's safe to say that I'm the biggest Maci Willis compact disc store in America. And all of those CDs are sold to me from Meacham Records!"

"Maci," Silverman interrupted. "Your best days are gone. Let's all agree on that. But we at Meacham are just trying to make your current days better than they are. And with the bulletproof glass, you'll sit on a cozy and darling little stool or comfy chair or whatever you want and sing to people. And it'll be safe"

"And if they miss my glass show, we can always package me in cellophane, and stand me up beside a Kmart meat counter. I could even be a 'blue light special.'"

Silverman realized the conversation was as deadlocked as the Lincoln Tunnel during rush hour. It was time to play his trump card.

"Maci," he said, his tone sharpened. "You go back to your big show, ever, and you run the risk of getting killed. And, knowing that, well, it puts me and Meacham Records at risk of liability. I know that sounds cold, but that's just how it would be. So we're not going to place a great deal of money into your next tour, not unless you do it our way. And if you tour your way, it'll be without us. To be frank, you're in the music business, and the keyword is *business*. Now you can do this my way, or you can do without. I'm sure you'll want to think about this."

"I'm already thinking," Maci snapped. "I'm thinking about how I can get your greedy ass out of my house. Leave now, or I'll call the cops. Believe me, they know the way to my address."

Silverman rose, and nodded at the buxom blonde, her cue to rise as well.

"We can find our way out," he said.

Within seconds, he opened the door for his companion, and then took his own step into the doorway. Slowly, he turned to face Maci, still sitting across the room.

"You'll receive a notarized and official letter from Meacham's legal department," he said, dryly. "After more than two decades, you're no longer part of Meacham Records. Good luck finding a new label. Given your situation, I doubt that many would be willing to work on your terms."

Maci was sure his slamming of the door echoed unduly long. The next sound she heard was his driver starting a limousine. The car purred from her front door and out of earshot.

Maci was suddenly alone once again, wrapped in hollow silence. She was used to it. Already crying, she was trying to convince herself that she was fine.

16

"A big house is a prison when you have no one else around and no one is expected," Maci said aloud. After all these years, she still made a habit of talking to herself when alone, sometimes in hopes that a line or an idea for a song might surface from her solitary prattling. But now, in her exhausted state, her jabbering seemed crazy, and she wondered if it had been all along.

"I have nothing on my hands except time and wrinkles," she said, still talking to herself.

Both mental and physical fatigue were beginning to take their toll. Were it not for the oppressive wave of exhaustion, she would have had no feelings at all. Now, minutes after Silverman's ultimatum, she just wanted to be anyone other than herself.

Again her mind drifted to the recurring paradoxes that filled her stagnant hours: If millions of people loved her, why wasn't there just one person who loved only her? And if what she wanted more than anything else to have someone by her side, why did she feel most natural when she was all alone?

She'd often shared those haunting and conflicting thoughts with her psychologist, but got no answer. Or, perhaps an answer was suggested, but didn't ring true.

"The Last Word in Lonesome is Me," she half sang, recalling the title of a Roger Miller song. She suspected her young fans had never heard of the song, or of Roger Miller.

She wondered if he was alone when he died at age 56. And if he too didn't want to see the fans who wanted to see him. Some people saw him as the eternally funny man, but Maci believed differently.

No one finds pending death amusing, she thought. And the funniest people are usually those who are trying hardest to mask the pain. Roger didn't want to be seen while suffering. Adoring fans can be so insensitive, and don't realize there's a real person behind every persona.

Everyone dies alone, she remembered someone saying, even if surrounded by people. Death, she thought, was the final remedy to incurable loneliness.

"I need to call Max," she said, as a force of habit, momentarily forgetting that he was in jail. Her words surprised her. She'd always called him when she needed consolation. But that was over now. She knew his evil conspiracy was wrapped around her, so maybe she was partially at fault, she thought. She shook her head. Her psychologist had told her that, despite her wealth and fame, she was like so many other women with low esteem. She partially blamed herself for any and every bad thing that happened in her life. The doctor said it was all rooted in early pain from sexual abuse.

Her thoughts shifted to Max. She suspected he was in solitary confinement and not among the jail's general population.

"How could he walk among other prisoners?" she said, smiling while still talking to the walls. "My fans in jail would beat the daylights out of him for what he did."

Her eyes were open but unfocused, and arbitrarily floated like a lazy breeze sweeping across the room. Her thoughts had become disorganized, but at least she was cognizant of that much. Each notion was initiated by its predecessor, and she couldn't control either. She let her mind drift.

Then, as her cognizance turned blank, her memories involuntarily sneaked back to her father and his repulsive rapes of her. To escape, she forced her thoughts into other territory, anyplace where she could focus her frail attention.

Turning on the television, she heard a man shouting loudly, and presumed he was angry. Then she heard him say "Jesus," and she instantly categorized him as another "Cash for Christ" televangelist. Like all of the others, he was groomed like a maître d at an overly pretentious restaurant. His hair was as meticulously coiffed as Silverman's, and he wore an Italian suit worthy of a mafia don.

She hated television preachers. She also knew that wasn't much of an indictment, as she hated mostly everything these days. Like a parrot with only one thought, her shrink had repeatedly told her that people always hate universally when they hate themselves.

The minister called himself "Reverend," and Maci wondered where he attended seminary. She remembered an old tabloid newspaper ad that offered a doctorate of divinity for one dollar. Holding their faux-parchment certificates, buyers often pretended to be clergymen, and used the cut-rate credential to get the ministerial discounts on airlines tickets. She watched the guy on her television, and could picture him doing that.

"Better watch yourself," she muttered to him. "The only time Jesus resorted to violence was when he went after the money changers in the temple. You're treading on thin ice. Book of John says so."

Suddenly, her mind rushed vividly back to her child-hood days spent in church, a place where she could escape her dad, and her home. The haven where she would take refuge among the men in bibbed overalls and women in print dresses who closed their eyes and opened their hearts as they praised their God, the same one she would have praised, had He kept her dad away from her.

She remembered craving the kind of peace enjoyed by those simple people who listened to sermons every Sunday. She adored the poor parishioners who had the need for spiritual salvation, and the faith to believe they could have it.

She wondered how they could believe God could love them, or love anyone for that matter. She finally decided that they were certain in their convictions because that's all life afforded them. Standing in her mansion, she'd told herself that she would gladly trade her wealth and fame for their innocence and decency. She muted the television screamer, whose irreverent blasts seemed like a sarcastic insult to sincere believers.

Maci watched the silenced preacher as he began to cry. Even without hearing his voice, she knew his cries were not for salvation or love, but for donations and tithes.

"How can anyone believe in anything, when things always prove to be phony," she said.

For the first time that day, she wished someone were there to answer her.

***

Each evening, sundown brought its own grand production to Maci's estate, as light and shadows danced through the soaring oak trees, many of which were hundreds of years old.

She often strolled the lush grounds, her refuge of tranquil sanity, where small animals frolicked. Sometimes, a familiar doe would surface, and eat out of her hands. When Maci closed her eyes, she could hear the 150-year old musket fire from Confederate and Union soldiers, many of whom left bullet holes in the bricks and mortar on her stately mansion.

As darkness began to seep into the house, Maci flipped several switches after she walked through the matching front doors. In the light, she ambled through her home, taking in its history and majesty and beauty.

She wished she could share it with a loved one, but doubted she ever would. Even when someone showed up to ease her loneliness, it was never long before she began to tire of his company. In the end, she realized she simply couldn't abide companionship.

"Talk about a quandary," she muttered. "It's like saying I want to go swimming, but I refuse to get wet."

As she climbed the stairs to her room, she realized her cleaning women had probably quit during the chaos of the past weeks. Maci hadn't been there to pay them, and she was certain the crowds of reporters and fans had frightened them off.

"Those women need their money, and I've messed that up," she said. "Maybe I'll just send them a check for no reason."

She realized she didn't know their addresses, or even their last names, and dismissed their quitting as just two more people to add to the list of those who've left her. And like the others, it was her fault, she was sure.

She toweled her hair dry, not caring if its remaining dampness would moisten her pillow. It would take more than that to keep her awake; even as she lay back, she could feel the fatigue thoroughly overtake her like the darkness engulfing her Franklin Road estate.

Within minutes, she was in a deep sleep and drifting toward dreams.

Suddenly, a blast like a small explosion, with shattering glass fallout, shook her from deep sleep. Immediately bolting up and onto one elbow, she instinctively reached for the lamp only inches from her head.

The light sliced the darkness like lightning in a July sky, leaving her squinting through unfocused eyes. As she adjusted to the brightness, she was able to make out a pool of glistening reflections on her bedroom floor.

"What the hell?" she screamed, as she took in the array of broken glass surrounding a solitary brick.

Slipping into her shoes, she stepped lightly over the broken shards and picked up the brick, onto which was banded a folded sheet of paper.

She saw before she felt the shaking of her hand. As she slipped the paper from beneath the rubber band that held it to the brick, she simultaneously walked toward her phone.

Unfolding the paper, her body froze as she read its contents:

WE'RE OUTSIDE. OPEN THE DOOR OR WE'LL KNOCK IT DOWN. YOUR ALARM SYSTEM HAS BEEN DISCONNECTED.

She grabbed the phone to call the police, but found it silent. Scanning the room for her cell phone, she remembered she hadn't placed a call all day, and had no idea in which of her fourteen rooms she had left it.

Through her closed bedroom door, she heard the pounding on the main entrance. She looked at her clock. 10:14. Leon was gone. Darkness blanketed her grounds, and tonight no alternate guard happened to be on duty.

Panic set in as the pounding downstairs grew louder. Her body filled with a burst of adrenalin as she raced from her bedroom and sped down the stairs. She slowed her pace as she approached the front door, fearing her footsteps would be heard on the porch, despite her plush carpet.

The twin doors seemed as tall as a tower in the darkness, as she stood helplessly before their frame. The knocks came again, this time delivered so forcefully that they seemed to shake the doors' massive oak panels.

Instantly, a flashlight shone through the vertical glass on either side of the twin doors.

"I see you standing there," someone said, his voice deep and loud. His volume told Maci he wasn't afraid of being heard. There were no neighbors, not for a half-mile in either direction. She thought about the trees and bushes that would also filter whatever sounds were made.

"No one is going to hurt you," he said. "If we were going to hurt you, we wouldn't have woke you up with a brick. Now open the door. We just need to talk."

The voice was loud, but didn't seem overly aggressive or angry, she thought. For a moment she contemplated slipping out a back door or window. But the voice had said "we." What if someone was waiting elsewhere on the grounds?

Uncertain of what might happen, Maci found herself walking toward the door. Slowly, her fingers turned the lock. Good or bad, the open door would finally put an end to the pounding.

Slowing pulling the creaking door, Maci peeked through the crack that revealed a silhouette illuminated only by moonlight.

"The cops are on the way," she yelled, "I've already called them."

"No you haven't," the voice replied. "Your landline is down, and you can't find your cell phone. You never can."

"Max!" she yelled at the voice, discernible to her in day or night. "What are you doing here?"

"Turn on the lights," he yelled, as if the house were his.

Switching on the lights, Maci was taken aback by Max's disheveled appearance. He had seemingly aged a year in twenty-four hours, and he reeked of body odor.

"What the . . . ?" she started to say. Again, Max tried to cut her off, but Maci decided otherwise.

"Why aren't you in jail?" she screamed.

"Are you kidding me?" he said. "Have you been sleeping under a rock? The judge set bail for $1 million, which means I only had to post a hundred grand. It took my lawyer all of ten minutes to deliver a cashier's check."

Maci realized that his voice had softened with each sentence, and the last was spoken in a civil tone. She decided to choose her words carefully to sustain the calm.

"I've been staying away from television mostly, and I haven't gone online," she answered. "I'm just trying to tune everything out. For all I know, the Martians have landed."

"Now, just why are you here and how did you get on these grounds?"

"If the cops or FBI weren't following Ears, they sure weren't following me," he said. "Ears is a fugitive from justice, I'm not. I've been processed and have a preliminary hearing date. Do you understand?"

Maci's face went blank. Max knew she wasn't satisfied by his two-sentence explanation, but was too tired to explain anything else.

"Getting in here was easy," he said, his tone now actually consoling. Max told her how he and Ears had been riding up and down Franklin Road until no headlights were in sight. Ears then drove him to Maci's security wall where it extended to the adjacent woods. There, he'd climbed a small tree, carefully dropped to the top of the wall then hung over it to the short drop to the ground below.

"Your wall is more decorative than protective," Max said, as he watched her lips tighten.

After landing, Max ran toward Maci's house, while dropping to the grass whenever he heard cars passing on Franklin Road. Squatting on the lawn behind the wall, he was invisible to motorists and passengers, and felt like a burglar who had no intention of stealing.

"Sorry about the brick," he said. "Overly dramatic, I know. I just didn't want to risk you calling the police on me. And I couldn't call you, because your phone might be tapped. Lord knows all mine are."

"Usually, when you misplace your cell, you call it and walk to the ring," Max explained. "But you couldn't call it this time. As I said, you have no landline. I disconnected it."

"So," Maci said. "Looks like you took great pains to plan this. Like you've planned a lot of things lately."

"Maci . . ."

"So what are you even doing here, Max?"

"Maci," he said. "I'm sorry. What I did was horrible. And what I tried to do was even worse. I can't begin tell you how sorry I am."

"How long have you been practicing that apology?" she asked.

"Maci," he said, clearing his throat. "My lawyer tells me I could get as much as twenty-five years in prison for conspiracy to commit murder. But, he says, I could do less time if you'd take the witness stand, and ask for my leniency. I need for you to tell the court that you asked me to do whatever I could to revive your slowing career. And that I just came up with a stupid idea that was designed to get news coverage—and not actually work."

"Maci," he begged. "I need you. We've been through everything together. And I am totally in the wrong. Can you help me? Can you do this for me?"

"Let me get this straight," Maci said, measuring her words. "You and Ears tried to have me killed so you could sell more records, and you had me sign a life insurance policy with you as the beneficiary. And you want me to make a judge and jury think I'm deranged enough to think what you did was okay?"

"Maci," Max begged. "That's all I can come up with. If there's a better way, I'm open to it. If you have a better idea, I'll do anything you say."

Maci looked into the eyes of a broken man, a man who once held sway over her life and career. She thought carefully, then spoke.

"There might be something else. Wait right here."

He heard her hollow footsteps cross the floor as she walked toward a small table near the couch. With her back to him, she quickly spun around to face him. It was then that he saw the 9mm automatic pistol in her hand.

"Maci!" he exclaimed as she leveled the gun toward him. "What are you doing?"

"Max, hear what I say, and focus on my eyes," Maci said, her voice void of emotion. "Ask yourself if I'm telling you the truth."

"Max, I've got the safety off, and my finger is on the trigger. The only thing between you and death is the twitch of my finger.

"Notice my calmness, Max. This is the calmest I've felt in weeks. Now get out of my house, or I'll kill you, and right now. And if I do, I won't even go to prison, not after everything you've done."

"Maci," he said. "After all we've been through?"

"We've been through one thing too many," she said. "But I'm not going to talk anymore. Leave, Max. Leave now."

Trembling, Max knew she was aiming directly at his heart, and the nine-millimeter would make it explode inside his chest.

"I'm leaving, Maci," he said calmly. "But I want you to think about what we talked about. I asked nicely. I begged. I need your help, and I have friends who know where you live, and I've got the money to pay them. Get my drift?"

"LEAVE!" she screamed, her voice suddenly a hybrid of demand and terror.

Max turned around, opened the door, and flipped on the outdoor light before stepping out. The glare blinded him to the world beyond the porch.

Maci felt the sudden spray of warmth on her face and saw the crimson speckles on her blouse. Max was falling backwards, and even seemed to bounce ever so slightly when his body hit the floor. She unavoidably watched as a pool of blood quickly widened around his head.

A wave of panic swept through Maci as she fearfully looked down at her pistol. The view confirmed what she'd already known.

Her gun hadn't been fired.

In fact, she hadn't heard any weapon fire, and investigators later said the bullet came from a .306 rifle shot from approximately 200 yards away.

The coroner said Max had died instantly, and never felt his body strike the marble floor.

And the noise from the rifle's shot was no mystery either, the FBI agents said.

It had been just another sound lost to the night on Nashville's busy Franklin Road.

17

Helicopter searchlights turned Maci's grounds into a sea of white brilliance. For a moment, she felt as if she were walking into the spotlights of an outdoor amphitheater minus a few thousand exultant fans. Her hands cuffed behind her back, she stood motionless and wondered why a policeman hadn't placed her in the back of a squad car. Maybe because she wasn't a person of interest in the death of Max Abernathy, she prayed.

Her prayer was answered. Within minutes after a forensic team's arrival, they told investigators that the fatal wound had come from a high-powered rifle positioned beyond the gates of Maci's estate. The bullet had gone through Max's head and had left pieces of his skull scattered on Maci's front porch and foyer.

After declining her right to legal counsel, Maci watched a forensics expert swab liquid across the backs of her hands to reveal they bore no traces of gunpowder residue.

"Am I under arrest?" she said loudly, hoping someone would respond.

"No ma'am," said an officer who appeared to be in charge. "But we'd like to talk to you downtown at the station. It appears as though you're the only witness.

"We're fully aware that the victim was earlier released on bail today," he continued. "You're considered a person of interest because you have a potential motive against him."

"I understand," Maci said. "Totally. I'm eager to talk right here if it'll help solve who did this. It wasn't me. I'm the one who called the police as soon as I found my cell phone upstairs. I'll even, I'll take a polygraph, if it'll help."

Maci was ushered through a quagmire of busy policemen, and placed in the back seat of an unidentified police car. For more than two hours, she anxiously awaited for the coroner and investigators to remove Max's body from her blood spattered home.

Knowing she had a reputation for defiance, Maci determined to try her best to maintain a level of calmness. Intrusive reporters shouted questions through the car's glass, but Maci ignored all of them, including those she recognized and had known for years. She simply lay dormant on the car's seat and closed her bleary eyes, wishing she'd grabbed her signature wig to hide her thin, matted hair. To her dismay, the world would once again see the real Maci Willis, and strip away the illusion of glamour that she'd nurtured for decades.

"The crazy and troubled country singer is at it again," Maci said, impersonating a make-believe and sarcastic news anchorman, while shaking her head.

She was still reclined in the back seat when the police car turned out of her driveway and headed north on Franklin Road and eventually through Music Row en route to the downtown police station. Looking upward through the window, she gazed at the parade of towering trees, a vista that soon segued into neon signs atop liquor stores and nightclubs. Inside some, customers were probably listening to her recorded songs on jukeboxes and sound systems, while others sang along.

She even saw a marquee for a karaoke bar, and visualized women howling her tunes on an elevated stage, while she invisibly passed by inside an unmarked sedan.

"What a peculiar thing," she whispered below the car's purr. "They all love the woman who's never loved herself."

"What did you say?" asked a detective in the front seat. "Did you say something?"

"Nothing," Maci replied. "Nothing that mattered."

"I thought I heard you talking to yourself about something."

"Yeah, well," she said, her voice unduly steady. "I was asking how I'm supposed to dry my tears with my hands locked behind my back, and where do I go because I'm busting to pee."

"See" he slowly replied. "I was right. You did say something."

Neither said another word until they reached the police station.

When the car finally came to a stop, Maci weakly emerged from the back seat while a beefy hand clutched her arm. Lost and looking around, she found herself surrounded by a fleet of squad cars and surmised she'd been driven into a garage beneath the police station. She audibly breathed a sigh of relief; no reporters were anywhere in the secured lot.

The plainclothes detective apologized for her handcuffs, claiming he didn't know she'd been wearing them, as he'd entered the car minutes after she was placed there.

"I never would've put you in handcuffs," Ms. Willis, he said. "Someone made a mistake. You're a witness, not a suspect. I'm sorry you had to ride that way."

"Really?" she said. "Do you also have some oceanfront property in Wyoming to sell me?"

He smiled, and so did she. After looking both ways, he said something about having simply done his job.

Two uniformed officers joined the undercover cops, and Maci was escorted to an interrogation room, a stark, compact cubicle with four bare walls, a bare table and a single chair in which she sat. Once seated, she realized the five-person arrangement had its own psychological motives. Everyone around her was standing, making her feel like a guilty child surrounded by a disciplinary committee. The more she looked upward at their downward gazes, the more she became willing to confess. But she had nothing to confess, and little to say.

She realized why non-professional criminals confess to things. It was just to break the screaming silence. She'd had enough silence, and decided to take the lead in a forced conversation.

"Let's see," she said. "I'm sitting here surrounded by a bunch of grown men who have absolutely nothing to say. I'm rich, single and good-looking, although not right now. That said, I've rarely seen a man that didn't have at least *something* to say to me."

The cops were obviously trained to withhold reactions. But the youngest officer, perhaps a rookie, slightly smirked, and turned his face to hide his reaction.

She was about to mention his suppressed giggle, but a cop with bottled water stepped into the room, and said he hoped it wasn't too cold.

"Someone actually spoke!" she shouted. "Alert the media!"

"Ms. Willis," said one of the plainclothes cops, "you already know that given the ballistics' report and reports of the shooter's position, and the entry of the bullet, that you're not suspected of shooting anyone. But it's no secret that you and Max Abernathy were less than friendly."

Maci said nothing. The tone of the detective's voice told her that, while he admitted she didn't do the shooting, he was reserving judgment on the possibility of her of hiring someone to do it. After all, revenge was a powerful motive. So was self-defense, if she felt Max wanted to prevent her from testifying against him.

"Is that true?" he asked.

"Officer?" she said.

"Detective," he retorted.

"What?"

"Detective, detective, I'm a detective!"

"Whatever," Maci replied, rolling her eyes. "If you want me to call you detective, you should act like one and notice what's obvious."

"Are you sure you want to go this route," he said, his voice lifting. "We could resume this interview in a couple of days. I'll be rested by then, but you won't. A lot of women in jail would really enjoy your company. The women's jail is about a seven or eight minute walk from here."

"What would be the charge?" Maci asked.

"Loitering!" he snapped. "You could sue me, and you'd win. I wouldn't care, but meanwhile, you'd be locked up with some strong and lonely women."

"I get it!" Maci said, her voice as serious as she looked.

"I didn't hire a sniper because I don't know one, and I don't know anyone else who does, except maybe for Max," Maci began, suddenly wanting to spew information.

"If you had looked beside my bed on the second floor, you'd have found a brick with a typed note beside it. Max threw that package through my window. Go back. You'll find broken glass in the carpet, a hole in the window, and probably Max's fingerprints on the typing paper. He told me to meet him at my front door. He'd obviously come across my grounds, rather than up the driveway as any invited guest would do. And obviously he didn't come to be killed. He came to talk to me in person."

For additional security, Max had severed her landline phone, Maci explained.

"How do we know that you didn't dismantle your house phone?" asked one of the uniformed policemen.

"Seriously? As if I'd know how to do that?" Maci said incredulously. "Look, I'm not mourning the murder of Max Abernathy. He conspired to have me killed! But in no way did I know Max was even on my premises until he threw a brick through my window. Either the shooter knew Max was coming, or, the shooter had been following him. Or the shooter was Ears Sullivan, who drove Max to see me. Ask Agent Hathaway or Shale at the FBI. Not long before Max was killed, he told me that he'd been driven to my property by Ears. Maybe Ears dropped off Max, then shot Max from across the street for whatever reason."

No one replied, and she took the quietness as her cue to continue talking.

She pointed out that Ears had reason to kill Max, as Max had gotten him into this mess to begin with. Plus, the police were probably trying to get each of them to testify against the other.

"Max won't be testifying against Ears now, will he?" she asked.

"We still don't know Ears' location," one cop said quietly, as if to remind the others. "We contacted the FBI because, after all, this is a federal case. Agents initiated a silent dragnet for all of the major recording studios in Nashville. No luck."

"So what?" Maci said, interrupting. "He has a cell phone, and it's always turned on. I mean, come on, you guys know how to do that."

"It's activated right now," said one of the detectives.

"Ears bought a one-way ticket to Memphis on a bus. He put his activated cell phone under a seat, then got off the bus before it departed. His phone arrived in Memphis, but he didn't. The Memphis police and FBI had surrounded the entire station."

"I'm sure the FBI has alerted airports from coast-to-coast about Ears' passport," the detective continued. "That means he can't leave the country. And there are probably searches underway for entry points into Mexico and Canada."

Maci shifted again in her steel chair, and realized no position was comfortable. Her writhing had become incessant, and she felt like an amusement for the lawmen who'd watched her squirm for more than an hour.

"The way I see it, gentlemen, is that I've been a helpful citizen during this late night and early morning vigil. We all know that I'm not guilty. I even volunteered to take a polygraph, but you guys didn't want it. 'Not at this time,' you said.

"So, all of that tells me that you need to either call my lawyer, or take me home. You all know where that is. You've been there. And ten- to-one odds say you'll be back."

A detective told a uniformed officer to honor her wish, and each thanked her for her cooperation. She didn't relish the idea of being taken home in a police car, but at least she wouldn't be wearing handcuffs.

18

At morning's first yawn, Maci's sudden smile told her she was happy, and she waited for her memory to tell her why. She wiped the waning sleep from her groggy eyes that focused on her ceiling fan and crown molding. She was home, that warm and invincible place. And she'd managed to sleep late without one cop waiting downstairs, or a single brick blasting through her window.

She made a mental note to contact a glazier.

The reflection of aluminum foil she'd temporarily spread over the window clearly violated the room's decor. She smiled widely at its ugliness.

She envisioned what the otherwise stately window must look like from Franklin Road. Retro-frat house chic, she concluded.

She inventoried her slightly groggy mind, and it returned scattered images from the previous days. She saw her world as a roller coaster that repeatedly struggled to reach the top, only to dive into a bottomless abyss. Instantly, she determined to exit her life's turbulence, and restore it to at least a facsimile of sanity.

She wanted to call a family member to comfort her, but she didn't. The reason was simple. There wasn't one.

Her cowardly mother and abusive father had died years ago. She had no idea if her only sister, Sadie, was even alive, as she'd been placed in a foster home soon after Maci had run away.

"Mom caught him naked and on top of me," Sadie had told Maci. "I told Mom he'd been doing that to me, and he'd done it to you, and she should have listened to you years earlier."

Their mother told Sadie she'd raised two liars.

Maci had committed her little sister's words to memory, the last words she ever heard from her only sibling.

Maci asked herself who else she might call to hedge her budding loneliness. Only one name came to mind. But he couldn't talk to her, as his dead body had been removed from her front door only hours ago.

"It's true," she thought to herself. "Max was the person I loved and hated, and then hated even more. And now I already miss him."

She tried to comfort herself, like a widow mourning her late husband. The analogy was fitting, she decided, as her relationship with Max was like a marriage.

"We never had sex and we always argued," she said. "Just like a marriage."

But the analogy stopped short in her mind. It wasn't like a widow and spouse, or even like a lost love. Max loved the money she generated for Meacham, and she loved the money and career that Meacham gave to her.

"Commercial love is better than none at all," she thought, despising herself for already missing her tolerable nemesis.

Maci shook upon seeing herself in her bathroom mirror. She used the toilet, then placed her open palm across her eyes to shield herself from her disheveled reflection as she exited the room. She plopped back into her bed, and surrounded herself with more pillows than she needed.

She decided to broach the scheduling of future shows, or even a tour, anything that would get her on stage, as a way to dilute her depression. Just imagining herself singing in front of her band and above a crowd lifted her spirits.

Her bedside clock showed 11:03 a.m. Ronnie Stone, her booking agent, would have returned his overnight calls and emails by now, and would be ready to indulge his celebrity clients. As a young man, he booked shows for jugglers and mimes into small circuses, and thirty years later knew every reliable promoter for major touring shows throughout North America. Ronnie would no doubt get her and her band a performance date quickly, maybe even by week's end. Once he realized her life was settling down, he'd probably assemble a tour.

"Look how quickly Ronnie got me those promotional dates that Max wanted after the first attempt on my life," she said to herself. "Too bad the first stop resulted in a suicide. I'll get him on the line and tell him ole Maci isn't stuck at the bottom; she's on her way back to the top."

Knowing that talking aloud was her conduit to composure, Maci was reminded of her cliché about working to live, but mostly living to work. On this sunny morning, the words had hit home in ways they never had. Counting Max, she'd cheated death on three occasions, and the trio told her she was meant to live. But the only way she could do so and hold her sanity was to do what she loved, what she did best. She needed to work.

She wanted to laugh out loud, but didn't. She'd talked herself into happiness, and that was enough.

"Good Morning, Vibrant Talent Agency," said Sharon Rose, Maci's friend of fourteen years.

A former wannabe singer, she had come to Nashville in the early nineties. During her twenties, Sharon had tried to climb the ladder of success by sharing her body more frequently than her music. Nicknamed "Turnstile," a few people on Music Row joked that she should put up a revolving gate to accommodate the arriving and departing men who frolicked with her between the sheets.

Sharon actually recorded three songs with a major record label, but rejected the sickening sexual antics of the label's distribution head. As a result, her recordings were ultimately heard only by her family and friends. Now the trio of her tunes existed only on cassette tapes in an age of digital music, and gathering dust that would probably never be wiped away.

"Hey Lady," Maci replied to Sharon's greeting. "Let's get a Silver Eagle bus, and sing our way across the hinterlands. You hit the high notes and I'll hit anybody who doesn't like them."

"Hi Maci," Sharon said, dryly. "Do you want to speak to Ronnie?"

Maci was surprised at the lack of amity in her old friend's voice, and she wondered if Sharon still regarded her as a companion.

"Is that it, 'do you want to speak to Ronnie'?" Maci said, chuckling. "Girlfriend, you and I haven't talked for months. I wanna know if you've finally found 'Mister Right.' If so, does he have a brother?"

"Maci, uh, Ronnie and the lawyers said I'm not supposed to talk to you. Let me connect you to Ronnie."

Holding the phone, Maci listened to Vibrant's hold music, and heard her own rendition of "I Saw the Light," Hank Williams' song about overcoming sorrow after finding happiness through Jesus.

She wondered how many people had been inspired by her version. She considered the irony as she remembered how miserable she'd been the day she recorded it.

The tune ended, and was immediately followed by the opening notes of "Cold, Cold Heart." Maci thought about the coldness of the powerful men in the country music industry, and how they have their way with female singers, then toss them aside.

As the song ended, she realized she'd been on hold for five or six minutes. It was more than enough time for Sharon to connect her to Ronnie, unless he didn't want to talk to her.

"That definitely isn't the case," Maci thought. After all, whether in or out of controversy, she was still Maci Willis, and her performance booking commissions had been enough to pay a big chunk of Vibrant's overhead for decades.

"I'm just being paranoid," Maci said softly, and realized Sharon might have heard her. Maci felt her face growing warm and knew it was beet red.

"Maci," Sharon finally said, sounding friendlier than before. "Ronnie is really busy right now. But he wants you to check your mailbox. Your gatekeeper signed for a letter that was delivered yesterday."

"What letter?" Maci replied, curiously.

"I'm not at liberty to say, and I can't keeping talking to you. I might get caught."

"Caught? What the hell? What's going on, Sharon?"

Maci's voice was interrupted by a dial tone that somehow seemed mysteriously lonely, like a distant freight train's whistle on a quiet night.

Once again, she involuntarily considered the remote prospect of Vibrant Talent Agency's dismissing her, but it was unthinkable. Not even businessmen on Music Row would drop an artist who'd built that much of their business. Something was going on, but Maci wasn't sure if she wanted to know what it was.

Then, suddenly and unexpectedly, her landline phone rang. Maci glanced at the screen, which curiously listed her own number.

Wondering who'd repaired her house phone, Maci picked up the receiver.

"Good Morning, Miss Maci," said Leon, from the gate.

"The mailman done left you a registered letter that I signed for yesterday. I didn't call you about it then, what with all the police and goings on. You want me to bring it up to the house?"

"Yes, please," she said. "Now. And place it under the doormat. I'm heading downstairs to get it right now."

Downstairs, Maci's bare feet on the marble floor felt cold but invigorating. Peering through the front door's peephole, she saw Leon's three-wheel scooter putter to a stop. Impatient, Maci met him in the driveway where he insisted he would have put it under the welcome mat.

"No problem, Leon," she said, smiling. "Don't be doing any wheelies on that golf cart."

His friendly laugh was as loud as a lumberjack's yell, but Maci had no time to respond. That would only prompt more small talk, and distract her from the letter.

Once inside, she tore opened the envelope and let the scraps fall to the floor.

Dear Ms. Willis,
    The board of directors of Vibrant Talent Agency has enjoyed representing you for twenty-three years,

and is grateful for the commercial success that we have enjoyed together. The board regrets its decision to cease representing your future concerts, television appearances, motion picture roles and any other theatrical production. Sadly, your recent controversies represent a level of potential liability that we do not wish to place upon Vibrant and its staff.

We will waive your outstanding performance fees, and wish you all the best as you seek new representation.
All Best,
Ronnie Stone
senior booking agent and president
Vibrant Talent Agency"

Maci felt as if a tidal wave of paralysis had swept through her. She gazed at the single sheet of paper which unwound a relationship that had stretched back nearly a quarter century. She tried to collect her thoughts, but could only scream like an unfairly jilted woman.

"I have no booking agent, I have no record label!" she yelled.

Always the survivor, she impulsively began listing her options, and rapidly asked and answered her own questions.

"Be calm Maci," she said to the empty house. "You're a little scattered now but you can get on the phone and call the promoters you've worked for previously. They know you draw big crowds. Your friends are gone, but you still have your name. No one can take that away. Just be calm, girl. All of this is happening fast, but you can fix it fast. You can fix it—fast! Your friends are gone, but you still have your name."

Even a flustered Maci could realize that she was repeating herself. She took a deep, exasperated breath.

"Brett," she said. "I just need to call Brett. Precious Brett. He's been my bandleader for going on twenty years. I sang at his wedding! I know he hasn't called me through all of this because he didn't want to disturb me. Yes, Brett, I'll call Brett."

Opening and slamming her household doors, Maci was delirious while yelling for his number.

"It has to be on one of these damn scraps!" she shrieked as she rustled through her desk drawers. Scraps of paper floated downward like confetti. She began to curse the crumpled papers, madly throwing pieces into the air without bothering to read them.

"His damn number is somewhere in this pile!" she yelled as she dropped to her knees and began to sob. Her wailing grew louder until she could cry no more, and she listened to her desperate gulps of air that sounded like a drowning swimmer.

"Maci," she said calmly to herself. "You don't need to find Brett's phone number. It's in your cell phone. Think, girl. Think."

A minute later, her mood swung to optimistic anticipation the instant she heard Brett's voice on the phone.

"Brett, honey, how are you?" she said rapidly, not waiting for his reply. "Baby, I need your help. Meacham took my record deal, and Vibrant won't book me anymore. It's all happened the in past week, or days. Can you believe that? I mean, I've made those bastards a mountain of money, and now they don't want me, just because a couple of people tried to kill me and it wasn't my fault and then Max got killed in my house but I didn't do that either otherwise I'd be in jail. You know me, Brett, you know it's all true. How are you doing, Brett? How are your kids?"

She paused and tried desperately to slow her rapid breathing.

"Okay, I'm glad the kids and your precious little wife are doing fine," she said, then realized Brett still hadn't said anything beyond "hello."

"Okay, I'm talking too fast. I'm just so excited to get back on the road with you and my wonderful band and incredible dancers. We don't need these big shots. You call everyone in our group and tell them we're going to go on the road, just like we always have, and I'll call you in a few days to tell you of all the places we're going to play!"

"Brett, are you there? I knew I was talking too much. Brett honey?"

"Maci," he said, in a voice as somber as hers was frantic. "We need to talk. Most of the band has taken other gigs."

"Other gigs? You mean I don't have a band?!"

"You missed a lot of dates when you were in the hospital and on that publicity tour. And Ronnie didn't pay the band for shows they didn't play," Brett explained. "Then you did that comeback show, that outdoor gig outside Bridgestone. But you weren't paid because it was a free show. Well, Ronnie wouldn't pay the band or the dancers or the crew or anybody, even though they'd been without pay for a while. Your lead guitarist and bass player and steel guitarist left. One is doing session work on Music Row, another moved back home to Oklahoma, and the other is playing for another artist. And the dancers? Forget it. They all have husbands or boyfriends or kids. As a group, they voted to get off the road."

"My God!" Maci screamed. "That's loyalty these days, I guess. How many times have I paid some musician's rent because he drank up his money? Or some girl background singer who wanted an abortion? Why didn't you tell me about these flakes, and why didn't you replace every one of them? Nashville is overrun with unemployed musicians. You could have found people to work on stand-by, to go on tour at the sound of the bell, because they know Maci Willis will always get work. Why didn't you tell them that?"

"I did, but nobody wants to work for someone who might draw gunfire."

The last sentence hit Maci like a piano falling from a high rise roof.

"Music Row players are afraid to work with you in a dark arena," he continued. "They're afraid they'll stand in the line of fire. So you're going to have a hard time finding musicians."

"No, *you're* going have a hard time finding them," Maci blasted. "You're the bandleader, so get me a band and I'll have us a date somewhere in two weeks."

"I can't," Brett replied, his voice now slightly louder. "I took a job myself. I'm playing for Gabe Wendell, and we've got a big show at McCormick Place Friday night in Chicago. We're in St. Louis the next night, and in Dallas on Sunday."

"Wait a minute," Maci said, her voice breaking with anger. "I sang at your wedding. I sang at your wife's daddy's funeral. I paid the down payment on your first house. And I paid you more than my other musicians, because you're the leader."

"I know, Maci, you did a lot of good things for me," Brett said. "But the night that guy came on stage and fired a pistol, well, I almost got killed. It seems like death is chasing you. I'm grateful. But I'm sorry. I'm out of here."

Bawling uncontrollably, Maci stared vacantly into space. She held the phone to her ear long after Brett had left the line.

19

noher sundown came, triggering another trip up the winding staircase and into her bedroom, the sanctuary that let her escape the end of another day.

"If it weren't for bad luck I'd have no luck at all," she hummed. "Not much of a lullaby, but it'll do."

Finally in bed, only the thinness of her closed eye lids hid her from her raging world. If seeing is believing, then not seeing might let her detach herself from her latest round of heartbreaks.

She turned off her telephone, then pulled the heavy quilt over her face to mute the brightness of her overhead lights. The maneuver was easier than rising from bed, then walking to flip a wall switch. The emotional fatigue was overpowering her, and the smallest gestures had somehow become large tasks.

As always, her cellphone was lost wherever she'd last used it. She didn't miss its ring. People couldn't tell her bad things if they couldn't talk to her; shutting down both of her phones meant she was safe.

But she was wrong.

Suddenly, she felt something intrusive in her bed. Acting on reflex, she touched its presence against her thigh, fearfully hoping it wasn't an animal or insect.

Disappointed but relieved, she soon recognized the feel of her cellphone and its silent vibrations.

Under the bedding, she pushed the phone away from her, then placed her hand near it. She felt its subtle humming against the mattress.

She was tempted to answer it, but not before glancing at the caller identification screen.

"*Viewpoint*," it read above a 212 area code. New York City.

She recognized the caller ID as that of America's most powerful and highly rated news magazine. She wished that someone, anyone, was on hand to answer for her.

What if *Viewpoint* wants to ask about Max? she thought. Or the kid who jumped to his death? Or my dismissal from Meacham? Oh God, what if they want to ask about Max and whoever killed him in my living room, and why I'm not in jail?

The questions punctuated her mind like an automatic rifle dots a target. The phone, meanwhile, continued to vibrate.

With one ring to go before voicemail kicked in, Maci frantically again debated whether to answer. To her surprise, she yanked the phone from beneath the covers and fearfully answered it.

"Hello," she said, a slight quiver in her voice.

"Ms. Willis?" a voice kindly asked.

"Yes," Maci said. "Who wants to know?"

"This is Charlotte Stiffelman at '*Viewpoint*' in New York."

"Are you needing some more human fodder for your show?" Maci fired, and instantly regretted her tone.

"No," said Charlotte, still friendly. "I'd simply like to ask you a few questions for tomorrow's newscast during *Morning In America.*

"How did you get my number?"

"Well, as I said, I'm with '*Viewpoint*,'" she said, in her same, amicable tone.

"Yes, you did," Maci retorted. "I don't know which is more threatening, '*Viewpoint*' or the FBI. But I've got a feeling I'm going to find out fast."

"There's no cause for alarm," said Stiffelman. "I just want your take on a few things that transpired today."

Feeling her brow furrow, Maci wondered just how a woman a thousand miles away knew that she'd lost her band, or why she even cared. Hating the feeling that she was on the defensive, Maci decided to take control of the call.

"What was your name again?" Maci asked.

"Charlotte Stiffelman."

"Well, Ms. Stiffelman," she said. "I really don't think losing some of my musicians is newsworthy, do you? I mean, the stock market isn't going to plunge, and World War Three won't erupt just because a few band members decided to abandon the ole gal who'd paid their bills and kept their secrets about cheating on their wives. In Nashville, for every musician who leaves a job, there's ten more who'll take his place."

"I guess you're recording me."

"Yes," said Stiffelman, "I am. But I had no idea you lost some of your band members. I'm sure you'll find replacements. There must be a lot wonderful musicians who'd love to play for Maci Willis."

Maci paused, bewildered. "If you're not calling about my players, why are you calling me?"

"Ms. Willis, I'm calling for your response to today's ruling by the Federal Communications Commission regarding your recordings."

"What are you talking about? What about my recordings?"

"Ms. Willis—I don't want to be the bearer of bad news, but the FCC today banned the playing of your music on all American radio and television stations. The ruling said your music had initiated two deaths, instigated by your songs' subliminal suggestions. And that your songs must now be vetted to see if they contain subconscious messages that are harmful to listeners, especially those with homicidal or self-destructive tendencies.

According to the commission, your songs may be out of the public arena for a year, maybe two. Many of our viewers in the morning will want to know if you feel as though this ruling has jeopardized your career."

Maci's throat closed as tightly as a vise on lockdown. The more she tried to speak, the more she panicked.

"Call my publicist," Maci finally said, gasping for air.

"Ms. Willis," said Stiffelman, her voice concerned. "Are you alright?"

"Call my press agent," Maci said, again forcing her exhale.

"Ms. Willis—are you talking about your publicist at Meacham Records?"

Maci realized the futility of the question the second the words left the caller's lips. Maci had no publicist, as her former publicist was a paid employee at Meacham, the record company that had just shown her the door.

"I've been under a lot of stress," Maci finally said. "I don't have a publicist because I don't have a record label. Just like I don't have a band, a manager, a producer or faith that my shitty life will ever change. But that's off the record. Call back tomorrow; I'm sure an even bigger disaster will have happened by then."

"Ms. Willis, your thoughts about the blacklisting of your recorded music?" Stiffelman said, obviously uninterested in Maci's hardships.

"What do you want me to say, that the damn songs were recorded in the wrong keys anyhow?" Maci said, sarcastically.

"You call me at bedtime to announce the worst thing that could happen to a recording artist. And you want me to comment?"

"Do you intend to appeal the commission's decision?" Stiffelman asked, attempting to overtake the dialogue.

"Now let me see," Maci said, pretending to weigh her words carefully. "After two attempts on my life, I realize how short life is. So I really want to spend more of my time in a room full of lawyers. Especially ones that bill by the hour. That way it'll only take ten years to get results. Hell, it would be easier just to sue Meacham for everything they got, since one of their people put the subliminal words in my songs. Get a court order to make Meacham re-master everything without the creepy stuff. That'll only take five years."

"Is that your official statement, Maci?"

"I don't have an official statement," said Maci. "How can I have an official statement without a publicist? Don't you know anything?"

"Three months ago, I was riding a career crest. I had opening acts, but my name was at the top of every marquee, and the lines were around the block. Then someone I didn't know tried to kill me. Then another guy I didn't know tried the same thing. Then my record company fired me. Its president and my longtime producer was arrested then murdered. His assistant is somewhere at-large. Are you still listening, Ms. Stiffelman?"

"I am," was the dry reply.

"Yep, my label dropped me and my band quit me. I can no longer make new records, and now the FCC won't let radio play my old ones.

"I ask you, Ms. Stiffelman, did you sense my being at fault for just one of those tragedies? Really, do you see me being at fault for any of that stuff?

"No," she replied.

"Of course you didn't! Because I *wasn't* at fault! Now, that's my official statement, and you can play that on tomorrow's *Morning In America*. And you can also tell your viewers that there's no sunshine remaining in the life of Maci Willis. I've recorded a lot of sad ballads. But not one of those make-believe songs is as painful as my real life. Good-Bye, Ms. Stiffelman. Good-Bye."

Maci lay down and stared at the ceiling. "The ceiling needs painting," she said to no one. She told herself that she needed a makeover too, from head to toe. She wanted to hide inside sleep, but didn't dare, as she feared waking up and facing the same set of circumstances once again.

Her mind totally numb, she thought about the terrifying catastrophes she'd amassed, knowing full well that any one would have crippled most people.

"I may be tougher than I thought," she said to the ceiling. "And if I am, why do I feel so bad? Life sucks, but I keep bouncing back for more. It's just that simple, it's just that hard."

She thought she heard an unusual sound, and hoped it was an intruder, and hoped he had a gun aimed at her head, and hoped he could shoot accurately.

She fell into a numbing trace, until the morning sunlight peeked through her blackout curtains. Her eyes were open, and she didn't remember having ever closed them.

As if catatonic, she casually rolled over to face her digital clock. 6:55. "Morning In America" would be on in five minutes. She saw her television tuner on her bedside table; she had five full minutes to debate whether or not to reach for it.

Her better judgment lost out, and she clicked on the television. The show's trademark emblem filled the screen, and her face soon took its place.

"This morning we'll share an exclusive telephone interview with the legendary and embattled country star Maci Willis," said the announcer.

"I wonder what I said last night?" Maci said. Deciding she didn't want to see, she turned the set back off. She hoped her question would be the last words she'd hear after finally falling asleep, then waking to dread yet another day.

+—❧ ☙—+

Maci's bedside clock flashed "7:47 p.m.," abruptly telling her she'd been asleep for twelve hours. She wondered what happened on "Morning In America," but not enough to view the show online. She wondered why so many people are entertained by other people's misfortunes.

Ravenously hungry, she couldn't recall when she'd last eaten. Her stomach was as empty as her spirit, and both needed something to keep them going.

Weak, she stumbled down the stairs, intoxicated from fatigue. Knowing she was still groggy, she fumbled for the wall light switch but failed to find it. She squinted when her refrigerator light flooded the kitchen.

Maci peered intensely into her nearly empty refrigerator just long enough to read "McDonald's" backwards. She grabbed the crumpled sack, but wasn't brave enough to peek at its week-old contents.

She sighed. She'd have to go out for food. She thought about the hassle of a drive-in window, and perhaps overhearing radio news about the banning of her music from airwaves.

By now, millions of people knew about her songs' boycott, and she wondered if they were sorry that they couldn't hear her anymore. Or, did they care at all?

Grabbing her purse, she stepped into her garage, turned on the light, then wondered why her car wasn't there. Pressing the automatic opener, she watched as the rising door revealed her BMW.

She had no recollections as to why the car was outside, but didn't have the patience or the stamina to try to solve the mystery. She was suddenly too anxious to eat and, besides, misplacing 4,000 pounds of steel and leather just didn't seem significant when compared to how the rest of her month had gone.

"I just don't care anymore about anything," she said to herself.

Walking closer to her car, she saw a conspicuous package wrapped in heavy brown paper sitting on the center of its roof. A white envelope was tucked under the string that bound the parcel.

"Great," she said, shaking her head. "What are the odds of this being something that will make me happy?"

Her eyes scanned the grounds in all directions, hoping to see or hear who'd left a gift on her sedan's hood. Hints of curiosity and fear begin to rise in her mind. She wasn't threatened by the package; more than anything, she just wanted to know who had left it it.

"What if it's a bomb?" she asked no one.

"Nobody leaves a note on a bomb," she answered. "So, I'm safe after all."

Her hands began to shake, and she realized that she was getting used to the sight of her quivering fingers.

"Here I go again," she said, her voice rising. "Have I gotten to a place where I fear everything? It's just a dumb box wrapped in paper and tied with a string."

Tearing open the envelope, she pulled out a greeting card She saw nothing on its front page. The interior of the card was also blank, except for some tiny scribbling in the bottom right hand corner.

"I did this to me," it said, "imagine what I'll do to you if you talk."

She fumbled madly inside her purse for her cell phone, hoping she hadn't misplaced it inside again. Tissues, makeup, car keys and other odds and ends fell from her upturned bag. Her cell phone finally fell, then bounced twice on the asphalt. She prayed to herself that it wasn't broken.

She steadied her fingers long enough to dial 911.

"I think there's a bomb on the hood of my car!" she said, before the dispatcher finished his greeting.

"Get away from your car and find shelter," he said. "I have officers on the way."

"I didn't give you my address," she yelled.

"Isn't this Maci Willis?" he replied.

"Good grief, have you guys been here so often you recognize my number?"

"Guess so, ma'am," he replied. "Get as much distance and protection between you and the bomb as you can. And be sure you open the gate for the squad cars."

"You even know I have a gate?"

The dispatcher ignored her small talk, and she heard him dispatching a squad car.

Maci ran under her raised garage door, locked herself inside her brick house, then hit the button that opened her estate's gates. Inside the lighted guard booth, she saw her second-shift security man cup his eyes and peer up at her house. She knew he'd call if her car didn't come down the driveway shortly. He had no idea the police would soon be arriving.

"But what about the box? And the bomb?" she asked herself. "What if it's more powerful than the dispatcher thinks? I can't just stand here and wait for the damn thing to blow up my house with me inside it." She pressed her phone's redial button.

"9-1-1," said the dispatcher. "What's your emergency?"

"Where are those cops," she blurted. "Pony express won't do. This thing might blow up everything on my property."

"Officers and the bomb squad should be arriving soon, Miss Maci," he replied, his voice urgent and slightly annoyed.

"Oh hell, I'll open it myself," she shouted.

She heard his panicked voice shout, "No don't, Miss Maci, no no . . ." as she abruptly disconnected the phone.

Her hesitation overridden by curiosity and fury, Maci jerked the brown paper box from her car's hood, and shouted that it must hold the lightest bomb ever made.

She looked among her purse's scattered debris for a cutting tool, and spotted her fingernail file on the pavement. Within seconds, she was sawing at the package's binding string until it broke.

Like a child on Christmas morning, she began furiously tearing the brown paper from the flimsy cardboard box that was so light, she was sure it was empty.

She shook the container, but heard nothing.

As she removed the lid from the box, the shaking in her hands returned.

Inside she found a thick bed of cotton, on which was a circle of dried blood. Inside the circle lay a human ear.

20

Police sirens and swirling lights engulfed Maci's driveway with a level of noise that would rival a tractor pull. She wondered if clashing Confederate and Union armies had generated as many decibels on the same land during the civil war.

Given their recent history of investigating crime at her address, she knew the police would be prepared for the worst, and running on pure adrenalin. But this time, they needed to maintain a degree of calm. This time, they'd been summoned to diffuse a potential bomb.

Blinded by their cars' headlights and hoping to lessen their aggression, Maci decided to resort to humor.

With one hand, she waved the square box holding the ear.

In the other, she held her purse.

"Don't I look like a human scale?" she yelled while grinning. Make light of things, she thought. All would be fine.

"Drop everything! Drop everything right now!" a voice demanded through a loudspeaker. With the glaring lights still focused on her, Maci couldn't even see who was speaking. Afraid, she wanted to see someone, anyone, to put a face with the voice.

"There's no danger!" Maci replied, shouting in an attempt to override the engines in six cruisers and a bomb squad truck. "You guys won't have to save me tonight. There's nothing here except something weird."

"Slowly, put everything down and lay on the ground!" the voice continued, now aggressive.

"Hey, it's me, Maci. I'm the one who called you. But it's a false alarm."

"For the last time, drop your possessions and lay flat on the driveway."

"'For the last time' yourself, damn it! I called you about a bomb but there isn't one. Will one of you step into the light and let me see you?"

Thinking that seeing is believing, Maci laid her purse on the asphalt, and innocently began to raise the lid off the box. Instantly, she heard the pounding of feet racing up the driveway before she saw the silhouettes of four policemen storming toward her with pistols drawn.

"Hey!" she screamed. "I'm the one who called the police and . . ."

Her sentence was cut short when two officers tackled her to the ground.

"What the hell?" she yelled, at the officer on her back. "Get off me! You weigh more than a damned Buick."

"Take it easy," came the reply.

"Are you a sumo wrestler?" she fumed, her face pressed against her driveway. A second officer, his face also behind her, forcefully slapped a handcuff on her tiny wrist and, in one motion, cuffed the other.

"Why the handcuffs!?" she screamed out of control. "Look in the damn box. That's somebody's real ear, and you guys should suspect who's, just like I have."

Both officers stood up, then lifted her petite frame as she continued to squirm and thrust.

"Stand still!" came the earlier voice from the loud speaker. "Stop moving, or you go back to the ground!"

"I won't move an inch. Now will you tell these gorillas to take these cuffs off me so I can make a few calls and have them all fired?"

"For the final time, stop resisting!" The voice had now grown overly hostile and Maci realized she'd gone too far. She simply needed to obey, and let them do whatever they were there to do.

With two officers still holding Maci on either side, she watched a policeman behind the blinding lights step into view, then cautiously enter her space. His weapon was in its holster, and his gaze locked directly on hers. With high powered flashlights, he and other officers assessed the stuff that Maci had strewn from her purse. Beside her belongings was the small box, whose lid had flown off when Maci was tackled.

The container's content included a liner of heavy cotton and a crimson stain that resembled dried blood. One officer found the threatening note nearby, and read it aloud when told to do so by the officer in charge.

The policemens' flashlights still sweeping the scene, one beam locked on a small white object on the blackened asphalt.

"Good God!" he shouted upon realizing he'd found a human ear.

"I tried to tell you guys," Maci interrupted. "But you were too busy slamming me on the ground and putting me in shackles. Did you listen to my records and decide that I secretly wanted you to kill me?"

"We need you to step back out of the crime scene," said one of the officers near her.

"Look. I came outside and happened to see a box on the hood of my car," Maci said. "It felt too light to be a bomb. I didn't stop to think it would be an ear."

"Do you have any idea who that ear belongs to?" she finished.

No one spoke.

"Don't you have any idea?" she continued. "Seriously? Have any of you even heard about what's going on in my life?"

No one replied.

Maci sighed. "Jim Sullivan, my old recording engineer, is nicknamed Ears."

"Of course we know your story," replied the same officer.

"Well," she continued. "Max, my producer, was killed minutes after Ears apparently drove him to my house. I believe Ears is Max's murderer."

"Yes, we're aware of that allegation."

"Ears was arrested and released on bond," she resumed. "Because Ears is alive, I might have to testify about his role in doctoring my recordings. My testimony would go a long way toward putting Ears behind bars."

"Max's testimony would have done the same thing," she said.

"But Max was murdered. I think Ears killed Max to prevent him from testifying too. Who else would it be? Long story short, the note and the ear are telling me that I'll be killed too, if I testify."

"Have you seen Mr. Sullivan since his release?"

"No," she replied. "But Ears is serious about killing me, and to show me how determined he is, the idiot cut off his own ear."

The lead officer told one of his crew to kill all the car lights, including the red ones. He told Maci making a false bomb report was a serious offense, but from what he could tell, her only crime was interfering with a police investigation, and that he didn't want to arrest her. Instead, he warned her not to disrupt the crime scene any further during the next day or two.

"We'll need time to process this scene," he continued, almost sympathetically. "I'm going to get all of these guys and the bomb truck back downtown. I'm going to call the police chief, and tell him your predicament. If he says I must arrest you, I'll be back with a couple of officers. Personally, I don't see anything here except impatience by a woman who's been shot at before, so it's understandable that she's gun-shy."

Moving slowly, the motorcade eased down Maci's driveway and toward the road.

From a distance, Maci saw people with notebooks and cameras. At least one television crew, and possibly a second, added to the bottleneck of press and curiosity seekers in her driveway. Initially the journalists stormed the cops like piranhas. Through the otherwise still night, the reporters' shouts could be heard all the way to Maci's hilltop. No quotes, but at least they got footage of police vehicles departing her front gate.

"That's what journalism boils down to today," Maci said. "Pictures that fill 30 seconds. It doesn't matter if you have anything to say, as long as you have pictures."

She thought the second shift guard deserved an explanation as to why the cavalry had stormed in and then departed, leaving the mass media in their wake. Activating her cell phone, she rang the front gate.

"This is Leon," he answered.

"Leon, you're not supposed to be working this late."

"Well, I had to stay. The other guard didn't show up."

"You must be the most loyal man in the world. Turn out the lights and take the rest of the night off with full pay. But there's one request."

"Yes, Miss Maci, what's you want."

"Please go somewhere and bring me a giant platter of food.

I haven't eaten since last night."

"Yes ma'am," Leon replied. "I'm on my way to get your vittles. But I don't knows why."

"What do you mean?"

"Miss Maci, if I had to live with all your doins on that hill, well, I'd have done lost my appetite a long time ago."

In seconds, Maci saw the guard shack's interior light go off.

At last, food was on the way.

For an instant, the sheer silence prompted Maci to wonder whether she was actually in her own home. There were no shots. Or yelling. Police and FBI agents weren't congregating on her driveway or performing field forensic tests in her living room. Trinkets and mementos adorned her bedroom, but not a single ear. And not a single sound.

"I could sorta get used to this," she said.

Yawning then stretching, Maci fondly reflected on the previous night's menu of barbecued ribs, potato salad, sweet rolls and apple pie. Leon had never brought her a bad meal.

"Funny, that old man is paid less than anyone else in my organization," she said to herself. "Now, he's probably my last remaining employee. And when he brings me food, he won't even let me tip him. Instead, he just rambles on back to his old guard shack." She wondered why he seemed happy, or how a person could be content just to sit in a small cubicle all day.

"If Max were alive, or if my bandleader were still in charge, I'd promote Leon to president, and let him fire both of them."

Hearing her own voice made Maci feel slightly alive. Once again, she asked herself about the wisdom of regularly talking to herself. She couldn't decide if it was good or bad, so she simply rationalized by telling herself that she was the best company she'd ever had, and maybe the only company that knew when to shut up or leave.

She wondered what her psychologist might say about her monologues. Then she realized she'd never know, as she'd fired the doctor a short while ago.

"It's just me and my memories in a giant old house, and poor old Leon in the guard shack," she said, thinking that the idea of a night watchman might make a good song.

Maci surprised herself when she suddenly dialed the guard's direct line, and Leon picked up after one ring.

"This here is Leon," he said, trying to sound official.

"Leon, didn't you know it was me?" Maci said. "I'm calling on the direct line. So it had to be me."

"I knows that, Miss Maci," he replied. "But just because I knows you, well, that didn't mean you'd know that I was me. Maybe one of the other guards might be covering for me."

"Leon, has anyone ever been your daytime substitute down there?"

"Oh no, but some day somebody might. A lot of big shots has come through this here gate. How you know one of them might be a Hollywood movie director, and make me the next movie star? Or Denzel Washington might need a substitute for his love scenes."

Maci laughed, and Leon joined her. Pausing, Maci instantly realized that their brief joking was the best time she'd had in days.

"Leon, if I pay you more, you should get a full set of false teeth, but please don't run off to California to be a movie star," she said.

But the line fell briefly quiet.

"Miss Maci," Leon finally said. "Yous don't need to pay me no more money. I wouldn't leave you no how. The way I sees it, I'm your last friend. So I ain't about to go nowhere. I just couldn't do you that away, Miss Maci."

The lump in her throat feeling larger than a baseball, Maci said only that she'd call him right back. She didn't want to embarrass him when he cried, and his breaking voice had told her he might.

Her phone turned off, she looked over to the empty side of the bed. She sadly acknowledged that half her mattress had never been dented, not even by a dog or cat.

She thought, as she often had, about the irony of constantly sleeping alone despite entertaining millions of people. Now, even her broadcasts would be no more, just like her bedmates never were.

Her parents gone, her sister nowhere to be found, Maci knew that her memories were as unwelcome as they were indelible.

"A living memory is useless to a dying soul," she said to herself.

She realized the danger of lingering on her past; there was a point where it passed reflection and turned to sorrow and she felt herself rapidly approaching it.

"Well, let's just not go there tonight," she said.

Once again, she rang the guard shack, and spoke before Leon could utter a syllable.

"Hey Buddy, are you still there, or have you gone to Hollywood?"

His friendly chuckling amused her again, at least partially.

"Leon, I want you to come up to the big house right now. Lock the shack, and put this sign on the gate. Have you got a Sharpie and paper down there?"

"Yes 'em, I surely do."

"Okay. Write ths: "Maci Willis is alive where she chooses not to live. Not today.""

"That don't make no sense, Miss Maci."

"Write it just as I said, and make the letters big, and hang them on the gate. Then come up here. Oh Leon, first go get you and me some breakfast. Sausage and eggs seems good, with orange juice and milk."

As Leon hung up Maci couldn't remember when she last showered and made herself up.

"Why should I?" she said. "I haven't been out lately, except to the police station. I noticed that high fashion wasn't en vogue in there."

But for Leon, she decided to shower, and to do it quickly before he rang the front door bell with food.

She donned a smart Versace pantsuit, and even wore one of her signature wigs. She once again thought she was as striking as Dolly, except she wasn't as pretty and didn't exhibit two assets.

"Other than that, I'm a spitting image," she said, laughing at herself.

Her doorbell's ring broke the silence like Big Ben on a cloudy day. Maci yelled for Leon to come inside, and loved the way her friendliness floated throughout her foyer and living room.

Downstairs, she and Leon tore open the food sacks, and she scolded him for trying to gather the scraps for the wastebasket. In no time, crumbs of toast were falling across the table and onto the floor, as she and Leon told stories about the house, and all of the years he'd stood inside the guard shack, rain or shine, hot or cold.

Only then did she realize that this was the first time he'd ever been inside the main house, although he'd often peeked around whenever he'd delivered her dry cleaning or meals.

"Leon," she said, secretly wishing for wine with breakfast.

"You're the most important person who's ever sat at my table."

"Oh Miss Maci, why you go on like that?" he replied.

"It's true, Leon, it's true. All of those other people came because they wanted something, and they left when they got it. But you have never even asked to be here. And you've never asked for anything. Hell, you don't even take money when I offer it.

"Do you remember that time when the tourist bus came by, and one of the passengers insisted she needed to use my bathroom?"

"I sure do," Leon said, and you was gonna let her come up to the big house, and instead she done jumped in the Koi pond to relieve herself."

"That's right," Maci said. "Do you remember what she did next?"

"Yes, Miss Maci. She wanted me to ask you to let her come up to your bathroom after all. She wanted to take a shower cause she'd been in water that somebody done peed in—her!"

"I'll bet that bus driver made her ride in the back row after that," Maci laughed.

"Remember when some woman got dressed up like me, and stood in the street with a sign saying she was my sister?" Maci resumed. "People stopped to take pictures with her, but she wouldn't let them until they paid her ten dollars. That old gal probably made more money that day than I did."

"I knows for sure she made more money than me!" Leon said.

Maci suddenly felt safe inside a coat of sentimentality, and the wrap became the prelude to a joyful morning filled with laughter and love, the kind among people whose celebration of memories births more memories.

The banter continued until Maci became hungry again, and sensed that Leon was too. She asked Leon to go buy more food.

"That's two meals in one morning," said Leon.

"I know, but who's counting?" she replied. "Better yet, why not bring your wife and children when you return?!"

"Oh Miss Maci," he said, reeling. "Is you serious? My wife ain't never even been inside the guard shack. She might fall plumb over if she gets to come in the big house."

Quickly opening a kitchen drawer, Maci grabbed three hundred dollar bills and told him to bring enough to feed whoever he chose to bring.

Like the unspoken words of a grateful child, the moisture in the old man's eyes expressed his humble thankfulness.

"I'll be back, maybe in an hour, cause the food got to be cooked and my people is going to take time to primp."

"That's fine Leon, but nobody needs to dress up," Maci said. "I just want some people, real people. Like you."

Perhaps it was the instant contrast of laughter to silence. Or maybe the temporary refreshment of someone who'd saved her from again sinking in a sea of solitude. For whatever reason, as she watched Leon leave, Maci was ambushed by an overwhelming wave of isolation.

She instantly wished she'd recorded the chatter and fellowship that had filled her house with sound and her heart with glee only moments ago. She'd rather replay every word than to sit while waiting in desolation.

Frantic, she trotted to her giant flat screen, an appliance she'd ordered to entertain guests that she never got around to inviting. She knew why. She hated being by herself. But even more, she hated being alone among people.

She fumbled with the hand held remote, and an old, black and white movie appeared, one she'd seen as a child. Wanting nothing to remind her of that part of her life, she quickly changed channels.

As she surfed by random clips of other shows, she kept scrolling, hoping for some palatable form of electronic distraction until Leon and his clan arrived.

Suddenly, she heard her name spoken by a television announcer. On the screen, she recognized a piece of the brick wall that surrounded her estate.

The camera slowly panned her lush grounds, while the announcer kept talking about someone having broken the rules of his court bond.

"Police captured him early this morning after spotting him with a conspicuous bandage over his ear," said the newsman.

"He was scaling Ms. Willis' security wall when authorities pulled him off the wall and down to the ground. Police found a nine millimeter pistol in his possession. According to the police, the suspect had apparently severed his own ear, and bandaged it himself."

"Police have been unable to reach Ms. Willis," continued the newsman. "And reporters' calls have gone unanswered."

Shaking her head, Maci made a mental note to reactivate at least one of her phones.

"This is just the latest in a string of bizarre incidents that have plagued the legendary singer for the last two months."

Maci pressed the mute button, then sat numbly while repeating the announcer's last sentence about the horrors that have recently overtaken her. Her life had always required effort, even when things were going well. But with the latest intrusions, she felt that living was a task that she no longer cared to do. As if speaking could ease her misery, she continued to softly babble.

Once again, she was talking only to herself.

21

A fragment of peace miraculously came to Maci. She didn't know how or why, but she didn't care. She was too busy celebrating its arrival. Looking out the window as she brushed her teeth, she could see the mating of doves on her estate, feel their unblemished love, and not fall into uncontrollable tears.

For the first time in months, she could sense the burden of her emotional load slightly lightening.

Inexplicably, she felt her energy returning, and with it came a growing desire to move fast and far, and right now. She felt as if she were breaking away from the recent calamity, and decided that fleeing the scene would free her further.

"There's no future in my past," she said. "I need to move on."

Picking up her phone, she dialed her lawyer.

"Hi Jeremy, this is Maci Willis," she said, surprising him at home. "Hope I didn't disturb you, but not really, not with all of the inflated fees you've levied on me for years. Do you still hold that power of attorney on me?"

She discerned his loaded pause.

"Uh, Maci," he said, startled. "Say, how are you this morning? You took me a little by surprise. It's really nice to hear you. I've thought about calling you, what with all of the mishaps that have befallen your life. And I . . ."

"That's okay, cause you would've charged me outrageously for the call. Besides, you're a civil attorney, not a criminal attorney, and you thought I didn't need your services."

"Actually, I think we probably need to talk about Meacham Records," he said.

"Maybe later," she said. "Right now, I just need a friend. Or a reasonable facsimile. So be a friend and just charge me an hour for this five minute call, okay?"

"Maci," he laughed nervously. "What can I help you with?"

"Jeremy, do you still hold my power of attorney?" she asked again.

"Well, uh, sure Maci. I think. I mean the hardcopy is in my safe at the office, but I can probably call up the electronic . . ."

"Never mind. I just wanted to be sure that you still have the thing, and hadn't sold it on eBay. I want you to bring it to my house, and bring the deed to my house and any other paperwork needed for me to sell the entire estate, including the main house and outbuildings and all of my furniture and clothes.

Everything that's under my roof and on my grounds . . . I want to sell it all."

Jeremy's silence lingered again, this time to the point that Maci had to ask if he were still on the line.

"Yes, I'm here. Are you saying you're going to sell everything?" he asked.

"I just told you I am," she answered. "Yes, I want to sell everything, and I want to sell all of it for one dollar. I've heard people say that my accepting a single dollar will make the transaction binding."

"Are you sure you want to do . . . ? What are you thinking?"

"Let me finish," she said. "Now, sell everything to Leon Smith, my gatekeeper. I'll leave the dollar on my kitchen table. When you write up the contact, be sure that you also bind me to pay his property taxes for as long as I live. Also, tell him he'll find a list inside the kitchen cabinet for a plumber, electrician and all around handyman. Tell Leon I'll call those guys every month to see if he's incurred any debts with them. I'll pay them. Put that in the contract too."

"I want that old man to be the only $15 million estate owner in America who doesn't have to pay for any upkeep."

"Maci, I know you've been under stress, but are you sure you know what . . ."

"I'm sure you knew I was under stress, and I'm sure you didn't come around. After all, you're a big shot Music Row lawyer, and you didn't want to scare your other clients by associating with a crazy women. Funny, I was your first client, and I brought you most of those you have now, except for those two who went to prison under your counsel. Tell me, are you still dating the warden's wife?"

No reply.

"Now, do what I just said. Do it now, and do it right. Otherwise, Leon and his family will be here, and they'll wonder if the food they bring will get cold before I come back. They're polite that way."

"But you, Jeremy, will be here, and you'll tell them I'm not coming back. Not ever. Tell them to eat their paper-bag meal with millions of dollars worth of real estate as their dessert. And Jeremy, I'm still Maci Willis, and I can still get a call through to the Tennessee Bar Association. Blow this off, and I'll report you."

"Maci," he said. "If this is what you really want . . ."

"Of course it's what I want," she said. "Why are you still on the line? Why aren't you heading to my house with the deed? My computer and printer are in my office if you need them. I can hear you breathing. Inhale, and don't exhale until you drive up my driveway."

Click.

She listened for a moment at the electronic hum of her landline, and she began to hum along in perfect pitch. Then she hummed high harmony, and then bass, all the while smiling to herself. That monotonous dial tone was lifting her spirits more than anything since she'd survived the first attempt on her life. After taking a quick shower, she hurriedly gathered a few clothes and three wigs. The modest ensemble would be enough to see her through the next chapter in her life, the beginning of the end of her celebrated life as a Nashville star and American icon. A new life awaited her on the first inch of concrete leading from her estate.

She had never before simultaneously felt so ecstatic, relieved, terrified and reckless.

She noticed that she'd spent thirty-two minutes preparing to flee the magnificence of her mansion. She hoped Leon and his family didn't get sick inside central air-conditioning. She thought she should leave a note explaining the use of the bidet for his wife. How on earth, Maci wondered, would Leon and family work the numerous television remote controls? She wondered if they'd ever used a wall thermostat.

They'll learn, she thought to herself, somehow they'll just learn.

The front gate opened automatically as her sedan approached it. She remembered she'd forgotten to bestow her three others cars to Leon, but felt little guilt about the oversight. Besides, she could fix her mistake when she talked to Jeremy again, and probably many times thereafter. She knew that her fairytale escape from all that remained wouldn't really end like a Hollywood movie. After all, she couldn't really sever herself from her old life with only one call to her lawyer. She'd have to talk to him to wind up the loose ends after her whirlwind escape.

"I feel like I'm eloping," she said. "But just with myself."

Stepping from her car, she eased into the guard shack and feverishly scribbled a note.

"Leon, the gate is unlocked. Just push it open and drive up to the house. Tomorrow, you're going to need to hire a new gatekeeper. You and your folks enjoy your breakfast. My lawyer will arrive soon and he'll give you a surprise. Listen to him, but don't give him any food. Tell him I said so. And Leon, you were my first and last gatekeeper, just as you were my first and forever friend. Love, Maci."

She pushed the note into a Federal Express envelope she'd grabbed from a stash inside the shack. She wove the package inside the wrought iron, and hoped no one would steal it. If they entered the house, they'd soon face an Ivy League lawyer, Leon, his wife and no telling how many kids. The image of that scene made her smile, then laugh out loud.

She hoped that something like that would actually unfold, and wished she were present to see it. But she wouldn't be there. Not today. Not ever again.

⁑ ⁑

Maci drove with blind faith that the four wheels spinning beneath here would escort her to a place with uplifting surprises and no stress. She wondered if this feeling was a bit too idyllic, but quickly rejected that notion. Now on the precipice of liberation, she preferred idealism over reality. She'd had enough of the fans, touring, deadlines and getting shot at. She might never again know riches or fame, but at the moment, she didn't care. She insisted that her new world would hold only one priority: happiness.

Headed South on Interstate 65, she began formulating the next step of her plan: To disappear, despite the fact that she had been one of the most reported news stories of the past two months.

She wasn't an officially missing person, so local or state police wouldn't be looking for her. Come nightfall, she'd pull into a truck lot and steal a license plate. She'd place it on another car whose plate she'd also steal. Eventually, her car would exhibit a license plate that belonged to someone who didn't know his plates were missing. If stopped, she'd swear she had no idea who put improper plates on her car.

Yes, that was illegal, she admitted to herself. But no one would get hurt, and no car would be stolen. And she would be emancipated, the psychological bedrock of burgeoning happiness.

As always, she decided no one would recognize her without her wig and absentee cosmetics. Minus her makeup, she'd always thought her face resembled a gaunt mannequin.

"Who'd take a second look at that?" she said.

Her non-Maci garb had always worked. She'd never been recognized inside a Cracker Barrel, where they sold her CDs, or in a Waffle House, where she sang from the jukebox. Once, while eating at a counter, a man next to her said he loved the Maci Willis song blaring from the nickelodeon. She told him she liked it too, but thought that Maci woman was a bitch. He angrily insisted she wasn't, and didn't speak to her again.

She hadn't broken any laws, yet, as far as she knew. But still, cruising down the highway at 75 miles an hour, she felt a little like Bonnie minus Clyde, not being where she should be, going places she shouldn't, and all while vaguely incognito.

"I must be free," she said. "I'm singing, and not getting paid for it. So, yep, I must be free!"

She pushed back her sunroof, rolled down all four windows, and let the wind finish drying her hair while it slapped her grinning countenance. She turned on her car's radio, cranked the volume to its maximum, and sang along with Kathy Mattea, "eighteen wheels and a dozen roses . . ."

Like the thrilled truck driver in that song, Maci was going home. But there was a difference. That driver knew exactly where he was going and who he'd see. Maci knew no one would be waiting for her, and wasn't even sure if her old childhood home still existed.

But still, she was moving, and that was the first step on the long journey of finding then liking herself. She was certain she'd flourish and her heart would thrive, someplace where gunmen and mass media were never seen.

Her eyes began to moisten, and she blamed the blasting winds whirling inside her car, instead of the mixture of emotions flooding her heart and mind. She blinked rapidly and tuned the radio to find anything that had a beat. Seeking still more distractions, she activated her car's windshield wipers, although it wasn't raining. She turned on the air-conditioning, although it was useless against the inside winds. She situated her rearview and exterior mirrors, although all were correctly posed.

Her impulsive getaway was increasingly thrilling, but deep down a glimpse of reality told her that things might not change for the better for a long time.

"Keep busy, Willis!" she shouted. "Don't even think about circumstances! Keep singing. Turn the dial some more. Find a song that's fun to sing."

She wondered if fate had intervened. A choir was singing "Oh Happy Day," and their jubilance about Jesus and His washing away sins infused her like a melodious transfusion.

The singers reminded her of her childhood's tiny, country church where she went every Sunday morning and to midweek services as well. There, she found her emotional bastion, a public hideout where her depraved father never entered. There, the memories of his filthy hands on her vulnerable body were eclipsed by the soothing warmth of fellowship and trust.

The parishioners didn't know her dark secret. They didn't even suspect it, or at least she'd always believed. Sometimes, they asked her to come home with them for an after church lunch which they called "dinner." She always called her dad for permission, and he always said no, and she always went anyway.

Because she'd disobeyed him, she knew he'd beat her once she came home. But the beating meant he wouldn't touch her sexually, and it was a tradeoff that Maci could accept. Not even her deranged dad wanted sex from a child he'd just battered.

"He taught me how to watch, to watch and pray..." the song continued, filling the interior of her sedan. As the noisy wind drowned out her voice, she rolled the roof glass in place and raised the side windows. Cutting back the air heightened the hymn's volume, as if its blasting harmonies would surely reach the portals of heaven. Even Maci's loudest voice was lost to the radio choir. She loved singing amid the unity.

"So what if the voices are recorded," she thought. "But I can feel them with me now. Surely God put this song in this car at this moment."

And so it continued, hours of a private, one-car concert where Maci heard songs she'd hadn't heard since childhood, that horrific time and place she'd suffered until escaping. When one radio station faded into static, she'd find another, and nostalgically remembered the abundance of gospel music that filled the rural South.

"Amazing Grace," "Joshua Fought the Battle of Jericho," "How Great Though Art," "I Come to the Garden Alone" and

"Just a Closer Walk with Thee." It was as if God Himself was the programming the play list, or so it seemed to Maci. And for the moment, her car was her very own beloved church, a moving temple whose anthems were her Heaven on earth.

She began calling everything "wonderful," and realized the adjective had been absent from her vocabulary for months.

"I can't remember when I last said it, and I can't remember when I felt it," she said, raising her hand skyward.

She sentimentally wondered if the wooden church of her childhood was still standing. She was certain most of its members were not.

"But the church house might still be there, and its members' children might be there, maybe," she said, resuming her monologue.

She seriously doubted her hometown could be located on her GPS. And she was certain it had no directions for the town's tiny and lone church. But she was determined to find it, even if the church was now merely a vacant yard.

Maci eagerly awaited the next highway sign; she'd paid no attention to directions all day and nightfall was approaching.

No matter how remote, the route would take her to other routes, which in turn would take her to her birthplace, Mt. Larson, Louisiana. From there, she'd find her way to the church house. She wondered if she'd be able to find the same path she'd walked years ago. The search might take a day, maybe even two.

"I don't care," she said, staring into the rearview mirror to bask in her smile. "I don't care how long it takes. I've got a new life. And in this one, I've got all the time in the world."

She glanced at her Rolex wristwatch, but decided not to read the time. Instead, she opened its clasp and hurled it out the driver's window. Once again, she stared into the mirror, and laughed out loud at her glorious smile.

22

Majestic oak trees drooping with moss line the Louisiana highway, separating it from the brooding swamp that lay just beyond. Maci heard the amplified sounds of bullfrogs, and felt the silence of alligators submerged beneath the pungent yet serene marshes. She shivered at her childhood recollections of men riding inside teetering pirogue boats that floated only inches above the waterline. There, reptiles large and small occasionally raised their beady eyes, mirroring reflections of the dull moon, a powdery light that barely penetrated the dark, humid sky.

Years earlier, she stood on the bank of a slough whose water amplified the conversation of two alligator hunters who floated perhaps fifty yards away. She recalled a rifle blast that shattered the air, followed by cursing and a gator's frantic, death-knell thrashing. Squinting through the darkness, Maci had watched the spindly men hoist the gator into their long, flat boat where the monster momentarily revived. At point blank, the hunter fired another deafening round, tripping an eerie exhale that marked the giant carnivore's last moment of life.

Forcing her mind back to the present, Maci turned off the highway and onto a blacktop road, then partially lowered her driver's window to enjoy the hiss of her radial tires against the asphalt. The swamp found her before she found it: the air smelled of stagnant water, although none was in sight, and she remembered how Louisiana's elevated humidity left all things sticky and some people struggling to breathe. She switched her radio to an AM station, where she was greeted by the deep Southern drawl of an announcer who, without background music, urged his "friends and neighbors" to buy from Fred's Seed and Feed, where birds eat to sing, and hogs eat to die." This was immediately followed by another commercial for Henry's Barber Shop, where "we cut everything above your shoulders except your ears."

As she drove, her mind shifted from the good-hearted announcers to bone-chilling fear. Ahead a rural mailbox jutted out toward the road, marking a long gravel drive that lead to a house. She didn't know the distance, but she'd counted 993 steps from the mailbox to the porch when she was twelve years old. She remembered counting her paces while singing loudly, then easing into silence as she approached the front door. Her childhood home was not a place worthy of songs; she could still imagine the torn screen that admitted horse flies, and often leaked the screams of her sister. Each time she heard the sob, she was filled not only with pity for her sibling, but also with an unspoken fear that the same fate would be awaiting her shortly after she stepped through the door.

She remembered how her pace would slow as she approached the porch, and how she tried to quiet the sound of the crunching of gravel beneath her feet. But her efforts at silence were often sabotaged by her terrified but muffled sobs about what she'd suffer next. Whenever her dad heard her approach, he'd whip her for making noises that might alert his wife. That meant he wouldn't get the privacy he needed to force Maci to take her turn beneath him.

That was decades ago, but the memories had never died. Today, as the old house came fully into view, she could see that it was direly in need of paint, even more so than the day that she'd gathered all her courage and hitch-hiked to New Orleans where she caught a bus for Nashville. The yard, once cut with a manual and reel mower, was now lost to horse weeds and sunflowers, and home to small birds and a choir of buzzing insects. Stepping cautiously from her car, Maci stood erect, momentarily entranced by the weathered state of the dilapidated dwelling. She gazed at it, as if her fiery eyes could burn away its hateful memories, and allow her to enter safely. Hearing a whisper of movement, she glanced down at a rat emerging from nearby weeds, then saw it scramble off to safety upon seeing her.

The tall growth brushed her naked arms, and soon they bore redness as she slowly but purposely crept toward the house's sagging porch. For the first time in years, she stood before her childhood home. She approached it with reverence, as if she were drawing near a gravestone, but could not understand why.

Her trepidation running in high gear, Maci approached the rusted screen door and its rotted wood frame. She pondered the wisdom of climbing the three worn, wooden steps. She decided she wouldn't be seriously hurt should she fall through them. She sighed with relief when she reached the highest step, and then renewed her caution as she lightly walked across the sagging porch.

Pulling open the tattered screen door, she delicately stepped through the doorway and into the crumbling abode. Seeing the cracks in the floor that exposed bare earth, she remembered the poisonous copperheads and rattlesnakes that often sought out the shade and cool moist dirt beneath her. Intuition told her to turn around, to sprint from the termite-infested habitat of her nightmarish memories. But she hadn't driven hundreds of miles simply to turn around. She pressed forward as warily as an infant facing a growling dog.

Columns of sunlight peeked through holes in the roof where birds had flown in and out, as evidenced by withered nests meticulously perched in the crown molding. Outdoor winds had invaded the house, piling leaves high enough to conceal the baseboards. Strewn pages from pornographic magazines lay amid additional debris, which included empty cans of dog food. Maci guessed that transients and their pets had made a campsite of the house, a theory validated by the countless and scattered beer cans, whiskey bottles and wadded cigarette packages. Lifting her hand over her mouth, she almost vomited after spotting a pile of feces in a corner that visitors had used as their makeshift bathroom.

Making her way past the living room, she tiptoed into the kitchen where the chipped range and refrigerator were gone, leaving only their deep imprints in the thin linoleum. The wooden cabinets that had been battered relics when she was a child were also missing. She assumed they'd been used for firewood on chilly nights.

As she crept silently through the house, Maci was filled with the sense that she was being violated, not sexually but spiritually, by the ghosts of these despondent people who'd intruded on the site of her painful, private memories. How dare they add further to the violations that had happened here? Her dad had created an overflow of her disgusting memories. She didn't need more from humanity's dregs.

Leaving the kitchen, she crept into the hallway that led to the bedroom - her father's bedroom. She didn't understand the obsession that led her there that forced her to look for something she hoped she wouldn't see.

"This makes no sense," she said to herself. "But I've got to stand up. I've got to enter that room."

She realized the words were the first she'd uttered since entering the decaying dwelling. She was sure that she was mentally sound and in control, despite the horrific surroundings. She turned the corner into the darkened room and to her astonishment beheld the bed, the first piece of furniture she saw. The linens were gone, and a torn, shapeless mattress lay crookedly over rusting box springs. The palate bore a large and faded stain of blood she instantly knew was hers. She'd left it there when she'd lost her virginity to her drunken, smelly father. Given the filthy mattress' sagging contour, she assumed the invaders had used the bed throughout the ensuing years. She surmised they'd slept in soiled clothes under equally soiled tarps or blankets. She shuddered at the thought of the rain and wind that must have raged though the rectangular openings that once framed glass windows.

Maci had never shown much compassion for the less fortunate; after all, she had been one of them and had managed to lift herself up. Now, standing in her childhood home, she was consumed with fury at the unseen people who'd dared to rest on the very place where she'd suffered her father's unspeakable attacks.

Now, their intrusion would add just another layer to the painful recollections of this place. Upon seeing the squalor and tattered state of the home, she knew she would retain a feeling of further violation forever.

"What was I expecting?" she screamed, her voice resounding in the near hollow rooms. "Did I think I'd get some kind of healing? That I'd see this room and instantly forgive him? What was I thinking?"

Suddenly panting, Maci charged from the bedroom, down the hall and toward the front door. She hit it with as much momentum as her 120-pound frame could muster, and the screen door instantly burst open upon impact. The door's outward swing hit the outside wall, and rebounded off Maci before she could leap off the porch and beyond the steps. Upon landing, she fell to one knee, and then staggered to her feet. Without looking back at the house, she began running at full gait toward her car.

While in motion, she fumbled in her blue jeans pocket for her keys, and found the one that would start her car before she reached it.

She slammed the transmission into reverse, and stomped the accelerator as her body hurled against the steering wheel.

As the car skid to a stop, she struggled to fasten her seat belt. Snapping the buckle into place, she again pressed the gas pedal, and again the car sped backwards. Without slowing down, she forcefully turned the steering wheel and the car revolved 180 degrees without losing speed. Almost smiling, she sped down the gravel road, and the noise of small rocks hitting the car's undercarriage sounded like hail on a tin roof. Her speedometer registered 73 miles per hour when she approached the asphalt. There, she locked all four tires, filling the air with gravel and billowing dust.

She gave the car a hard left, and didn't realize she'd knocked down her childhood mailbox until she looked into her rearview mirror.

"That looks like my life," she yelled above the raging engine. "I ran over a mailbox like my father ran over a little girl! And now, both are old, and broken forever!"

⊹⸻❧ ☙⸻⊹

A flashing neon sign contained a burned out letter "t" above the Mt. Larson Motel, and Maci could read "Mo el" from a quarter mile away. It was the type of place she referred to as a "stop and flop," during her early touring days, and now knew it was probably as good as any other bad place in her hometown. She wondered if her room's television set would be black and white, or if the proprietor even knew that television had been "colorized." She giggled at her sarcasm.

As the sky grew darker, Maci realized that she'd spent more time than expected at her crumbling childhood home. She wondered if sickening sights ever prompted other people to linger, too.

Pulling into the motel lot, she parked her car and soon registered as Ruby Laine.

"This place should be called the "Mites Motel," she said to herself upon leaving the lobby. "But it won't be stained in dried blood. Or if it is, it won't be mine."

Walking to her assigned room, she rubbed the brass key between her fingers. Until now, she hadn't realized that rural motels still used metal keys that could be copied at any hardware store. She wondered if the previous occupants had kept a key to this same room. Uneasy, she thought about asking for her money back. But, she'd just been told that Mt. Larson didn't have another motel, and she was too weary to drive to another town.

She envisioned beige walls over a flat carpet and an old portable television set. Her mind's eye conjured up the image of a bathroom containing only one sink, and a half-used roll of tissue paper whose last sheet was folded to a "v" to suggest that it was new.

Upon entering the room, Maci realized that her predictions were a bit off. Instead of flat carpet, she found scarred tile. It was dirty yellow with a dull glow, the result of many coats of wax buildup. She wondered if guests were expected to enter while wearing shoes or ice skates.

The showerhead was partially clogged, but its water was hot, and it ran on any and all soiled skins that stood beneath its spray. She wished she could cleanse her mind just as easily.

Later, Maci listened to the rusted faucet dripping onto the bathtub's scarred and stained porcelain. She turned on the room's hair dryer, but quickly unplugged it the second it spit sparks.

"Guess I'll drip-dry my 'do' again," she said, sadly staring at herself in a cracked mirror. "Too bad I'm not a star anymore and Max isn't alive. I might create a hair-do fad that could only be styled from naturally hot air. For that, I'd only have to stand in front of Max."

Her private jokes were of little consolation.

Still, they were better than silence, and they diverted her mind from the still fresh images of her childhood home.

For the second time, she entered the room's lavatory and spotted her makeshift shampoo—a flat tiny square of cheap motel bath soap. From nowhere, she flashed on her old days when she and her band members routinely pulled pranks on each other. Once, while having a drink after a show, she told her drummer that one of those waxy squares was white chocolate. He popped the entire thing into his mouth where it lodged in his teeth's upper plate. He began yelling at the bitter taste as his saliva turned to foam.

"Your life used to be fun, for a while," she now said to her reflection in the mirror. "You're talking a lot tonight. Doesn't it feel good? Since your music career is ruined, maybe you could be a talk show host. At least you'd always have a celebrity guest. Which would be you."

Suddenly someone outside started a motorcycle, and the noise was so loud it sounded as if it were in her room.

"I hope that thing doesn't backfire," she said. "It's liable to blow the door down."

Walking to her car, she peered through its windows to find a few hanging clothes, but couldn't see too far beyond the heavy tinting. Her car keys still inside the room, she decided to stroll the main street of Mt. Larson, down to the greasy spoon cafe whose weather-beaten sign stood bright against the dimming sky.

She began the two-block walk, and her leisurely gait prompted a potpourri of nostalgia. She recalled the teenage boys who drove around the little restaurant, honking their horns to impress the girls in short pants and halter tops who lingered in the dusty parking lot. The cafe had marked the first time she'd ever eaten in a room with a cash register in it, and she remembered turning each time its bell rang, to see who was getting ready to leave.

Maci's continued gait took her past empty stores including a vacant storefront that was once an antique shop patron-ized mostly by rich women who came from New Orleans or Baton Rouge while waving crisp, hundred dollar bills. They wore designer clothes, wore tasteless but expensive jewelry, and spoke with a formality that labeled them as city folk. Almost to a person, they blatantly thought they were hustling the small town merchants because of the cheap prices they offered. As a child, Maci thought the store's marred lamps and squeaking pedal sewing machines were nothing but junk. After all, she and her school friends lived in houses filled with those things. She grew confused whenever snooty, well-dressed customers bought Mason Jars for three dollars apiece, not knowing her dad bought them for a fraction of that from a Montgomery Ward catalog. She looked through the defunct store's smoky window, and saw its relatively bare floor littered with random items like a car tire, manual wash-board and an ironing board without a cover.

"It was valuable when the shop was opened, but now that the store is closed it's just junk." she said.

She sauntered past the old grocery store, and saw nothing but empty food crates scattered on its similarly dirty and cracked concrete floor. She didn't even try to estimate how many times she and her mother had bought groceries there paying partly with cash and partly with food stamps. She recalled how each month, when the government coupons were depleted, her dad would mow lawns or do handiwork, bartering for his customer's food stamps as pay.

"When Mom got to the checkout counter, I always got a free stick of Doublemint gum," she said, her quiet tone gradually lifting her spirits.

Other lifeless establishments lined Mt. Larson's main street, but they now stood as silent as a cemetery. She suddenly understood the term "Ghost Town."

As she entered the Mt. Larson Cafe, the door creaked loudly enough to prompt everyone to repeat their ritual of raising their heads to see who'd arrived. Feeling uneasy, Maci was certain she was the first outsider the cafe had seen in months, or maybe even in years. She decided it would be nice to eat minus gawking fans, and without anyone knowing her identity. But that anticipation soon vanished.

"Well good lands!" shouted a heavy-set woman with white hair. "It's Maci Willis as I live and breathe."

"It sure is!" yelled an old man wearing bib overalls and a flannel shirt.

"I declare I never thought I'd ever see her again, not since she became a big star and forgot her raisin'!" said a spindly waitress wiping her hands on her apron.

The room became an ill-tuned symphony of screeching chairs backing from tables on the shopworn linoleum floor. People were laughing and slapping each other's backs as they left their plates on their tables, and converged around Maci as if she were family. Instantly, Maci knew that to them, she was.

She told herself they must have taken her years of absence personally, but she was the only person in the room who harbored that thought. These were her old fans, her original fans, who were first and foremost old friends, seasoned people whose love and loyalty overlooked her arrogance.

"Do you know me . . . ?" said a wrinkled woman whose makeup was thick as a blind hooker's. "I'm Ida Lea Jones, honey, except I'm Ida Lea Wilson now cause Everett died. You remember Everett, my first husband, and when you and me got into it because I thought you was flirtin' with him? You was just being friendly, but I wish you had been flirtin'. Cause that whore Jenny Lynn stole him five years later anyhow. Let me tell you, honey, I wish that cow would a gotten him the first morning after my wedding night. Know what I mean? I'm so proud to see you back in these here parts."

Maci could barely understand IdaLea, as the old-timer had pulled Maci's head firmly to her large and sagging breasts, smothering her left ear in the process.

But her words churned Maci's memories, and she began to remember in vivid detail Ida Lea's jealousy, and the ancient remarks that snowballed into a fist fight. Maci even remembered how Ida Lea had won by sitting on her, and refusing to budge until Maci cried "uncle." Maci began to giggle and Ida Lea laughed out loud. The embattled singer was glad the old woman had a sense of humor, and even happier that Ida Lea had won the battle for Everett. Maci remembered him as a harmless hillbilly who carried a tin can filled with Prince Albert tobacco that he rolled and chewed during their only date. He then asked her to kiss him and she replied that she would, but only if he never took her on another date.

For the first time in years, Maci remembered that she'd also told Everett she'd rather kiss a carp than him, because it was sure to have a cleaner mouth. He told her she had hurt his feelings, and that he wouldn't come back until they healed. Maci wondered if he was still pining when he died.

Everyone surrounded her table to fawn over her. Even the owner came from behind the counter, as well as two cooks who emerged still sweating from the kitchen's open flames.

As each person competed to dredge up the best Maci memory they could remember, she heard a story she'd long forgotten, a yarn about the time she and a friend had to stay after school for putting industrial putty in a teacher's chair. The seat stuck to the teacher's bottom, and a janitor had to use a hammer and chisel to crack the rapidly hardening substance.

Maci heard another forgotten tale about the time she went skinny-dipping with everyone in the ninth grade, and another about the time she sold someone a dog that she claimed had a pedigree, but in reality only had worms.

As she listened to each story, she realized how one man, her dad, had ruined an otherwise idyllic childhood. The more the people talked, the more Maci wondered if, under different circumstances, she might have been happy to never leave Mt. Larson. Without her father's actions, would she have been content to stay? Or would something else have led her to leave, to seek something bigger or grander and to never return?

As the reunion segued into nightfall, Maci continued to take in the loving folks' sentimental tales of old times. Some stood in line to use the pay telephone, something she hadn't seen in years. Each time coins were dropped, Maci heard the caller tell someone on the line to "get down here to the cafe, Maci Willis has done come home."

The laughter and tears created a glow of peace and joy that increasingly warmed the room. Realizing that Maci hadn't eaten, a cook put out a spread that overflowed with his best dishes, complete with homemade bread and pie.

Maci ate all she could, and felt embarrassed as everyone else had cleared their plates. Then it was back for one last course of sentimentality, and Maci tried not to notice how many of these blessed people stared at her through glistening eyes.

Tired and parched from happy tears, the worn-out singer accepted a ride from Ida Lea, whose car was filled with four other people. Five or six cars followed behind them, en route to Maci's motel two blocks away. Upon the caravan's arrival, everyone stepped from their vehicles, and resumed the telling of old tales.

And not once did anyone mention Maci's celebrity, or the deaths and scandals about which they had surely heard. These folks were as discreet as they were kind; it was as if they knew that she had come to escape her pain, and they had taken it upon themselves to shield her against it. To a small degree, Maci wished she'd never left Mt. Larson. To a larger degree, she didn't realize that a piece of her never had.

23

The long drive from Nashville, the terror at her childhood home and the cafe table reunions created a psychological cocktail that propelled Maci into her favorite hideaway, dream-driven sleep. Imaginary trumpets, shouts and singing became the soundtrack of her trance-like slumber, and escorted her into a vivid world that her subconscious beheld, but couldn't enter. Like an out-of-body experience, Maci was again looking down on herself, and wishing someone inside the dream would silence a meddlesome ringing that resonated in the distance.

Slowly edging into consciousness, she'd barely opened her eyes before comprehending the stale, musty smell of the cheap motel. And the ringing wasn't inside her head. It was inches from it. Clumsily fumbling about, she acknowledged that it was possible to escape every facet of her old life, with one small exception: Telephones.

Still more asleep than awake, she grappled with the receiver and noisily knocked the phone's base onto the floor.

"Whoever's on the end of the line just got an earful of artificial thunder," she thought.

"Louisiana Tornado Watchers," she answered, hoping the caller had a sense of humor.

"Hello, Maci?" someone said inquisitively.

"Are you calling to remind me of my name?" Maci responded. "I'm gone, but I'm not that far gone"

"Uh, Maci?"

"That's what my mother named me. What's your name?"

"Maci honey, I hope I didn't wake you up."

"Of course you didn't. I was already awake to answer the phone."

"Maci honey, it's Ida Lea. Would you like for me to call back?"

Feeling like ten pounds of rudeness inside a five-pound sack, Maci was now mostly awake, and instantly remembered the almost sacred sentiments that were showered on her by Ida Lea and others the previous day and night. Those stellar people had had no idea Maci was coming to Mt. Larson, yet they gave her an impromptu tribute that would've taken Meacham Records weeks to choreograph. And all the while, they had the decency not to mention her recently publicized traumas, Maci realized again.

When people's love is spontaneous, it's genuine, she thought. And love therefore made their hospitality even more heartfelt.

"No, don't go, Ida Lea," Maci finally said. "I'm glad you called. I really had a good time yesterday. All of you folks made me feel like the homecoming queen at my high school. The one I dropped out of, then drove a car through the principal's office. Remember?"

"Well now honey, we'll not talk about some things, but you are a queen in the eyes of everyone in Mt. Larson. Course that ain't many is it? I'll swear we could have a town meeting inside a walk-in closet. But some of these here folks have got your pictures a hangin' on their walls at home. Maybelle Hawkins has even got a big ole poster that you supposedly signed. But all of us knew you didn't sign it. We think Maybelle signed it herself, on accounta your name is spelled 'M-A-C-E-Y.' Poor thing, she can't spell a single word, except 'y-e-s' when some man is asking. If you know what I mean."

The ease with which Maci laughed made her wonder again if she might have been happy had she never left Mt. Larson. She loved people like Ida Lea and her friends, simply because they'd loved her, especially at a time when she needed it. The notion crossed her mind that at some point in the conversation, Ida Lea would surely ask for something. Maci was used to that; it was a lesson she was taught on an almost weekly basis in Nashville. But in Ida Lea's case, Maci was determined to grant it, whatever the request.

"Ida Lea, what can I do for you this morning?" Maci said, finally taking the lead. "I'd be happy to give you my mansion and three cars, but I already gave them to my gatekeeper before I came to Mt. Larson. What do you need?"

"Maci honey, I hope you're a teasin' cause I don't need no money or nothing. I've got eternal life. And I hope you do too. And me and last night's folks was a hopin' you'd go to church with us this mornin'."

"Go to church?" Maci thought to herself. "This early? Listen to some harping preacher? I'd rather have somebody give me a tonsillectomy with a fork."

She presumed Ida Lea meant the little country church house where she, Ida Lea and most of the previous night's friends had grown up. Still holding the phone, she realized that church was where she, like so many other country singers, had first discovered her talent, first raised her voice in song, and first realized that, even in a room full of other singers, there was something about her voice that set it apart from all others.

But there was a price for this bliss: She had to sit through a sermon. As kids, she'd listened weekly to an ill spoken, windbag preacher who told everyone they were going to hell if they didn't stop sinning. According to the preachers, sinning meant anything that hinted of fun.

For the most part, preachers didn't tell her of all the things that faith could empower a person to do. They were more apt to list the actions that faith didn't allow. The preacher said Maci wasn't allowed to wear makeup, slacks, or go to a roller rink over in Stonesville, or go bowling. Smoking and drinking alcohol were unforgivable sins. And motion pictures were strictly taboo. All of those things were worldly, according to her preacher and the others who'd passed through her formative years.

Maci once revealed to her Sunday school teacher that "Bambi" was a movie.

"Would watching a cartoon about a baby deer send me to hell?" she had asked.

"'Bambi' would send you directly to hell!" the teacher exclaimed. Her spiritual guide said that seeing "Bambi" would be a sin because anyone who saw that movie would have to enter a dark and sinful movie theater. The teacher knew for a fact that teenagers hold hands and kiss on the lips inside such places.

She also said that patronizing "Bambi" financially underscored Walt Disney, the cartoon's creator. Once again, she knew for a fact that, "Mr. Disney drank beer and engaged in all manner of sin out there in Hollywood."

"So Mr. Disney is going to hell too, just like the people who enjoy entertainment inside movie houses, and people who drink the devil's brew - beer!" the teacher finished.

"Well Ernest and Homer drink beer under the bleachers, and they look up the girls' skirts," Maci replied.

The teacher gasped, said nothing, then wrote a note to Maci's parents saying they should force Maci to love God and not anything or anyone else except kinfolks and the saints at Mt. Larson Church.

Maci had read the note, and saw a scripture that said something else about God's children not conforming to the ways of the world.

Drunk, her dad cussed as he quickly threw the note away, then told Maci it was her turn to go to his bedroom. She wondered if seeing "Bambi" would send her to the same hell where her father was surely destined. She didn't pose that question to her spinster Sunday school teacher.

Maci dreaded returning to that little church and the backwards thinking of that time. The cafe did more for her yesterday than any church ever could, she thought. Her empty spirit had almost foundered with the cafe's nourishment to her body and soul.

"Ida Lea," Maci said, "did the church ever get a proper name, or does the sign still just say 'Mt. Larson Church House'?"

"Oh it's the same, honey. But them hell and fire preachers that us kids growed up on has done gone or died years ago. Most of them quit because they didn't get no salary, they just got love offerings. Trouble is, for most of them the love was small, and the offerings were even smaller!"

The aged woman cackled into the phone and Maci instantly knew that her promise to grant any request would soon be filled. She'd half expected Ida Lea to ask for a new used car, or help with a medical bill. And, to be frank, Maci would have preferred either of those to an invitation to church. But, a promise is a promise, Maci told herself, even when the other person didn't hear it.

After all of these years, she was going to go to church. She presumed she'd have to drink a lot of hell-bound beer just to stand it.

Her car's passenger window completely down, Maci basked in natural fragrances floating across open pastures as she rode with Ida Lea to the end of a dirt road where other cars and trucks were parked in single file. Maci leaned forward and peered across the field to see if the unmarked path she'd walked as a girl was still there. It was.

"How many times did we walk and skip that narrow path up to the church house?" Maci asked, glancing toward Ida Lea.

"Ain't no tellin,' Ida Lea replied. "Remember when we was in fourth or fifth grade, and Leroy Somers told us to go ahead so he could pee, and directly we heard him a screamin' cause a bee had stung his thing?"

Howling with laughter, Maci reminded Ida Lea about the time they were late for church, and Luke Johnson and Johnny Lee Griffin didn't think anyone would be walking the path.

"I remember that!" Ida Lea said, laughing. "They was tryin' to learn to smoke and drink moonshine like they was men. They'd done rolled their own cigarettes, and didn't have no filters."

"Right!" Maci returned. "So Johnny Lee smoked his cigarette to the end, and when he inhaled again, it went down his throat. He was yelling and jumping up and down and Johnny Lee tried to put out the fire and told Luke to take a swig of the Mountain Dew! That stuff is pure alcohol and combustible."

"I'll say it is!" Ida Lea responded. "And when Luke swallowed, he spit out so much fire that it singed his eye brows. I guess that ain't funny, is it?"

Maci couldn't reply, as she was roaring with glee at the memory, and asked Ida Lea not to tell anymore stories. More laughter might make her pee her pants.

"Then I'd have my bare butt hovering on this bare path!"

"You could sell tickets for that," Ida Lea said, "if you sang while doing it."

"I hope you folks have indoor plumbing at the church house after all of these years," Maci laughed.

Well we don't, so you'll just have to sit on that same old creaky outhouse seat like you did when you was a girl," Ida Lea responded.

"Forget it, I think I really would pee my pants before I'd sit on that nasty thing. Remember how wasps would build nests in there, and we'd be trying to hurry up our business before we got stung?"

"Good land, Ida Lea, now that it's the twenty-first century, you folks need to join the twentieth century, and get some running water and an indoor toilet."

"Running water from where, Gerald Hatchet's pond? It's dry half of the time and his cows break through the fence and walk all the way to the river and I declare that must be six or seven miles from here."

Bathed in the friendship that only reunions can bring, the two women continued to walk to the beat of their heartfelt laughter, while slapping mosquitoes and looking out for an occasional snake.

Then Maci saw it, the tip of the steeple that rose above the swaying weeds and towering trees that had surrounded the church house since it was built in 1872.

Stopping abruptly, Maci stood in awe at the steeple that she thought was incredibly high as a child. It seemed so much shorter to her now. But regardless of size, that steeple standing among wild foliage was still the symbol of the House of God, a definition that she'd never realized as a child. In those days, she went to church and endured the fanatical rants of her preacher primarily to escape her father, knowing he could never hurt her there.

Today, she was going as a favor to an old friend, and for the thousandth time she was glad the friend knew nothing about what her dad had repeatedly done to her. Back then, Maci often wondered why Ida Lea never asked why she was crying whenever she left the church house and started her journey back home. She assumed Ida Lea was like all of the rest, and had no idea that anything so repulsive could exist in a town as small and close-knit as Mt. Larson.

Getting closer to the church house, Maci was spellbound by the white wooden frame that glistened under the rising rural sun. The outdoor temperature wasn't yet hot, although the sun had dried the dew.

"The church house looks like it's just been painted!" Maci said affectionately.

"It has," Ida Lea replied. "We done put on two coats just last year. That's the third time we painted it since you left."

"How on earth did you get up to...?" Maci tried to ask.

"We carried long ladders over our heads walking the path to the church house. Some of the men hefted boxes of paint cans. Us women brought fried chicken and fixins'. Come nightfall, we'd go home and come back the next day til we got the job done, including the steeple and the whole rest of the building."

Silenced by her amazement, Maci felt her pace begin to slow, simply so she could absorb the striking vista. Easing closer, she stepped onto a lush and deep carpet of grass. To the best of Maci's recollection the lawn was nothing more than an extension of the dirt path when she was a child.

"I know that, honey," Ida Lea said. "But Homer Sills built a tool shed—see it over there? He done stored grass seed then spread it and it growed. Then he bought a lawnmower and a weed eater. He and his boys sprayed weed killer and fertilizers and now they mow this here yard every week in the spring and summertime."

Upon reaching the door, Maci heard friendly chatter coming from inside. Like Ida Lea and her, the parishioners had walked that same quarter of a mile from their parking places to this hidden sanctuary in the woods.

Maci slowly walked into the one room dwelling and instantly smelled the aroma of wood varnish emitting from time-hardened pews and floors. To her, the odor was wonderful, and reminded her again of the safety she found in this parish where no one threatened her. Instantly, she darted to the seventh row where she'd once used a pocket-knife to engrave her name. The etching was partially filled with varnish, but still legible.

"You probably don't remember me," said Leroy Somers. "You and I was friends, and you used to . . ."

". . . help you dig worms so we could catch bluegill in Hatchet's pond," she said, finishing his sentence.

"Maci honey, I'm Mary Belle Winston, and you and me used to play like we was . . ."

". . . beauticians." Maci blurted out, completing Mary Belle's sentence. "We pretended we were beauticians, and stole our mothers' lipsticks, then used water colors for eye shadow!"

Maci hadn't anticipated her ability to recollect so many names, let alone attach them to faces that had changed so much over time. Occasionally she'd meet a divorcee who had returned to her maiden name, rather than keep the name of a former cheating or abusive or worthless husband.

Most of the room's hair was gray or white, and Maci wondered why the women didn't get wigs or dye their locks a shade or two darker. Facial wrinkles were veritable crevices, and lined most countenances, including Ida Lea's. If placed delicately, Maci was sure she could embed a playing card on Ida Lea's deeply furrowed brow. She thought she could place five more in Mary Belle Winston's.

Yet none of that mattered to the prodigal daughter returning to Mt. Larson Church House.

If love was a train, it was moving at 100 miles per hour for Maci Willis. And she hoped to never get off, not even if it derailed.

⊹─⸙ ⸙─⊹

The looming Reverend James L. Houston dwarfed the pulpit like a teacher sitting at a first grade student's desk. The pastor's flashing brown eyes were deep and sparkling like chestnuts glowing in a fireplace. When he looked at Maci he looked through her.

His voice was deep and loud like the blare of a tuba. His twenty-something, blonde hair was mildly tussled, as if he had just come in from a walk on a slightly windy day.

He wore a navy blue blazer, a button down collar and no necktie. His skinny jeans pooled over his Nike LaBron James sneakers. His casual look was a clear contrast to the aged men of the congregation, who'd removed their caps to reveal white foreheads and various degrees of balding above sun-darkened faces. Many wore unfashionable neckties under bibbed overalls.

Maci braced for a modern rendition of a same old and fiery lecture about sin and God's hate toward people who didn't obey the Bible's demands, and how they'd go to hell. Hopefully he wouldn't mention "Bambi."

To her surprise, Houston's words weren't hostile, but compassionate. And the sermon wasn't about God's fury, but about His love. To Maci, the presentation resembled an honor student who coincidentally believed in God.

She felt herself focus, and couldn't remove her eyes from this countrified sage who ministered just twenty yards from weeds and bugs. Somehow he fit in, as his lilt felt as natural and comforting as the sustained chirping of crickets and birds. She yearned to hear more, and wondered if this disciple in denim could ever be a friend to a worldly person like her. She wondered what he'd think if he knew of her hardened soul and explosive temper, and of the fact that she held no remorse for either.

She wondered what he'd think if he knew she'd persuaded a mentally challenged man to jump to his death.

The young preacher continued, and Maci silently saluted the optimism within a naive oracle who'd never faced the harsh realities of her childhood, or dwelled in the chaotic, competitive career she'd chosen. She hadn't felt the minister's type of naivety or innocence ever since her father raped her. She hadn't felt purity or felicity since. All of her adult life, she'd bravely been able to face the world while fueled by her hatred of virtually every male in it. She'd heard that love conquers all, but preferred to psychologically conquer every man through her talent, wealth and disdain. Not since her father had she been in bed with a male. Not once.

She likened that preacher's stance to John Wayne's, and wondered what he might think if he knew she was closer to Satan than he was to Jesus, assuming either really existed. Meanwhile, the undaunted speaker kept preaching in humble tones like a loving daddy's with a little daughter. Unavoidably, Maci remembered never having heard that sweet and reassuring kindness from her drunken father - ever.

Turning his congregation into an open forum, Houston temporarily abdicated his role as shepherd, and for a moment became one of the flock. He simply was diametrically different from the screaming preachers who'd held court within those very walls when Maci was young and impressionable.

Houston allowed people to interrupt his presentation with their opinions and direct questions. Not one statement was ignored, not even when contentious.

"You say that God is a good God," said a longtime church elder. "If that's true, why does He let hard working people get bad off and sick when they need to work just to get by?"

"I have no idea," said Houston. "But let me ask you a question. Remember that same God let his only son die a slow and agonizing death. I'm not here to second-guess why God did that either. But I'll say that letting His son die was even worse than letting people become unable to work. And I'll tell you that the same God who allows such pain will comfort those who suffer, whether they've lost the ability to work, or lost a loved one. That doesn't mean God will erase their sorrow, because sometimes He won't. Often, the best He'll give you is time, and time is supposed to heal everything. I don't agree with that. But while time might not erase the pain, it will lessen it."

"How come God didn't let it rain much last year, and most of us done loss our crops to drought?" someone else asked.

"I don't know," Houston responded. "Why did a merciful God once destroy the earth with water? You know, Noah?"

Maci gasped, and felt her back push against the pew, when a woman asked, "What makes you think you're a preacher when you don't have the answers to a lot of our questions?"

"Jesus was a preacher, and He didn't have all the answers either," said the parson. "Remember the night before he was crucified, He asked God why he had to die the next day! If I were Jesus, I'd have asked the same question. There he was, just a carpenter from Nazareth who'd spent three years spreading the word of God, and doing incredibly kind things to people, and his own father allows him to bleed to death on a cross. How do you explain that? Not even Jesus could!"

Totally out of contrast, Houston's voice suddenly rose aggressively. Maci was startled by the transformation, and the body language of others said they were too.

"I don't think you've got all of the answers, preacher!" someone interrupted, loudly and clearly.

"You don't think . . . ?" Houston said, his smile dropping. "I know for sure I don't have all of the answers. The fact is some of you folks have read the Bible all of your lives. I suspect that some of you know more about the Bible than I do. There was a time when I wanted to call on some of you veteran believers. But I'd only been preaching for three weeks, and none of you really knew me, since I drive over here from Wellsville and I was supposed to minister to you, and not the other way around."

Something was wrong. People suddenly sat still. Even the creaking of the pews stopped.

"I just couldn't find...I couldn't find any kind of peace after my seven-year-old daughter ran into the street to chase a stupid softball . . ."

Now, the room was loud with silence.

No one knew much about Houston's past, and feared where his story was going next. People heard his voice tighten, and then break. They saw his eyes fill as he burst into the uncontrollable sort of crying that can only come from a heart broken beyond repair.

"That driver, he could have stopped! But he was so damn drunk that he didn't. And when I got to her the blood was running from her nose and her mouth and her eyes and she said, 'Daddy, where is Jesus? Am I going to go see Him now?"

"Know why I didn't answer her?" Houston yelled at the congregation. "Because, I didn't have any answers to give!"

"I had no answer, so I lied, and the last words she ever heard came from her dad who told her she was going to be alright! But I knew she wouldn't be alright, not anywhere this side of heaven. Know what else? I yelled in front of a dozen curiosity seekers and the cops who came. And I, this so-called man of God, told God I didn't want to go to His heaven, except to get Sadie and leave! I didn't have any interest in some big shot God who claimed He created heaven and earth. I told Him I'd let someone else take my place in heaven if He'd just let Sadie stay on earth, if only for a little while! But nothing happened. It took four cops to tear away her little body from my arms!"

When his voice stopped, the overpowering hush filled the church like an empty tomb. The congregation sat spellbound, perhaps twenty adults and as many children, their blank faces afraid to look at the broken man, and more afraid not to.

"There's a scripture in the Bible," the preacher said, choking back his tears. "It's Isaiah 55:8. And it was written long before Jesus ever walked this earth."

"It says, 'For my thoughts are not your thoughts, neither are your ways my ways, said the Lord.'"

"Does that mean we can trust God even though He lets tragedies happen? No, it means we *must* trust God, or we won't get through this minefield called life. Our time on earth can be hard and full of pain. But that scripture is the 'out clause' in this contract with God and His promise for eternal salvation. And I trust God to keep His word and you know why? Because I must. Otherwise, I'll never see Sadie again. And once I'm in heaven, I'll get in His face and ask just why He let her die a brutal death during her short and precious life on earth."

Maci felt the silent unity among the room's people, all of whom seemed dazed by unspoken confusion, yet somehow comforted by faith, and by a verse scratched in another language on a parchment thousands of years ago.

"Is there really a merciful God?" Maci whispered, not caring that others might hear her.

"Don't feel as though you'll go to hell if you disobey the Ten Commandments," Houston told the gathering, alerted by his renewed voice. "Christ died for your sins, including those that aren't listed in Moses' Ten Commandments, such as the love of money. All of those sins were forgiven for you when Christ died on the cross. All you have to do is accept that He did that, and accept him as your personal savior. Then, your sins are forgiven from your past, present and future. Then, you can pretty much do anything you want to do and still go to heaven. But I'm telling you folks, once you accept Christ as your redeemer, you won't want to live in any way that is contrary to Him. And I'm here to tell you that you'll never understand Him through logic, but you can feel His comfort through trust. I know of which I speak. Believe me, I know . . ."

The words touched Maci as explosively as a match touched to gasoline.

"This preacher, this all-American and unblemished preacher has been espousing abundant life and God's salvation and all of that stuff, and nobody knew he probably had as much or more pain than everyone in this room combined!" she said, again not caring who heard.

She watched a slow parade of people who put their calloused hands on a country preacher who'd officially come to pray for them. Many, including Maci, were softly weeping, but incredibly, no one seemed despondent.

Through all the drama, she somehow felt comforted, and for the first time in a long time felt something resembling peace. She wondered if she could actually feel that way forever. "It's too much to ask," she told herself. Still, she thought, stranger things had happened. Her miserable life had proven that.

24

Lunch hour at the Mt. Larson Cafe was as busy as Grand Central Station, excluding the trains and a few thousand people.

Upon entering the small-scale bedlam, Maci was again greeted by dozens of smiles and twice as many eyes. Everyone waved vigorously, as if standing far away, and Maci waved back. A cook wearing a white paper hat bolted through swinging doors simply to hug Maci. He thanked her for eating the pie he sent her on Saturday night, and promised to make her an entire dessert to take to her room later today. She knew he felt inferior, as he never looked into her eyes, and always down at his feet.

Through the horizontal window where food waits for waitresses, Maci watched the cook return to a commercial stove with tall flames. Even from a distance, she saw beads of his sweat reflect the gleaming fire.

"That might be me had I not run off to Nashville years ago," she said under her breath. "Maybe it wasn't entirely a bad thing after all."

As if she were the star of the staff, Ida Lea emerged balancing plates on her forearm, and weaved through the noisy crowd like a running back headed for the goal line.

"Maci honey, do you know a Jeremy Sinclair?" Ida Lea shouted above the crowd.

"Yes," Maci shouted, but not loudly enough.

"What?"

"I said 'yes,' I know him. He's my lawyer back in Nashville."

"Yep, that's who he said he was. I just wanted to be sure he was really your lawyer, and not a feed salesman. We have a lot of them guys call here looking for our cattle farmer customers. We try to screen the calls for the folks who eat with us. We gotta look out for our eaters."

Maci turned her head to conceal her smile. She wondered how many people protect friends from feed salesmen, and do it proudly? Once again, she wished her own life were filled with such stress-free simplicity.

"You're supposed to call Mr. Sinclair. He said he'd done called your cell phone a whole lot, but you didn't answer. Did you lose your phone, honey?" Ida Lea asked.

"No, I threw it out the window when I drove down here."

"Well, that was dumb. Now you'll have a hard time charging it."

Maci smiled, and the fact that Ida Lea was serious made her smile even more. Maci realized she was beginning a wonderful addiction to hometown small talk, and she loved it.

"How did Sinclair know I'm in Mt. Larson, and where I'm eating and where I'm staying?" Maci asked herself, then chuckled at her ridiculous question.

"In Mt. Larson, everyone knows everything about everybody, everywhere," she said to herself. The grapevine was both the biggest curse and greatest perk of small town life.

She finished lunch shortly after one o'clock, and the customary post-meal talk about anything and everything kept her in the restaurant until a quarter past three. She wanted to walk to her room, but a lot of feelings would be hurt if she didn't accept a ride, including her fellow passengers and the people inside both cars behind them.

From inside her personal convoy, Maci gaped at the historic homes with wraparound porches and spectacular flowerbeds shaded by giant Oak trees. She could understand why so many locals had never wandered from this place, a living postcard of the antebellum South.

She stepped from her crowded car, and hugged everyone who emerged from the other two. To her, the gesture made no sense, as she'd hugged the same people when they'd entered the motorcade just two blocks and three minutes ago.

Car horns and shouts of "bye Maci" continued, even after she entered her room. In the semi-darkness, her eyes were drawn to the blinking light of her bedside phone. As she sat down, she again became aware of the bed's musty smell.

"I can't believe I slept on that repugnant mattress," she said. It reminded her of another she'd recently seen, and she was half-tempted to step outside.

She instead forced herself to pick up the telephone, knowing that simply lifting its receiver would trigger a recorded message from Sinclair.

After two days inside in her safe and small world, she didn't want to speak to anyone outside it. But if Sinclair was calling, she assumed he needed something for Leon. Without listening to his message, she reluctantly returned his call, but would have preferred to floss her teeth with bailing wire.

"May I help you?" the lawyer asked.

Assuming Sinclair would recognize her voice, she playfully said, "Oh Jeremy, my husband knows all about us, and he's headed to your office with a gun."

The line went still.

"He's coming here? To this office? I told you this would happen!"

Silence was sustained, this time from Maci.

"It's Maci Willis, and you just got busted!" she laughed into the receiver.

"My God, Maci!" he yelled, "Tha- tha- that isn't funny!"

"Why is it that guilty people usually stutter?"

Sinclair dodged and changed the subject.

"Just where have you been?" he asked. "The world has turned upside down and your face is all over the news again."

"What do you . . . ?" she said, not expecting still another interruption.

"You have to get home. Ears was arrested. He waved his preliminary hearing and wants to go directly to trial, and his case is now in district court, but the district attorney doesn't want to schedule the proceeding until he can subpoena you to testify.

"I don't understand why they even need your testimony," he continued, "because Ears now wants to cut a deal and whittle the charges down from "conspiracy to commit murder" to "obstruction of justice." He could get twenty years but be paroled in eight. But the DA won't give him a deal because he now thinks he can make a first-degree murder case, if you saw Ears shoot Max. But you told me you didn't see the killer. Isn't that right?"

"Of course that's right," Maci said. "I *assumed* the shooter was Ears. But I never saw him."

"That's what I thought," Sinclair said, interrupting her again. "And another thing has come up. Do you know Fred Lemons?"

"I've never met him, but I know about Eziah Records," she said.

"Well, Lemons has called me three times. He's jumping to sign you to a record contract, and release a new album of your old hits. He wants updated versions. I think that will work, Maci. I mean, look how many times Johnny Cash recorded 'Folsom Prison Blues.' Look how many times Dolly recorded 'I Will Always Love You.'

"Lemons wants a 'comeback' album from an artist whose tragedies took her to the bottom. This could be big."

"You're kidding?" Maci said, hoping he wasn't. "You won't believe where I went on Sunday, and how I've been thinking about life and getting a new start."

"Did you go see a fortune teller?" asked Sinclair. "Those people are goofy. Don't take any of that stuff seriously."

"Not exactly a fortune teller," Maci said. "I went to a little church here in Mt. Larson. The same one I went to before I ran off to Nashville."

"Really? Why'd you do that?"

"I didn't want to, but this friend from when I was a little girl asked that I go, and I did. And I heard this preacher whose burdens are actually greater than mine. Only unlike me, he didn't run from his miseries. He faced them armed only with his faith. And what he believes is that God prevails, and sometimes God allows tragedies into our lives, but He knows what He's doing. And we just need to accept that, and totally trust God, no matter what He does, no matter what He allows."

"Maci," asked Sinclair, "did they serve a lot of wine at that church?"

"If you don't stop your sarcasm, I won't tell you anything else about the first and only spiritual experience I've ever had in my entire life. And just think how much money you'll make, because it'll take me at least a few billable hours to describe it."

"Well fine, but save it for when we have more time," he replied. "For now, we need to get you back to Nashville."

"Okay," Maci replied. "Jeremy, I really do look forward to meeting with Fred Lemons. Tell him I'll do the old hits, and insert two or three new tunes that I hope will hit, of course. But I'll only do that if he lets me do a Gospel album."

A few seconds of nothing passed.

"Really?" Sinclair asked. "Gospel? And what will you do with all of the money you won't make?"

"I won't record it for the money," Maci said. "I just know that when I blasted out of Nashville a few days ago, I didn't care if I lived or die, and truth be told, I preferred to die. Then I met a minister who pulled no punches about his tortured life, and like me, it was all because of circumstances he couldn't control.

"In my case, men were trying to kill me for money," Maci said, her words now steadily flowing. "But that preacher, his little girl died. Fact is, she was run over by a drunk. Yet that preacher had only one source of consolation and recovery - his personal relationship with Jesus Christ. And let me tell you, this preacher who's spent his life advocating Jesus actually wondered if He even exists, and admitted that to the congregation!

"I want to have that kind of honesty too. I want to have that kind of relationship with Jesus, and help others find it too. I mean, He must be the real deal. He's been around for two thousand years and more than half of the planet believes in Him."

"I don't know," said Sinclair. "That's something that Lemons isn't expecting. Maybe we broach that subject with him after the first record, and go from there."

"I know, this is out of the blue," said Maci. "But this isn't just some spiritual high I got just because I heard that preacher's heart-wrenching confession. He said that Christianity begins with a decision, and continues with surrendering to Christ. And that's a daily decision. And I'm going to make that decision just that often."

Maci felt the lawyer's antipathy seeping through the phone. Carefully, he said her personal beliefs were just that —personal—and advised her to keep them to herself until they'd built a relationship with Lemons.

She didn't reply, and she knew he mistook her silence for an agreement. But he was mistaken. He'd realize that soon.

As Maci wearily rolled into the Nashville city limits, she realized that she had no place to go, except the dump where she used to hide from herself, her life and the people in it.

She needed fresh clothes, and had racks of them inside her former mansion. She smiled upon calling it "Leon's Place." She wondered if it would be inappropriate to drop by the house she just gave him. Then she realized she couldn't call Leon or anyone else; she had no cellphone.

On the fly, she decided to drive to the estate's guard shack, and tell the new employee to ring the big house. She was sure Leon would be thrilled to see her.

Rolling into the driveway adjacent to the guard shack, she called out for the attendant to contact Leon in the main house.

"He ain't up there," a voice said calmly.

Surprised, she raised her eyes to meet Leon's.

"What in the world—what are you doing out here?" she said, stepping out of her car as Leon raced from the building. Her car remained idling as they locked tightly in the middle of the driveway, like two friends who'd been apart for years, not days.

"Where's your new man for the guard shack?" she asked, tearfully.

"I'm still the guard," Leon replied. "I done had that job for twenty years, and I don't want nobody else to have it Miss Maci. And before you say anything else, me and my family ain't the kind of people who'd be comfortable in that there big house you give us. We used to hollering at each other, and we cain't holler loud enough to hear each other cause of all them rooms. So we done moved into the guesthouse, and we felt more like we's at our old home, except the old home has air-conditioning that sticks out the window, and your guest-house don't."

Maci laughed, and suddenly remembered how long it took her to adapt to living in such a large home herself.

"Miss Maci, I ain't signed no papers to take no ownership to any of your houses or cars or this here land. All of them things still belongs to you. And they should from here on."

"We loved what you done for us, and we loved staying in your guesthouse, but we'd be better off in our old place, and we want to go there now that you're back. See, I knew you was coming back."

"You knew I was coming back?" Maci said, feeling the warmth in her own smile. "Why did you think I'd come back?"

"Cause you would miss me!" Leon said, laughing louder than she'd ever heard him laugh.

Returning to her car, Maci drove up the hill to her former and current home. She raised and lowered the garage door, then stepped into her kitchen, instantly noting a hint of lilacs in the air. The wooden floor wore a luster, the dishwasher was empty and the refrigerator was filled. There was no litter, and even the concealed waste bins were empty.

Ambling up the stairs to her bedroom, Maci felt as though she was touring someone else's estate. All dust had been banished, and even the glass on the photographs had been cleaned. On her bedroom lay neat stacks of freshly washed clothes and underwear. Her brassieres were fashioned to stand erect on her bedspread.

"Leon," she said, calling the guard shack. "Who cleaned my house so thoroughly? I know it wasn't my usual house cleaner."

"Oh no, Miss Maci, "it wasn't her at all. Me and my wife and kids done cleaned the place. We didn't want you to come home to no dirty house."

Maci could feel her sentiments rising again, and kiddingly asked about the laundry.

"Leon, did you have any problems with the washer and dryer? Cause I don't know how to work those things myself."

"Oh, no, we didn't use none of those hoity-toity machines. We done took all your things to my house. We done washed everything, and hung your clothes on the line.

"Say, Miss Maci, you probably done got some more dirty clothes from your trip. You want me to come up there and take them home? Cause you and me both cain't use your washing and dryer machines."

"Leon, that won't be necessary. And you tell your wife and daughters that they can have anything in my closet, but I should probably keep my own underwear. Bye now."

Bathing in the warmth of her home, Maci plopped onto the bed and drifted toward a soothing sleep. She couldn't remember ever feeling such tranquility. For the first time in days, she awakened naturally, and not to the ring of a telephone.

Leisurely gazing now at the ceiling, she seriously considered going totally old school, and never buying another cellphone.

The folks in Mt. Vernon would be proud.

25

Maci's thick bedroom carpet seemed like a sea of foam to her bare feet when compared to the cold linoleum of her recent motel room. Busting to pee, and without turning on a light, she dashed toward her master bath, landing perfectly on the commode, despite the darkness.

After flushing, she took three steps toward her sink and discovered that the semi-blackness prevented her from finding the faucet. Fumbling, she felt her way to the door where she flipped on the light switch.

The switch was silent by design, but the shower curtain wasn't. As if choreographed, the room filled with illumination the instant the rattle of curtain hooks slid across the horizontal rod and slammed against the wall.

Although her eyes squinted against the brightness, she nonetheless discerned the profile of a man standing in her bathtub.

He had no ear.

Maci screamed so loudly that she felt her throat contract.

The defensive tightening of her body fired a shooting pain through the side of her skull, as if she'd been penetrated by a nail.

She let out a piercing scream, and as she did the intruder slowly turned his face toward hers. She looked directly into his fiery eyes, as he looked longingly through hers.

"You're behind bars!" she yelled. "You're going to trial! You're going to prison! You're not here! You're not. ...!"

"The hell I'm not here!" Ears yelled, his booming baritone voice drowning her shrieks.

Slowly, he lifted one leg over the bathtub, then the other. Paralyzed by terror, Maci's eyes refused to look away. To gain focus, she moved her entire head. She glared at his face then scanned downward toward his feet, but her pupils locked at his right hand and the luster of the blade it clutched.

It was larger, much larger than a butcher's knife. She was sure it was made to slice large animals such as big game or livestock.

Ears took two steps toward her, the knife raised high above his head. Then, with military precision, he twirled the blade from aloft to a perfectly horizontal position.

Her eyes locked on its sharpened edge, she realized the blade was only inches below her eyes and aimed directly at her throat.

She stepped backward as he stepped forward, and the dance for her life took her out of the bathroom and into her bedroom, only slightly illuminated by the light still leaking from the open bathroom door.

Ears stopped, and Maci hoped that a miracle had halted his assault. Instead, with his face still locked on hers, he reached back and slammed the bathroom door. The minimal light yielded instantly to darkness like a grave's.

Maci couldn't see Ears or the knife in his hand. She turned, saw the electric numbers on her bedside clock, and knew that her bedroom door was less than fifteen feet away to her right. She ran rapidly, and crashed in the darkness into her chest of drawers.

The throbbing pain told her she'd broken her foot. Her next painful step confirmed her suspicion.

Turning left, she extended her clutching hands into the darkness to find something, anything that would guide her away from her bedroom, her pending death chamber.

A creaking sound told her that Ears had leapt onto her bed, and was now running or jumping across the mattress. She halted, hoping he'd leap off the bed in front of her, so she could roll under it.

The ebony darkness prevented her from bracing against his forthcoming fist, whose force felt as if he had used brass knuckles.

"Get out! Get out!" she shouted into the black pitch. He didn't respond, and his silence told her he wasn't moving. So she held her breath to listen for any sound, any hint of his whereabouts.

But her plan was pointless. Ears remained as quiet as he was invisible.

"Why are you here?!" she bellowed, and felt herself shake at her own cries. "I never bothered you! You and Max bothered me—you two tried to kill me!"

More silence.

"You're supposed to testify against me, and how I planted those subliminal messages in your records, the ones that told someone to kill you," Ears finally said. "You're testimony is going to be the final nail in my coffin, although I'm not supposed to get the death penalty."

"I don't want to testify against you!" she argued. Even though she couldn't see him, the sound of his voice gave her an approximation of where he stood. "I'm going to be subpoenaed."

"No you aren't, you're going to die, right here and right now," came his threat.

She felt the thrust of the blade, and realized its length seemed to extend from her abdomen to her spine. She prepared for the agony, but felt none. Instantly, she felt the soggy drench of her blood against her lower shirt, her panties and her bare legs. She had no idea blood was so warm.

Once again, she saw the lighted dial of her bedside clock, but was sure she was seeing it horizontally, and assumed she'd fallen beside it.

"This is it," she thought to herself. "I've been stabbed and I've fallen on my bed." As she felt more liquid drenching her, and reached toward the clock and found the remote that enabled her to activate her bedroom lights.

Hitting the "on" button, she braced herself and prepared to see Ears and his knife.

The harsh lighting revealed his absence. Her bedroom door was still closed, just as it had been when she fell asleep.

The wetness around her torso reeked of urine.

"Good grief," she said, raising her voice. "I've peed all over myself. I got so scared that I wet the bed, just like I did whenever I dreamed about my dad attacking me."

She slid off of her soaked sheet, and stood while urine ran down her legs. She started toward the bathroom, making wet footprints in her carpet.

Slowly, she opened the bathroom door and the lights automatically came on, just as they always had.

The shower curtain was in its place, and obviously hadn't been touched. She pulled it open, and no one was inside.

She'd always hated nightmares, but took comfort in knowing this one was over.

After rinsing in the shower, she changed her sheets and moved to the dry side of her bed. Instantly, she remembered that she was the first person to actually lie on that opposite side.

She waited for sleep, but knew it would be late in coming. By design, she'd left every bedroom light glowing.

26

The front row of Maci's comeback concert was a virtual Who's Who of Nashville celebrities, as well as some of the music industry's most influential people. The vibrant and slightly nip-and-tucked faces came for the usual reason – to see and to be seen. As always, the big shots escorted their spouses while their girlfriends watched on television or online.

In the second row and farther back, some audience members bashfully shook hands with notable but attainable guests, as well as the uniformed policemen whose faces they'd seen on TV. Nearly an entire row was filled by law enforcement officers who, at one time or another, had responded to the distress of Maci Willis.

A television reporter actually approached one undercover officer, asked a question, only to prompt a curt reply.

"What makes you think I'm in law enforcement?" he said, as the embarrassed journalist walked away.

Fred Lemons, sitting on the aisle, had given Maci the most lucrative recording deal she'd ever had, making her old Meacham contract seem like pocket change. Wisely, Lemons had recorded Maci's first single with lyrics containing autobiographical overtones that hinted at the singer's victory over all odds. In two weeks, the feel-good tune rose to number-one on country and popular sales, for both compact discs and downloads.

Twelve weeks later, due to public demand, Lemons released a second song, and both were on Maci's first album, entitled, "He's Alive And So Am I." To her joy, Maci had faced minimal opposition to record a faith-based song as her new label's initial release. To her it was a sign: The first miracle in her restored vocation.

Jeremy Sinclair, sitting next to Lemons, was conspicuously quiet, but his body language shouted volumes about his pride in assembling Maci's breakout single and album.

"Let him gloat," Maci said, off microphone. "He's earned it. He pretty much cobbled this thing together when I wasn't even in town. No telling how much he could've done if I'd been around to help."

Maci made sure that FBI agents Shale and Hathaway were also present and, without revealing their identities, told the audience about two agents who had served her as both friends and protectors in desperate times of need.

She similarly saluted Nashville's Metropolitan policemen Randy Sorenson, Ezra Sorenson, Keith Shultz and Chief Lester Patterson. She talked about Shultz's killing a man who was trying to kill her, and said that after working with Nashville's law enforcement community, she'd never live in another city. The audience responded with sustained applause.

Leon, his wife and four children were beaming in their best Sunday clothes, and never stopped smiling. Shyly, the six-member family rose in unison when Maci heralded them from the stage. Unaccustomed to bright lights, each frowned into a roving camera that relayed their faces to the giant over-head Jumbotron.

"I know I'm boring all of you by introducing my friends and the major players in my life. But I don't care," Maci shrugged, and the audience laughed loudly enough to let her know that she still had swagger.

"Some of these people, especially those in law enforcement, are a big part of the reason I'm here tonight. And the other reason I'm here tonight, is because of all of you," she shouted to loud applause.

Two more reserved seats were held for two people whom Maci thought wouldn't come. But she felt herself struggling to suppress tears as she looked down to see the faces of Ida Lea and the Rev. James Houston.

"You came here, you came here!" she yelled to them, holding the microphone behind her. "Come backstage with the others after the show!"

Overly excited, Maci actually forgot to introduce her friend and recent minister. One's friendship had influenced her old life; the other had led her to a new one.

"Now!" Maci yelled. "Did someone say we're here for a show?!"

The arena was suddenly without lighting. Maci's new band hit the first chord, and the sky instantly filled with confetti.

"And they're off!" yelled an announcer, through the public address system.

Maci performed thirty-two songs, and did four more during three blazing encores, much like she had on this very stage less than a year before. Then and now, the atmosphere was that of a circus, an assembly of super-charged children of all ages.

She closed her eyes and tapped her soul during the ballads, then danced again like Tina Turner in her prime.

The nine-piece band, despite only three rehearsals, was as tight as a high-performance engine.

"She had the pizzazz of the Rolling Stones wrapped into a solitary singer!" a reviewer later wrote for a national wire service.

"Someone once tried to kill her on the same stage where she killed her audiences," said a newsman the following morning on "The Best Day Show."

"She's proof positive that sinking to the deepest of depths can help people reach higher than ever before," wrote a journalist for America's largest weekly news magazine.

When the blistering and soulful show finally ended, the house lights rose and the Mayor of Nashville called Maci from backstage to come forward and accept the Key to the City. Having shed her stage attire for blue jeans, she faced a three-minute ovation. Once the crowd settled, the Mayor said she was the "poster person of wounded souls who'd turned into a radiant spirit."

"And someone else feels the same way," he shouted into the microphone, "and she's here tonight."

The United States First Lady Edye Clanton stepped from the wings, somewhat invisible amid eight men wearing suits, ties, earphones and concealed pistols.

"The President sends his congratulations," she told Maci and the crowd. "And Maci, since he couldn't be here tonight, might you come to Washington to help the nation celebrate 'National Maci Willis Day?'"

Two of the Secret Servicemen leapt toward Maci as she almost fell, overcome with bliss and surprise.

Members of the band stepped from the wings, waving their hands in a downward motion to silence the jubilant crowd. Finally, the crowd settled, then incredibly hushed as Maci began to speak. Her soft, humble voice was a noticeable contrast to her earlier vocal thunder.

"I thank all of you for coming. I thank the Mayor of Nashville and the First Lady of our beloved country but most of all, I thank Jesus Christ, the master of human restoration. God bless all of you. I'll be making a lot of music for you in years to come. Thank you . . . thank you."

Even more houselights were activated, and America's most celebrated female country singer carried two-dozen red roses that left a spotted trail of petals behind her.

She slowly ambled off the stage, surrounded by musicians, politicians, fellow celebrities and police.

Maci's re-entry into spotlights—and into hearts—was completed.

❧ ❧

The towering ceiling behind the Bridgestone stage amplified each weary step of Maci's high heels. Eziah Records had been host to an after party for their oldest singer and newest star, and VIP's had included Nashville's and some of Hollywood's most famous luminaries.

Now, staring at the strewn confetti, dirty plates and scattered glasses, Maci congratulated herself for playing the gracious host and staying at her celebratory soirée until the last guest had gone.

Alone, she walked up the few stairs and into the sprawling arena, which now seamed surrealistically silent without the blaring music and the cheering fans. With the exception of a half dozen janitors, the arena was vacant.

"Thank you, Nashville, thank you," she whispered as her vacant stare scanned the empty seats. Given the room's precision acoustics, she wondered if her salutation had reached to the farthest point in the auditorium.

Wearily, she teetered off the deserted stage, and walked down the steps to the floor. Previously, she'd never descended those stairs without gripping one or two muscular arms. But in the wee hours, she'd vowed not to leave her party until everyone else had departed, including the drunken stragglers.

Only her driver remained. He hadn't seen the show, so letting him stay didn't violate her promise to see the last guest out, she concluded.

Walking toward the musicians' exit, Maci felt guilty for leaving scores of dozens of roses on stage, pastel shades that would begin slowly fading by the time she fell asleep. Like the flowers, she too was wilting.

Stepping into the last remaining moments of predawn, she debated whether she should stay to watch the sunrise. With clouds drifting in, she told herself that its shine would be pale in comparison to the flashing neon marquees that still punctuated Broadway Avenue's abandoned nightclubs. Sidewalks that earlier were jammed with drunken partygoers were now gone.

"The audience has left Music City's Yellow Brick Road," she said to herself. "Only scattered beer cans remain."

She stopped, looked squarely into a sky still flecked with a few stars, and told God she hadn't known Him long enough to deserve His many blessings.

"Someday, I'm going to live with you among those stars," she said. "But right now, I just want to dream about all you've done and what you will do, and what you can do. Thank you, God."

Pivoting, she walked to the beat of her steps against the concrete, and delicately tapped on her driver's window. Dozing, he jostled when she knocked the second time. His blank face told her he was embarrassed, no doubt for sleeping on the job. To reassure him, she smiled more than she normally would.

"I'm sorry, Miss Maci," he said, opening the door and rising to his feet. "I could hear the music and all of the cheering way out here. And I saw the First Lady and umpteen security men walk by this limo. You must have had a great night."

"I don't think I could've asked for better," she said, realizing she didn't know his name. "But now, all I want to do is sleep."

"I'll get you home, Miss Maci," he replied. "Do you have anything to put in the trunk?"

"I don't, but thank you for asking," she said warmly. "Okay," he said, opening the car's back door.

Maci slid into her seat and slowly closed her eyes. She felt so tired that she thought she might nod off before they left the parking lot, and she did.

Minutes later, through his rear view mirror, the driver saw her slightly open her eyes as he accelerated the limousine up the ramp and onto the interstate. She mumbled a faint "praise God," and he decided the words were her habit, not a sincere prayer.

The driver watched her eyes peek above his seat, as if she were suddenly looking for the speedometer.

"Oh driver," she said, surprised. "You're going the wrong way. So many people know where I live. I just assumed you did too. I'm sorry."

"I know where you live," he responded in a self-assured voice.

"No, it's back there . . ."

"We're not going to your estate. We're going to your other house, the dump where you hide because no one, not even your penniless neighbors, know that the famous Maci Willis lurks inside. Guess what? Those neighbors have moved from their dumps. You've got the whole cul-de-sac to yourself. Now the nearest neighbor is a half mile away."

Maci was startled by the details the driver was rattling off, and instinctively knew something was wrong. Glancing again into the rearview mirror, the driver saw her fixation on the back of his head. Simultaneously, she looked into the same mirror, and saw his eyes widen upon connecting with hers.

"How do you know about my other house?" she asked.

"Because I've been there with you," he said, "I'm Isaac Thompson, but you don't remember me or my name."

"Where do I know you from?" she asked, her question directed as much to herself as to him.

"I drove you once before," he said. "Does Fayetteville ring a bell?"

"I, uh, I . . ."

"Come on now, Maci girl," Isaac said in an antagonistic tone. "Think. You were on the run, after talking that mentally impaired kid into jumping out of a window. You said you'd pay me six thousand dollars to drive you home, and you did. I kept it, and used it tonight to bribe the real limousine driver so I could take his place. I told him it was worth six grand to be able to tell folks I drove the great Maci Willis."

"Did you get to see any part of my show tonight, even a little bit, Isaac?" she asked nervously as she tried to think of words that would calm a man who had just accused her of instigating a death.

"That poor, stupid kid," she said. "Someone talked him into killing me. In my desperate defense, all I could do was talk him into killing himself."

"They said he was nuts about you," the driver said.

"Yeah, well," Maci said sadly, shaking her head. "He was nuts alright. Did you know him?"

"Knew him most of his life," he said. "Lester was my stepson, but I loved him like he was my own. I didn't even know he was dead until I got back from Nashville to Fayetteville."

Stunned, no words came to Maci. Taking a deep breath, she said the only thing that came to mind.

"I am so sorry for your loss, Isaac," she said.

"Shut up!" he screamed, and turned around to face her as the car sped down the highway.

"He was mentally ill. You could tell that the second he opened his mouth. Everybody could. He was obsessed with you, and you knew that. But you're a star, and you didn't want to face something uncomfortable like the rest of us do every day."

"Isaac, that's not how..."

"So you coaxed him to take his life so he wouldn't bother you. You rode with me all the way to Nashville, and didn't even tell me that you'd seen someone jump from a window. You didn't even call for help, but you could have told me, and I would have called 9-1-1. He might have survived then. But you didn't care. Just like you don't care about that Ears guy, and how he might go to the electric chair for killing Max Abernathy. Which he didn't do."

"What?!" Maci yelled.

"Because I killed Max!" the driver continued. "I was across the street in a tree. When Max stepped into the doorway, I thought it was you. I meant to kill you, not Max!"

Frantically, Maci reached for the car door handle, but found it was electronically locked.

"You didn't care for one minute about my precious boy, and now I live with his death every second of my life. You took his life, and you also took mine. I'd give anything if you'd taken only mine."

The purr of the limousine suddenly seemed louder to Maci. Silently hysterical, she noticed that they had left the city limits and wondered how anyone could possibly rescue her.

"You already killed the man responsible for everything when you shot Max," she said. "If you've seen the news stories, you know he was behind this."

"That was a happy coincidence," Isaac said. "But he was only half the problem. You were the one who talked my boy into killing himself. And you were the one who didn't call for help."

"I panicked!" Maci said. "Anyone in my shoes would have!"

Resuming her watch in the rearview mirror, she saw the first of two tears on Isaac's withering face, and watched as his mood shifted toward delirium.

"We ain't gonna make it to your crummy old house," he said, slowing the car and edging it toward the shoulder of the highway.

The limousine came to a halt, and jerked when Isaac shifted it into park. He left the engine running, and Maci assumed he'd pulled over to regain his composure before resuming their journey. Perhaps she could smother him with apologies, or promise to build a memorial to his stepson. But her credibility dissolved the instant she tried to open her car window.

"The windows won't open," he said, now emotionless. "Or the doors. They only unlock from up here. Nice try, though."

"I was just going to get some air," Maci said.

Isaac shook his head. "Show business people lie constantly, but they still do it badly. Why is that?"

"Well, I . . .

"Shut up! I don't care about you and the rest of your self-absorbed and shallow people! Let ME talk!"

"Your life is your career," he said, now breathing heavily. "And tonight you got your career back, so tonight you got your life back. That's how I see it. And since you took two lives—my blessed boy and mine—I'm entitled to take yours. I mean, that Bible you're pounding says 'an eye for an eye,' right?"

"It says a lot more . . ."

"What part of 'shut up' do you not understand?" Isaac raged. "I don't want to live any longer, and so I'm going to take my life. But not before I take yours. And you'll be fine cause after all of your newfound Bible talk, you'll go straight to the ever after. Then you be sure you apologize to Lester in person."

As he turned his body completely around, Isaac's left hand rose to the top of the seat, and for the first time Maci saw the pistol. Her heart filled her throat as she watched his forefinger slide across the trigger.

"You claim you're a Christian who prays to Jesus. Well, in another second, you won't have to pray *to* him. You can pray *with* him.

"Oh, Jesus!" she cried. With tears streaming down her face, Maci looked squarely into Isaac's eyes. One was closed, and the other focused on the barrel aimed at her forehead.

"Let's see if your God can save you now," he yelled. "Open your eyes you killer!"

Maci began to pray. "Our Father which art in heaven . . ."

"Shut the hell up!" said Isaac in a deep, demonic voice.

". . . hallowed by thy name. Thy Kingdom come, thy will be done in earth as it is in heaven . . . ," she continued.

Maci felt her hands clasped together as she repeated the prayer. The past year had brought many things her way and she wasn't prepared. But as she continued to pray, she felt a deep calmness spread through her. She couldn't control Isaac. He might kill her, or he might have a change of heart and let her live.

But whatever happened, she felt as if she were ready.

She saw the fire in his satanic stare, and heard the click of the pistol's hammer. Her entire life could end in the back of a car with the mere twitch of his finger.

"Are you going to pull the trigger, Isaac?" she whispered.

"Are you? God and I are waiting."